Michele
I wish you
didn't so much
time to read!
but I'm glad
you want to fit
this one

Michael

MICHAEL J. MARTINECK

Cinco de Mayo

Michael J. Martineck

EDGE SCIENCE FICTION AND FANTASY PUBLISHING
AN IMPRINT OF HADES PUBLICATIONS, INC.
CALGARY

Edge Science Fiction and Fantasy Publishing
An Imprint of Hades Publications Inc.
P.O. Box 1714, Calgary, Alberta, T2P 2L7, Canada

In house editing by Richard Janzen
Interior design by Brian Hades
Cover Illustration by Tomislav Tikulin
ISBN: 978-1-894063-39-5

EDGE Science Fiction and Fantasy Publishing and Hades Publications, Inc. acknowledges the ongoing support of the Alberta Foundation for the Arts and the Australian Council for the Arts for our publishing programme.

Library and Archives Canada Cataloguing in Publication

Martineck, Michael J., 1965-
    Cinco de Mayo / Michael J. Martineck.

ISBN 978-1-894063-39-5

        I. Title.

PS3613.A78632C56 2010   813'.6   C2010-904490-8

Printed in Canada
(k-20100712)

www.edgewebsite.com

DEDICATION

For Sarah, my real-life Other

Cinco de Mayo

Prolog

The headache hit everyone—6,379,157,361 people—at the same time. It was sudden and fleeting. Crackling through the brain, the pain was enough to stop people mid-bite or mid-stride, halt conversation or song, wake the sleeping, start babies crying, and make people—for one and a half seconds—forget everything else. Back aches, cravings, trains of thought, lines of argument, a partner's touch, great ideas—all seared away. There was nothing.

Then there was more. Not more hurting, that was gone and replaced with more feeling. More emotion, more memory—lots more memory. Of things one never did, places one never went, of a life one never led.

CHAPTER 1

ALISTAIR

Alistair Bache slammed his hands to his head, magazine flopping to his lap. Instant hangover? Stroke? Was he having a stroke? Valerie sprang up in bed, pressing the sides of her own head. Alistair thought he had woken her, but she squinted like the lights were too bright and that didn't make any sense. Nothing made any sense but pain.

And Lucy's crying. And Rebecca's crying.

The pain vanished. No residual—more of an afterglow. He was awake and feeling good, much to his surprise. Before the pain, he'd been too tired to turn a page.

Valerie was out of bed, running to the girls. He followed, confused. The girls never got sick at the same time. Simultaneous nightmares? The same moment as him? And the flash of a headache?

Lucy was four, Rebecca only two. They slept in the same pink room, in matching beds separated by a gulf of fluff and plastic. Valerie scooped up the smaller one and plopped next to the other before Alistair got there. They'd stopped crying. Both rubbed their heads and stared with glistening eyes at dark nothing.

"OK," Valerie whispered. "Everything's OK."

"My head hurt," Lucy said.

Valerie looked up at her husband.

"Head hurt," Rebecca echoed her sister, as she frequently did for no other reason than to play copycat. Alistair knew this was different.

"My head hurt," he said.

"Mine, too." Valerie hugged her girls tightly.

Alistair sniffed the air. He looked around. What could give everyone a headache at exactly the same time? What made a headache that left just as fast as it came? Gas leak? Carbon monoxide? Ludicrous. He'd never heard of anything like this. They didn't live in Bhopal.

On instinct, Alistair looked outside. They'd been in the house for five years, long enough to know all the squeaks and creaks and rhythms of their environment. It was an orderly neighborhood. That blonde lady walked her collie in the morning. That Sydney Greenstreet-like guy walked his daschund at night, defying blizzards, floods, locust, or anything. By 9:00 PM the suburb was dim, down to streetlights and landscape lights and the occasional blue TV haze from a bedroom window. Except tonight. Bulbs lit windows in every house.

"Looks like the whole neighborhood is up," Alistair said. The house lights gave him the creeps.

Protect. Defend. Circle the wagons. He wanted everyone under the covers, in the big bed, regardless of the fact that this made no rational sense.

"What's going on?" Valerie focused on him like she expected an answer. He always had one. He was adept at making them up when he didn't know the truth. Sometimes his answers were comical, sometimes insightful, on rare occasion correct. He knew what Valerie wanted. An outlandish lie was fine, as long as it soothed.

"Chemical cloud." Alistair put lots of certainty in his voice. "It must have drifted through the area. Came and went. Let's see if there's anything on the news. Come on everybody." He picked up Lucy; Valerie took Rebecca.

"MuB ich zum Arzt gehen?" Rebecca asked.

They stopped and stared at Rebecca's little rose mouth. Was that German? Alistair didn't know. He didn't speak German. None of them did, which of course, included two-year-old Rebecca.

CHAPTER 2

SUSAN

Susan Grove did not want anyone to know what she was doing. She sat, legs tucked under her, wrapped in a blanket, with two magazine-sized journals barely balanced on her lap. She was not ashamed of her ritual. Lots of people did it. She just chose not to tell anyone what she did every weeknight at 10:00 PM.

She pointed the Tivo remote and brought up that day's broadcast of Oprah. She hoped it was a good one. The journals were just in case it wasn't. She'd still watch it, but read at the same time.

Susan had no intellectual condescension for Oprah. She did not feel the show was beneath her in any way. Quite the contrary. While Susan knew, without overstatement, all that was currently known about the topography and neuroplasticity of the human prefrontal cortex, Oprah seemed to know about everything else. Oprah knew all Susan did not and was willing to share it.

The reason Susan never mentioned Oprah to any of her colleagues was stereotypical, in the sense that doing so would settle her into a stereotype. Susan did not want to be pigeonholed as another African American woman eating whatever Oprah ate, reading whatever Oprah read, and, most of all, following her spirit. She did not want to be 'one of them.' Susan had enough problems shedding unearned labels—she did not need another one.

She did need to know more about Oprah. Every show gave her a tiny glimpse into her success, not just in her nasty profession, but across her life. Susan was very good at grafting lots of little glimpses into a large, coherent picture. There really was no other way to see the human brain. Oprah's or anyone else's.

Extrapolating the big from the small was not always a gift. When it came to neurology, the skill proved useful enough to make her one of the most influential practitioners in the field. When it came to that guy from the pool that always gave her a hefty smile, it was a curse. Sometimes a smile—to paraphrase Sigmund Freud—was just a smile. It was not an overture to dinner, day trips, and a loving, respectful marriage that would warm her into old age. Oprah didn't make mountains out of cleft chins. Susan admired that trait and wanted to make it one of her own.

That had yet to happened. She never talked to the guy by the pool. She saw 70 reasons not to with every glance.

At 40, Susan had reached an age compelling her to attend a spinning class every other day, without question, and to eat more blueberries. The antioxidant data was not definitive, at least to her standards, but the downside was innocuous. She did not hate blueberries. She did not hate anything.

Except the pain in her head. Sudden, acute, severe, diffuse. No history of migraines. Intracranial bleeding was possible and terrible. She had to get to the phone. *What was a phone?* Oh my God, what was a phone? She was deteriorating rapidly. She told herself not to jump up. She begged herself not to scream. She could not help but cup her hands around her head. This was not how she was going to die. Not now, not tonight—alone on this couch watching Oprah.

The pain passed, like someone had wiped her mind clean. She felt...sparkly. She let herself sit up, dropping the journals to the floor. She was alive. She felt more alive than before the pain, as if her dopamine levels had abruptly doubled. That was an abrupt conclusion. There was 5-HT, and elevated norepinephrine levels could account for her lack of concentration. Guessing was not her nature.

She was not in her nature. She was in the bellybutton of the world.

Chapter 3

CINDY

Cindy hated Thursdays. She didn't care much for any of day of the week, but Thursdays were the worst. She didn't hate them like broccoli or subtitles—she hated each Thursday like an enemy. A serial killer or child snatcher or drug-dealing cop. She felt it first on Wednesdays as a shadow in the back of her head—a big, black cloud coming from the west. On Thursday mornings it was more of a twisting in the gut. As the day went on, the twisting got tighter and tighter. On Thursdays she nibbled lunch, skipped dinner, and by nightfall found herself unable to sit or stand. She had to walk around her three-room house, straightening, fluffing, folding.

She tried to look extra cute on Thursdays. Brad liked her jeans, with the black and white striped top that made her plum-sized boobs look more like peaches. She was not a natural blonde, but he'd never learn that. She had plenty of time to color each hair individually. She thickened each individual eyelash and carefully covered any spot redder than the rest of her face.

Cindy had learned not to overdo the make-up or the cleaning. It had to be just right. Invisible. What she really worked at was making everything look like it was no work at all. The unnoticed was safe. That's why fawns have spots in the spring or rabbits grow white for winter. The unseen goes free.

Brad slapped Cindy for the first time around their three-month anniversary. Cindy had turned 24 the night before. She'd had way too many Coors Lights and spent the day on the couch, drinking Squirt. Brad got home, kicked a pile of mail, grabbed her fucking disgusting sweatshirt and slapped her across the face. The honeymoon was officially over.

She had been too stunned to cry. He plowed into the bedroom and she didn't see him awake until the next night. Then he took her out to dinner, apologized, and she wrote it off. Everyone slips once in a while, right? The following Thursday she made damn sure there was no pile of mail on the floor by the door.

A month later he slapped her because the house was so fucking neat. He couldn't get comfortable. He was afraid to sit down in his own goddamn house. What did she do all day? If she had enough time to pick up every speck of dust in the living room, she didn't have enough to do.

Cindy had been a waitress when they met. Brad made her quit when they started dating. She didn't need to shake her ass for tips, he'd provide. After getting hit for cleaning too well, she thought maybe she did have a lot of time on her hands. Maybe she could pick up a shift. That earned her two more slaps. One for wanting to show off her stuff for a bunch of drunks, the other for insulting his ability to provide for his woman.

By month five she thought about leaving. The married Brad was so different from the dating Brad. As different as a bunny and a snake. She couldn't stand him touching her. A soft pet reminded her of the sting. If he came near her, she tensed up like she was going to snap. She never told him her thoughts, but he must have sensed something. He sweetened, smiling like the old Brad. Dark, strong, and shy. She remembered the things she liked in him: the jokes, the attention, the devotion.

He hit her again. Why was she all dolled up? Who was she trying to snag? Some guy in the neighborhood? That lineman who worked nights? While he worked his ass off, she whored around?

She knew when a hit was coming, as it started with his breath. Beer breath so thick you could practically see it, a golden spray of nastiness.

It was back to mom's after that. Mom was not too pleased. Her boyfriend was over and three was not what she, at least, had in mind. At breakfast, Cindy got the lecture about making things work, keeping your man happy, and how her mother didn't raise no quitters.

Cindy got hit for going to sleep before Brad got home. She went to her friend Lorna's for three days. Cindy got hit for burning Salisbury steaks. Back to Lorna's.

Brad said he'd change after that. Adjusting to married life, a new job, having things different in his house, that had been tough. He was tough, though. He'd fix things.

His house, Cindy kept repeating in her head. Every morning, she'd do something around his house. Not *their* house. Like she was a guest who wouldn't go home. This marriage wasn't going to work out. Brad could be wonderful, but only in sprints. He couldn't run the long race.

Cindy had $120 hidden in an envelope in a shoebox in her closet. That would get her to about the end of the street. Mom's was out; there was no Dad's. She had friends, half of whom were Brad's. Some of those guys wouldn't open the door if she was pounding, some of them would only if their wives weren't home. She had Lorna. She'd been leaning pretty hard on her lately. Brad knew all about that hideaway. Brad would beat on Lorna even more easily than he beat on her.

Brad sold her Ford Escort. She couldn't believe it. Sold it out from under her. How could he do that? Didn't she need to sign something? He said she didn't need a car and they needed the money. He never said how much he got for it. She started to cry and he raised his hand.

When Cindy was little there was this game called Payday. It was an old, worn board game at her grandparent's house. She and her cousins played it before the boring Sunday dinners. Landing on the 'payday' spot was the best. That was the day you got your money. You got closer to winning. Now, Brad had twisted that feature of life like he twisted her stomach. Paydays, when Brad went out right after work and got shit-faced and angry at nothing and came home swinging. Thursdays.

Cindy hated payday.

Chapter 4

ALISTAIR

Alistair could not relate this feeling to any real world experience. This bubbling panic from some unseen, amorphous, circling threat. At 39 years, nearly all of which had been spent in calm suburbs, he had no personal emergency history to call up and use. He had never ridden out a twister or crouched in a foxhole or huddled below in a perfect storm. *This was like a video game*, he thought. *Like getting thrown into a video game without ever seeing the box or even learning the game's freaking name.*

He kept this thought tight to himself. If he said it out loud, Valerie would remind him in the nastiest possible way that this was no video game. Not everything was a video game. Why was that always the analogy?

He retucked the girls under the blankets and reached behind both of them to stroke his wife's straight black hair. Valerie looked at him. He loved her dark, narrow face. Film noir beauty, to which he never believed he matched. Not that he was in bad shape. A little thickness around his belly. A little gray frosting the temples. Otherwise, he was still boyish. Not a beautiful adult, like Valerie.

The girls were quiet but alert. They stared at the small TV on the dresser, waiting for it to come on. Alistair wasn't sure he wanted it on. Maybe it would be best if he tried to get them back to sleep. The headaches were gone. Rebecca had said nothing else in a foreign language.

In a crisis, it's all instincts and training. Alistair didn't like his set of the two, but it was what he had. American suburbs. TV, the great unifier. He pushed the remote's 'ON' button, wondering which channel might be covering whatever had happened. Which one was best at chasing firetrucks?

Television was normal. A courtroom full of frustrated people and tense music. Fine. The world wasn't coming to an end, because there is no way the networks would be missing that. They would be cutting in and—

The TV screen stalled. A blue and gold 'SPECIAL REPORT' logo came up with a few frightening blasts of orchestral music. The four of them gazed at the screen, unblinking, hypnotized. Alistair could feel his cheeks cool from lack of blood and his chest tighten from the restriction, like his body was ready to mitigate the leaking should he lose a limb. Alistair was pretty sure this was how his ancestors had survived, by being able to endure punishment.

The 'SPECIAL REPORT' logo did not go away. They were supposed to herald the actual report. They weren't meant to just hang there on the screen.

"Change the channel," Valerie said and Alistair did.

"—barded with calls. We're asking everyone to please refrain from calling. We have no idea what has occurred."

The anchor sat behind the desk, tie up, jacket straight, hair perfect, and face a volatile mix of anger, bewilderment, and, Alistair thought, cold fear. Oddly, the image made him feel a wee bit better. His little family was no longer alone in its anger, bewilderment, and fear.

"Reports are coming in from all over the globe. Unexplained headaches—and, I will remain...remind everyone this is unsubstantiated—claims of new memories. There is no official word on this, but the calls we are getting here are eerily similar. We are trying to...ah...substantiate the claims."

A network reporter stumbled around for the right words. They were normally so polished. They normally had copy and teleprompters. While Alistair liked knowing something big was going on—not something small and all his own, not a noise he had to investigate in his basement— he was not happy to watch this guy's abject puzzlement.

"I can't forget to pick up Lu Chan's medicine on the way home." Valerie slowly turned to look at Alistair, half her face glowing in the TV light, the other half disappearing in shadow. "He's got a fever. I couldn't stay home today, like I should have, but I won't forget his medicine."

"Lu who?" Alistair's nose wrinkled. This was no time for nonsense. But, Valerie was a no-nonsense girl.

"Lu Chan," she said. "My 12-year-old grandson."

"You're freakin' me out."

"I'm freakin' me out. I've got this memory that's very important and it's pushing to the front of my brain, because I can't just rush home like I always do. But I don't work in the payroll department of Ling Manufacturing. I don't have to take two buses to get home. My name is not Mi Sung Lu. I am not 64 years old, and from Beijing."

Alistair could see only her right eye, filling with thick liquid. She was strong. She only cried at movies. The girls would break down if they saw her. They were lost in the TV, though. Thank God for the mind-numbing flicker of television.

Valerie tightened her mouth so only words came out. "What's your name, Alistair Bache?"

"Al," he said. "Or John. John McCorely."

Alistair couldn't believe he just said that. Even harder to believe was the feeling that it was absolutely true.

CHAPTER 5

SUSAN

Susan had no idea what had just happened to her, and that scared her more than the thing itself.

Her job was to oversee the cluster for Systems and Cognitive Neuroscience at the National Institute of Neurological Disorders and Stroke. She determined who got funding for what when it came to studying the brain. In that capacity, she took in and analyzed the preponderance of brain-related research going on throughout the world. She was an expert's expert.

And she was disoriented, invigorated, and more frightened than if a ghost haunted her living room.

Susan did her undergraduate work at Fordham and got her M.D. from Columbia University's College of Physicians and Surgeons. She never left the area around Lake Atitlan in the highlands. His people needed him there, with them, all of the time. It is both an honor and a burden.

His? Me? A man. Fifty-one? *Age does not matter. Are you holding your place in the world? That is what matters. Are you still worth more than you eat?*

Susan shot up. The night was tranquil. Oprah talked through the television. The spirits were running wild tonight. Some great stick stirring them. He'd never heard anything like this in any story.

This was not on the calendar.

These thoughts were more than disturbing, they were a form of dementia. There was, of course, no such thing as instant onset dementia. Nor was she a man named

Antonio from somewhere in South America that she could not pinpoint because he had never seen a world map. Susan planted her feet and folded her arms across her chest.

Once, 10 years ago, she had been this close to panic. Her patient was bleeding out into her hands. Missy Armstrong was her name. Susan would never forget it. There was so much blood flooding the area of the incision that she could not see the source. Each millisecond brought more blood and the young woman closer to death. There was, quite simply, no time. Susan stuck out her lower jaw, ground her teeth together, and swore no lousy little devil child of a leak was going to kill her girl. She cauterized her best guesses and saved Missy's life.

Anger was just another process of the brain. It could be used as easily and efficiently as happiness, peace, or love. There was nothing wrong, Susan knew, with a healthy dose of pissed off.

Susan got pissed off. She decided she probably needed medical attention. A good doctor never treats herself. In this case, with an obvious mental impairment, the reasons were tenfold. She wasn't even sure she could get herself to the hospital. She needed a cleansing. She needed to burn the cola bush and the smoke would chase the bad spirits away.

There she went again. Tears came into her eyes. Her brain was haywire. Spirit crap. Worse than Grammie ever laid down.

She had to call an ambulance. She picked up the phone, telling herself that it better be intracranial bleeding, because she did not want to look like a fool.

The phone was dead.

CHAPTER 6

ALISTAIR

The girls fell asleep. Whatever new memories they had were not enough to keep them awake. Alistair was very glad for that. He was not having the same luck. The more he dug through his new memories, the more he doubted he'd ever fall asleep again.

The news on the television was no longer news. Alistair joked that they were now watching the 'olds', the so-two-hours-ago. They should change the name to the Nightly Recent. None of the media had anything new. They just repeated the same couple of lines every ten minutes with a fresh reassurance that they were looking into tonight's events.

Valerie appeared to be watching the television, but Alistair could tell she was probing her mind. Thinking back on what felt like her life and coming up with things she had never known. He could see it on her face. *Perfect*, Alistair thought. *I hope it keeps her distracted for a while.*

He didn't want any questions.

He didn't want to be rude and not answer them, but he couldn't. These memories were John McCorely's, and Alistair knew John wouldn't like it if they got out. In fact, John would kill to keep them safe. He'd done so on at least three occasions.

Alistair sat, staring at the television, actively blocking out his new memories. John McCorely's memories of how he came to reside in the security housing unit of the supermax inside Pelican Bay Penitentiary.

Bars, walls. Use them. Keep it all out. Alistair yelled inside his head. He did not need to know John's most recent, overriding concern was the hit he'd ordered on an attorney named Joshua Parks. A fresh-out-of-school black guy who'd had the nerve to laugh at him. *Him!* John Fucking McCorely. Laughing at him was laughing at the whole Brotherhood—an offense punishable by death. Simple as that. Not even because he was black. John wished he could turn the bastard white and then kill him so the message would be more pure. This wasn't black-white shit, this was about the laugh. Period.

Because as much control as John had from inside the SHU—and he had a lot, controlling millions of dollars, hundreds of people, life and death—time was still impossible to intimidate and tough to buy. He wanted Joshua dead. Now. But these things took time. As of 9:23, John had no idea where in the pipeline his message might lie. The jolly piece of shit was still going to die, it was just a matter of days. A week at the outside.

Alistair pushed the thoughts down and away. This guy John was in a supermax. No contact with the outside world. It didn't matter that he wanted this attorney dead. *He couldn't do it, right?* And this guy was a psycho. All this might not even be the truth. Psychotic delusion. Someone or something or some event had jammed memories into his skull. Did that make them true? Was any of this true? Truer than a dream?

"Waking dreams," he said out loud. "This crap in my head. Maybe it's some kind of waking dream. A solar flare made all of our heads go nut job and create these enormously detailed dreams."

"*Ou Duan Su Lian.*"

Alistair felt the creep on his neck yet again.

"Go run that through Babelfish. I didn't learn Chinese from a dream."

He knew she didn't mean it to be mean. She didn't know her personal revelation was backing him up to the canyon.

John McCorely had committed his first murder at the age of 17. He was a clear thinker. He was the leader of the Aryan Brotherhood, and its 1,600 active members, because he could be smart or psycho or whatever a situation demanded. He didn't fantasize about killing people. He had it done. It was, for him, easier than calling a plumber. He'd have to look up the number of a plumber. If John wanted someone dead all he had to do was ask.

Alistair carried Lucy and Rebecca back to their beds. They'd sleep better there, not so much tossing into each other. Normalcy was the new goal. Anything nice and normal.

When he got back Valerie was sitting in bed. A new face was on the screen. Some male-model reporter.

"—shared. Strange as that is, Gordon, it's probably no stranger than anything else we've seen tonight. Phone lines around the world are failing. The systems were never built for this kind of use. But as people are realizing that they now share memories with another human being, they are reaching out to each other."

"What is he saying?" Alistair kneeled on the bed.

"They are getting reports of people who have contacted each other. These people got each other's memories."

"Each other's?"

"Yeah," Valerie said. "Like I...maybe I just didn't get Mi Sung Lu's memories. Maybe she got mine, too."

"Is that true? Is it everybody? Did this happen to everybody?"

"I don't know!" Valerie's eyebrows bunched up. She was not happy with his tone or his questions or something. "Nobody knows."

Can't call my guy, Alistair said to himself. Even if he had a phone, John would kill him for trying. No connections. No overtures. He and Valerie and the girls were only safe in anonymity.

'If I told you, I'd have to kill you.' This was no joke in the Brotherhood. It was an actual rule that got enforced. Alistair knew this, like he knew his address. Or John's cell block.

"Who is this John person?" Valerie asked. "Can you call him?"

"That would be..." Alistair fumbled, like he was caught in a lie. He hadn't even made up a story yet and he was already strangling from it. "No."

"Can you remember his number? I can remember Mi Sung Lu's, though I'm not sure I want to call her. Do you think? They're saying the phone lines are all screwed up."

"It's probably not true," Alistair said. "It doesn't make any sense that we would exchange memories."

Valerie laughed. It wasn't the happy kind, more of a frustrated release. "You think any of this makes any sense? There are no rules anymore, buddy. Start with that."

But Alistair didn't want it to be true. Having this stuff in his head, all of this blood-and-gore-garbage from John McCorely was awful. It was so bad, there was only one thing he could think of that would be worse.

The phone rang. Alistair and Valerie jumped, rocking the bed. Valerie looped her hair behind her ear and picked up the receiver.

"Hello?"

Alistair held his eyes on the back of her head. Bluish silver rippling across the shinny black.

Valerie began jabbering away in Chinese.

Alistair walked quickly to the bathroom. He was going to be sick.

CHAPTER 7

SUSAN

Susan tried her cell phone, but it refused to place her call. It was the first time she'd ever had trouble with either her cell phone or her land line.

The coincidence was too strong. What could give her a brief headache and debilitate two phones? Nothing. Outside of spirits.

"Damn," she said out loud. Spirits. She was going nuts— her brain was telling her the phones were out. An oddly specific form of dementia, but she'd heard of worse. She needed help.

Susan didn't know her neighbors all that well. She wasn't the type to stand out front watering her petunias. She rarely came home before everyone else was inside for the night. Quarter to eleven was not the time to meet the block club.

He knew all his neighbors. Antonio.

"My name is Antonio," she said. *I can name everyone in Cerro de Oro. I don't just know them, I know when they were born. When they were married. All the dates in their lives. I have to. I am the keeper of days.*

Susan grabbed a running jacket from her hall closet, pushed on her sneakers and ran out the front door.

"Oh." For the second time in twenty minutes, Susan was stunned to paralysis. She froze with her legs on two different steps, arms back, ready to don the blue satin jacket.

People were coming toward her. The woman from next door and her daughter, in their pajamas. An elderly couple from across the street, wearing robes. The neighborhood was a budding, lawn-bound suburb, with thin trees and big homes differentiated only by cosmetics and care. It was always docile, but even more so after nine, when the kids came in. Tonight the air was full of light and noise, where Susan had become some form of focus.

Susan's anger left. She felt no capacity for it, even though she needed it. She needed to be plenty mad at this whole situation or she was going to be something else, though she was not sure what.

"Dr. Grove!" the pajama-clad woman from next door called out. She advanced in a hopping run, tugging her daughter. She was spindly and mopey, as was proper for that age. Straight brown hair. Susan had a mental caricature of the girl with an over-sized magnifying glass held to her eye. Girl detective. Nancy Drew. The girl's name was Nancy. She was in her first year of high school. The mother—white, late 30s, healthy, artificial blonde, worked an office job. She exercised four times a week to keep that figure. In Susan's imagination she wore a jogging suit with a collegiate 'G' on the chest and she shook her head. G-naw. Gina. Her neighbors were Gina and Nancy.

"Dr. Grove," she called again, this time slightly puzzled. "How did you..."

The old couple hurried. They looked both ways as they crossed the street, but didn't stop. Susan could see the fear on their faces. It was the full, soft fear she always hated to see in older people. The recognition that the body was doing something it had never done before, signaling some new and final stage in life. Grammie had had that look all the time, near the end. Uncomfortable, horrible acceptance.

"We have headaches," Gina said. Nancy nodded.

"We have headaches, too," the man crossing the street shouted. *John and Esther*, Susan remembered.

"Had," Nancy added. "We don't have them anymore."

"I remember you are a doctor of some sort," Gina said.

"Yes," Susan said. *I am a doctor. I am an* aja 'ij. *I help the sun cross the sky every day.*

"Of some sort."

CHAPTER 8

CINDY

Cindy rubbed her temples. Instant headache—great. Just what she fucking needed. Brad would be home any minute and a headache was no excuse with him. If she told him she had a headache, he'd laugh and smack her and say 'Now you have a headache, Bitch.'

Rubbing her temples really worked. Cindy stood up straight and looked at herself in the kitchen window. It was black outside, so she saw her face clearly. Her dumbstruck, dumb-blonde face, like she couldn't decide what to order at McDonald's. Rubbing had never worked that well before. She felt great. She hadn't felt this good all day. Christ, all year.

She'd better check the status of the plane and passengers. They came first. There may have been a sudden loss of pressure in the cabin. That was not good. Gun shot, explosive device, malfunctioning seal...

There was no cabin to check. She was not on Swiss Air flight 404. 'Remember your training.' That got hammered into you at school. 'Fall back on your training. We prepare you for chaos.'

This wasn't chaos. She was alone in her kitchen and she'd never had any training in her life. Training? She never heard of the University of Basel. Why could she describe it—the stones, the oaks, the smell of the rain-soaked cigarette butts and coffee, that he grew to love?

He? What the fuck?

Cindy shuddered. It was one of those chills kids tell each other are from a ghost passing through you. She had a ghost blow through her like she was a screen door, and he left some of himself behind.

This was that moment in the movie when you start yelling at the dumb blonde, "Get out of the house! Run for your life!"

What was she going to do, grab a kitchen knife? Ghosts don't care about knives or running. In fact, missy, they ain't even real.

Cindy looked at her misty reflection in the window again. She was there. She could see herself and no one else. *Get a grip, Cin. Get a grip, Flor.*

Cindy's eyes filled up. Her name was Florens Auerbach, from Basel, Switzerland. He was 26 years old. She was going nuts. Totally, balls-out batty.

Brad had done this to her. The pressure, the fear, the crap he dished out finally caught up with her and pushed her over the edge. She was schizo, like that girl in that movie with a bunch of personalities. She'd made up a new one that was as far from Attala County, Mississippi, as she could imagine.

She needed help. She had to get to a doctor. Brad was going to love that. Like he'd be able to drive her tonight, or give her the money for the co-pay. She'd have to cut her arm off to get him to take her, if he even came home tonight.

Her mom was 20 minutes away. That wasn't so bad. Was this really an emergency? Sure, she wanted out of the house, but was that it? Could this wait? It wasn't like she was bleeding to death or anything. *Take a couple of deep breaths.*

'Keep the subject fully reclined and warm, encourage well-paced breathing to prevent hyperventilating. Distract and refocus. Panic is a state of mind.'

Oh man, how did she know that? First aid. Taking care of a troubled passenger. CPR? The location of the automated electronic defibrillator? She couldn't make this shit up. No, she could, because she'd tell herself that it was true shit even if it was total bullshit, right? Like the guys who think they're Napoleon or got abducted by aliens.

Cindy actually wanted Brad to come home now. He was a dick, but this was serious. Even he would recognize that they were going to have to do something about it. She didn't feel bonkers. This could be simple, like she was low on minerals or something, right? Like in detox when they give you injections of vitamin E. Simple as that. Even Brad was not so much the complete asshole that he wouldn't take her to the hospital for a shot of vitamins.

The truck pulled in the driveway, its headlights slicing though the front window, arcing across the whole house.

Maybe she didn't need to tell Brad anything right now. Maybe she could sneak out tomorrow and take care off this all on her own.

Brad banged into the house with as much noise as possible. Flinging the door so it smashed the rubber donut Cindy had put on the wall to keep it from cracking. Stomping his boots on the linoleum. Dropping his keys in a dish from three feet up.

"Man, I just had the weirdest thing happen," he yelled.

Cindy was right there. She didn't like to come running, like a dog left alone all day. Tonight she couldn't help herself.

"What happened?" Cindy asked. He didn't sound seven beers down. That was already the queerest thing to happen.

"Got this pain in my head. Just a bit ago."

Cindy felt that ghost pass through her again. "A sharp pain? All over?"

"Yeah. An ice cream headache, you know?"

"This is weird."

"No, that's not the weird part." He sat down on the edge of the couch. The look on his face was something new to Cindy. It was...she didn't know what to call it...troubled, without being pissed off.

"No, this is the weird part. I keep thinking I should call Sanjay. He's gay, like me. I know it. I should call him. Fuck! Can you believe this shit? I'm like this lonely queer in Allahabad, India."

"Brad—"

"Seriously. This is, like, disturbing. If I'm going to dream, why can't it be about a busload of cheerleaders? I should call this guy? What kind of fucking faggot shit is that?"

"I had a headache, too."

Brad looked at Cindy for the first time since he got home, his mouth open in a mouse hole shape, his eyebrows trying to meet up.

"When?" he asked.

"Just now," Cindy replied. "A couple of minutes ago."

"Bullshit."

"Really. It came and went like that." She snapped her fingers. Brad's face changed. The awe in his eyes darkened.

"And you had a dream about some fag who lives in a shithole and has, like, 14 jobs?"

"No. A man from Switzerland who got to see his first Formula One race this year. I don't even know what that means."

"You're dreaming about another guy." Brad sat back and unfurled his arms, covering the back rim of the couch.

Cindy said, "It's not like that."

"You just said you were dreaming about another guy?"

"Like your dream. It just came to me."

"Who is it?"

"You don't know him. At least, we never, well..."

"Well what?" Brad half-smiled, like he'd caught her in a lie. Or like he was half enjoying this. That was more likely, Cindy realized. He didn't want to think about the homosexual, the headaches, the freakishness of the whole thing. He wanted to get back to Thursday night routine: find something to get angry about, then pour it on.

"Something has happened to the two of us," Cindy said.

"So you like him?"

"I don't know him."

"He good looking?"

"I don't..." Cindy couldn't go on. She hadn't conjured up an image of Florens, not until Brad nudged her. She got a clear image of him, in the mirror, after shaving, and he was hot. Smoking hot. 6'2", blonde, blue eyes, with a jaw like the front of a train. His shoulders and chest were so smooth and shapely Cindy held her breath. She was making this up. That nailed it. This Florens guy was so flat out perfect he must have come from her imagination.

"You don't what?" Brad's upper lip disappeared. He had a way of stretching his mouth so much that the thin little thing vanished, leaving his white teeth gleaming. "I asked you if this guy was good looking."

"No," Cindy said, "he's not."

"Then you do know."

"Know what?"

"Him. What he looks like. You said you didn't know him."

"This is weird. Can't you feel it? Something strange has happened."

"The only strangeness is why my woman is dreaming about another man."

"You were thinking about some other man?"

"Not somebody I want to bang."

"Who said anything about banging?"

Brad stood, running his fingers through his hair. He took two steps, leaving him about a foot from his wife.

"That what you want?" he whispered. "This other guy banging you? Huh? Spice it up a little? Get something different?"

Cindy's muscles wound tight. Her heart kicked up. The whispering was always the warning. He liked to get quiet before he got real loud. When he thought she wasn't expecting it, he'd swing an open hand across her face.

"Why don't you go lie down, Brad?"

"Why don't you stop telling me what to do?"

"Really. We can talk about this—"

He swung.

Cindy caught his hand, grabbing his fingers. She bent the index finger back, brought her other hand around to his arm, turned, and forced Brad to the floor. She rammed her knee into his back before the cracking and screaming registered.

"Let go," he wailed. "It's breaking. You fucking bitch, let go!"

She wasn't sure what to do now. She—or he—usually had handcuffs or zip ties for this part. Subdue the assailant, then restrain. Restrain with what?

"Let me go!" came out of Brad with a spray of spit.

She didn't want to, but she didn't have much of a choice. She wasn't going to kneel on his back for the rest of her life. She hopped up and back, well out of his way.

Brad did a push-up and shook his head. "Bitch."

Cindy stood ready, hands open, one foot placed six inches ahead of the other, knees bent.

Brad stood. "What the fuck was that?"

"I don't know," she said. "That's what I've been trying to tell you."

"Come here."

"No."

"Get over here."

"Like I said. No."

Brad snarled like a dog. Cindy had never seen him so mad. She'd never seen anyone so mad. Florens had, once. A Scottish tourist, drunk, in a club. It was the only time he thought he might have to draw his side arm.

Brad roared, "I said come here!" He lunged, with his right arm locked in front of him. Was he thinking he could grab her hair? It was the silliest attack she'd ever seen. She grabbed his arm, turned and flipped him over her shoulder. It was nothing. He'd done all the work. Brad crashed to the floor, shaking the whole house. Cindy again bent his hand back, producing another scream. She guided Brad on to his stomach.

"I could do this all night," she said. "But I ain't gonna." She grabbed the lamp and yanked. The plug flew out and the cord leaped toward her. She wrapped the cord around Brad's wrists before he guessed what she was doing.

"Don't you even—"

"Too late," she interrupted him. "Done." She couldn't pull the cord out of the lamp, so she looped it through a couple of times, then around the leg of the couch. If he calmed down, he'd probably figure out that he could reverse the process and get out in a minute or two. That would be plenty of time.

"Alright." Brad had a chuckle in his voice. "I'm sorry. Totally sorry. I get it now. You can let me go."

Cindy slipped the wallet out of his back pocket.

"Come on, let me up." He forced a little laugh.

900 bucks. He spent like 200 already! In five hours on a Thursday night? She ran to the bedroom, threw the closet door open and dropped to the floor. She ripped her old backpack out of the mess, jumped up, and started jamming clothes in it.

"Joke's over!" Brad yelled. "Cindy? Joke's over."

She dashed into the living room. Brad rolled around, scraping the couch across the floor. He saw the backpack.

"Wait, wait. Where you going? You leaving me like this?"

Cindy scooped up the car keys. "I want a divorce."

She popped from the front door like a champagne cork.

CHAPTER 9

SUSAN

A knock on the door at 1:30 in the morning was never an overture to something good. Susan wanted to ignore it. She was stuck to the TV. It was the only source of fresh data and she needed data desperately. This was a monumental evening. She wondered why whoever was at her door wasn't gazing into his or her own television right then.

She was, first, a doctor. She didn't ignore bumps in the night, especially on a night like this. She got up and moved quietly to the front door, peering out the peek hole.

A soldier: young, stiff, armed. He had an armband, but she couldn't read it.

"Yes?" she called out.

"Dr. Grove?" the soldier shouted back.

"Yes," she called again.

"Sorry about the intrusion, Dr. Grove. I've been asked to escort you to your office."

"Office?" Susan should have guessed. She was so focused on the big splash of the evening, she hadn't thought about the ripples.

"We're here to take you to work, Ma'am."

The National Institutes of Health, in Bethesda, Maryland, comprised 27 organizations dedicated to public health. Under the auspices of the U.S. Department of Health and Human Services, the institutes served as both a clearinghouse for research—directing funding and other resources outside—and conducting its own internal research projects.

The campus was architecturally uninteresting to Susan. As it should be. The importance of the facilities was inside— 900 people trying to make the world a better place. She was not now, and never had been, a bleeding heart hippie, but she was proud to work there every day. This evening was no different.

Looked at another way, this evening was as different as you could get. She'd never been in the back of a police car before, let alone a military police car, with the lights flashing, going faster than she wanted to know. Her building was lit up. Not just the parking and floodlights that burned all night, every light inside was ablaze. The marine helicopter on the lawn completed the spectacle. Time's Square on New Year's Eve. This place had been built for quiet thinkers. Not the marines and their noisy toys.

The MPs dropped her at the front door. Another young man in army greens stood waiting for her.

"Lieutenant Joseph Scott," he said. "USAMRID. I've been assigned as your liaison, Dr. Grove."

Pale, but clean and sturdy looking. He ran or swam to keep that build. The breadth of his shoulders and lack of a tan said swimming. He was at least ten years her junior. Still, there were no boxy protrusions in his breast pockets. All the men in her life had been smokers, and they were all gone. She was prejudiced and freely admitted it. She pictured him with his chest way out, holding an army coffee mug, with a kilt around it. Joe Scott.

"Nice to meet you, Lieutenant Scott. Liaison, huh? Might I ask who we shall be liaising with?"

"Whoever you want, Doctor. You're in charge." Joe's face broke its serious blankness. He suddenly looked embarrassed. "Very sorry, Doctor. Communication is down all over. I should have realized you were probably not briefed. You are the head of a joint task force to investigate tonight's phenomenon."

Susan smiled. "I think you got the wrong girl."

"I certainly hope not." The voice came from the doorway, with a rush of cold air.

"Mr. Secretary." Susan tried to conceal a gasp. Lesley Corwit, secretary of Health and Human Services. She had met him twice before. Both times, she had been impressed by his ability to look considerably less that 72. He was wiry, but not frail; hair was silver, not gray. The tailored suits helped. In jeans bunching around his waist and loose yellow polo shirt, he looked more like a grandfather.

"I picked you myself," he said. "So I hope you're not wrong for the job."

"No, sir. I'm just...befuddled."

"Well, come in and we'll talk about it."

They walked down the hall. Joe followed a few paces behind.

"Amanda's out of the country," Lesley said. Susan knew the institutes' director was gone. Switzerland, for a conference. "Besides, this is more your bailiwick anyway. No time for politics or chains of command. The president's looking for answers. Hell, the whole world's looking for answers."

For the first time that night, Susan felt a little queasy. Cutting into someone's skull to start 11 hours of surgery did not bother her. Being the center of attention—the center of the president's attention—she couldn't think about that.

Lesley held open a door for Susan. Old-style charm. "I asked five people for a neuro expert to head this up. All five said I should be talking to you."

Susan stopped. She wasn't ready to cross the threshold. Her brain was still organizing and sorting, using huge amounts of energy. She didn't know if everyone was responding this way, but she was impaired.

"With all due respect, sir—"

Lesley cut her off. "I don't want to be a prick but you're going to have to respect me on this one. I wish I had time to give you a pep talk but there's a helicopter waiting to take me to the White House." He gently pushed her through the door, nodding to Joe. "This guy's got a phone that actually works."

The secretary of Health and Human Services stepped back and let the door go. Joe slid in before it closed.

CHAPTER 10

ALISTAIR

In October 2002, John McCorely decided he needed to have a meeting of the highest officers in the Aryan Brotherhood. There were 14 regional leaders in 14 different high-security prisons. Like John, most were in solitary confinement. They never spoke to anyone, stuck in cells 23 hours a day, with one hour alone in a concrete courtyard no bigger than a handball court. The U.S. Department of Justice figured splitting up the leaders and slicing them off from the rest of the world would eventually kill off the organization.

The result had been improved protection for the Brotherhood's leadership. No more turf wars, internal wrangling, or power struggles. No more looking over one's shoulder. There was no one there. The leadership was, for all purposes, safe.

It was more difficult to communicate, but not impossible. For instance, when John decided to have his meeting, he sent a note to Bo Borowick. The next day, Bo killed a fellow inmate in the yard. Bo did not know his victim's name. He and the man had never exchanged so much as a glance. Bo stabbed this man through the back, up into the heart in full view of 41 witnesses, including three prison guards. He was confined, charged, and given an attorney. Bo gave the attorney a list of 14 character witnesses, from 14 different prisons around the country. They would all be shipped in for the trial.

"Inside," Alistair Bache said, "blood is currency."

He could hear the line in John's voice. He remembered when John came up with the line, the moment of epiphany, the creative surge it gave him. It was almost like poetry. He could have been a poet. He could have been anything he wanted. Proven by the fact that he was the second most powerful man in the United States of America. He wasn't sure he could take out the president. Sometimes he thought of ways that he could, just in case, just to stay sharp, just to prove that he wasn't second. He was first.

The sky was royal blue, the first wash of light flooding out in front of the sunrise. Alistair watched it, trying to see the color change, but it was too gradual. It wasn't a flash and a headache. Not like last night's dawn of a new day.

He hadn't slept. He'd never tried to go to work without sleeping. He'd had some poor nights when the girls were newborns, but he'd never gone all the way without. He hadn't stayed up all night since college. And even then, it had been pretty rare. He was never one of the guys that had to cram. He was organized. On top of things. Conscientious. He'd never ordered a murder just so he could have a meeting.

Alistair didn't know if he was going to work. Would there be work today? Would anybody do anything today other than peel back through their own new minds, or watch CNN collect a bunch of guess makers and prod them for inane speculation.

They'd probably cancel daycare. If it wasn't already a staff-building day. They seemed to be closed every third day.

Valerie had managed to fall asleep. She talked to her...what? Brain sharer? Ultimate pen pal? *Valerie talked to her new best friend for a half-hour and then dozed off easily,* Alistair thought. *Happily.* Alistair presumed Mi Sung Lu wasn't planning on having Valerie's throat slit.

One of the big reasons for John McCorely's October meeting was the disappearance of one of his chief deputies, Roger Pfeiffer. Nobody disappeared unless the Department of Justice worked real hard at it. They only did that if the guy they were working for now worked for them. John was sure Pfeiffer wanted out of the Brotherhood. He was going to flip on them. And he knew them. He'd made it pretty close to the top.

"Blood in, blood out," John wrote. It was passed around to the rest of the Brotherhood, all holed up in the same transient block at Pelican Bay. They agreed to use all of their resources—and even the resources of rival gangs, if necessary—to put Roger Pfeiffer in the ground.

By rough reckoning, Alistair figured he knew about ten times more about the Brotherhood than Pfeiffer. McCorely had to have him killed, maybe Valerie too, just to be safe.

CHAPTER 11

SULTAN

Sultan bin Abdullah Al-Marzouqi sat at his usual table outside his usual café. It was Friday, not a workday in the Arab world, but more than half the usual patrons were not around, the people he saw every morning during the rest of the week. Without names or stories, they made up his landscape, dotted reds and blues against the white-plaster walls, streaked brown and yellow across the huge expanses of glass that stood in for architecture now—the people made this place familiar and his. Their absence was unwelcome. The sparse streets were not something he ever remembered...

Memory was the devil today.

Sultan had cultivated a group of friends that didn't talk much about current events. Politics, religion, controversy, strife—they were for others, like scuba diving. There were those who loved diving, couldn't get enough of it, and those who had no intention of depriving themselves of the only readily available thing left in the world. All the training and gauging, not to mention the swimming. Scuba was too much trouble. Just like politics. Still, Sultan and his friends refused to be completely ignorant. They kept their eyes open. To keep from wasting time on what some official was lying about, they simply talked of devils.

Every week or two there was a new devil: weather, America, oil capacity. The list was endless variations on the same theme. Sultan was almost happy to have a brand new devil prodding the news, especially one leaving every cleric, ruler, and CEO with his mouth agape.

He sipped his Gowa. Usually he had plain coffee in the morning, today he thought adding cardamom was poetic. This was a blending of two ground ingredients to make one strong but intricate concoction. Everyone was like this today. The world was Gowa. Sultan chuckled to himself.

He was no poet. He was 25, dark haired, dark skinned, contrasted by his bright eyes and smile. Sultan never had any trouble getting a second look from women. 'Chiaroscuro,' one of his friends had said about his face. The unusual friend that had actually paid attention in an art history class, probably under the delusion that it would help him pick up women. 'Women love that effect,' he'd said. Full of shadow, mystery and the hope of truth.

But Sultan was no ladies man. As with most of his friends, he was all chase and no catch. Cruising Corniche, throwing looks, acting like he couldn't be bothered to drive up and down the street all night, and ignoring the fact that he was doing just that.

"I'm very glad you are here," came a voice from behind him. Sultan didn't need to look up to know it was Zayed. He didn't need to turn to know Zayed waved to the waiter, signaling for whatever Sultan was drinking. They did the same thing every morning. The usual.

"Who did you get?" Zayed collapsed into the black iron café chair. Like Sultan, he wore jeans and a silk shirt. "A woman? That would have been spectacular. Can you imagine? The memories of a fine, young—".

"No," Sultan cut him off. He wasn't in the mood for Zayed's musings. Zayed, the Arab Michelin Man to his friends, was given only a miniscule fraction of the paltry attention women gave any man in this city. This reality made his fantasies grander and grittier. He never considered that they should also be proportionally more private.

Not that anything was truly private anymore.

"You will not believe the memories I received," Zayed said. "Please. Try to guess."

"Well, they are not from a woman," Sultan said as if just waking up. "You established that... so... that leaves...

Michael Schumacher. The only person in the world you care about who doesn't have breasts."

"Ah, Schumacher." Zayed's face flashed, like he was simultaneously scared and delighted. "That would be even more spectacular. Do you think you'd get the skills? Do you think whoever got his memories is on the road right now driving 180?"

"Sure, if that person's got a Ferrari. Or even a car. Think about the poor bastard that gets Schumacher's supreme driving prowess and gets into his 1984 Skoda and peels off down some pebbly rut. That person is a stain on the road now. Michael killed that poor bastard. There is more to Michael than the skills."

The waiter brought Zayed his coffee, along with another for Sultan. He could feel its heat over the morning's warming air. The Gowa's heat was moist, like Abu Dhabi's. They swirled in his world together.

"I'm not referring to a person," Zayed said. "You must guess the *kind* of memories I have."

"My friend," Sultan said, "the only time anyone ever says 'you must guess' is when the guessing is futile. You would never say that if I could actually guess correctly. Your game is designed to build drama and I have already had more drama than I can take today." He slapped the table hard, then pointed at Zayed, arm snapped straight. "Tell me your memories!"

A few people looked over. A few did not, too busy with their conversations or buried in their own thoughts.

Zayed smiled. He leaned over the table and his face became serious. "I woke up like everyone, but my memories were sharp. The vision was right before my eyes. I was in a tunnel. It was smooth, like a huge drainpipe, and I was falling upwards through it, toward this wonderful light. My name was Lu and I was dead."

Zayed collapsed again, the story having taken every speck of air in his lungs, as walking here had, as everything did for him.

"I traded memories with a dying man," he continued. "A man in the process of dying."

"That is more interesting than I would have guessed."

"It was peaceful. Lu welcomed it. There would be no more pain or sadness. The light was so beautiful, but not like a woman."

"Certainly not."

"It was a beauty different from anything I have ever seen."

"You've never been dead before."

"You mock?"

Sultan smiled. "No. It's just you, all dreamy. You should carry an armload of flowers."

"You mock. You mock death."

"I don't mock death or you or anything. I just don't understand. How could I, right?"

"This is a remarkable thing—to be that close to death. I saw the door opening. I remember dying as if I had done it myself. The vision was just like everyone always says. A beacon beckoning me forward...astonishing. I will assume you did not have an experience that changed your life."

Sultan looked up at the skyline. Slabs of gold and ebony stabbing pure blue. Jutting blocks of sand and stone. Spearheads of steel. The noise of the day had started— honks, squeals, jackhammers, motors, and motion. It was usual. Like he said he wanted. The usual.

"I don't know," Sultan said.

"What?" Zayed had lost the thread.

"My memories." Sultan closed his eyes. "I don't know what they are. I don't know what they mean."

Zayed stared at his friend. A group of men passed, chatting loudly about expected chaos in the markets.

"So," Zayed said, "you're sure you didn't get a woman?"

CHAPTER 12

SUSAN

"This is the opposite of brainwashing," Larry said. Dr. Lawrence Edelburg from Johns Hopkins. Susan knew of him, but had never met him. He looked a little like Groucho Marx so she pictured Groucho in a leisure suit— her mnemonic device for anyone named Larry, as in leisure suit Larry—playing hopscotch. Now, whenever she looked at the Groucho guy, she'd recall her mental caricature and remember Larry from Hopkins.

"What do you call the opposite of brainwashing?" he went on. "Brain contamination? Brain pollution?"

"A dirty brain?" Commander Ornell Reilly, from the National Naval Medical Center. Thomas Jefferson paddling —'oaring'— an aircraft carrier.

"I already had a dirty brain. Nothing was going to fix that." Both men laughed.

Susan forced a smile. She wasn't ready for ice-breaking boy jokes. Normally, she would politely pretend. She did not consider herself adept at mingling and fitting in. She was better at blending in with the wallpaper and tonight that was not an option.

They were in a large conference room. Two technicians played with video conferencing capabilities on the pretense that the world's telecommunications systems were going to settle down and start working right again. The table was spread with coffee and individually wrapped Danish, exactly the wrong refreshments for the health conscious and the tired, so naturally they were all gobbling the stuff up.

Susan turned to Joe. "Who else are we waiting for?"

"Why are we waiting at all?" Larry said. "Let's get down to business. What do we need to accomplish here? What's the goal?"

He was right, of course. Susan was leaning back on old habits. This was not a meeting or a conference. This was a task force. She had never served on one before. She had no idea if there was any protocol at all. With two high-achieving alpha males in the room, she decided to apply force to the task.

"Let's list what we know."

"It ain't much," Ornell said.

"It ain't nothing, either," Susan replied.

"Good evening everyone." Adam Covensievic. Susan recognized the whiny voice before she even looked up. Another neurologist, she'd known him for years. He was smart and knew it, and wanted you to know it, too. Nobody likes a know-it-all, Grammie always said, followed by jutting eyebrows. Gepetto, without the mustache, in a fig leaf. He worked here at the institutes. She didn't need the mnemonic device, but she enjoyed it.

"Hello, Adam," she said. Another white male. This was not her scene.

"We need to limn the parameters of the event. My first inclination is that some kind of transference between the hippocampus or the prefrontal cortex, or perhaps even both, of two parties, across distance has occurred."

"Why limit it to those areas?" Larry asked.

"Yeah," Ornell agreed. "Why not the kit *and* the caboodle."

"Subjects have received memories, both long-term and short-term."

"And not skill?" Larry cut in. "Have we determined that?"

Ornell spoke up. "There's been some work in mirror cells that may be applicable."

"Maybe, could be, who knows." Larry shrugged.

Adam sat down. "There is no mechanism for extracranial stimulation that can account for the transference, admittedly. However, I can imagine a combination of light and sound that might somehow—"

"What?" Susan said. "Make us all mind readers?"

"Certainly not." Adam's lips pressed into a line. "Let's start with what we know. Joe, get a marker. Let's make a list."

Joe took a box and stood by the gleaming white dry-erase board. Susan sat with her back to it. She wanted to stay in everyone's focus.

"According to television reports—"

"Oh," Adam chirped. "Is that how we're going to run things? Based on television?"

"Yes," Susan returned. "Television news adumbrates stories. I expect nothing more. For the moment we have nothing more."

"Adumbrates," Larry repeated. "I've got two people in my head now, and neither one of them knows that word."

"Lieutenant," Ornell yapped. "We're going to need a dictionary in here."

To Susan's surprise, Joe set the markers on the board's edge and started for the door.

"Later, Joe," she said. The men snickered. Susan got just a tiny bit pissed off, which was exactly the way she worked best.

"At approximately 10:23 local time, this evening, I received someone else's memories," Susan started. "The event seems to have happened to people all over the globe and about the same time. What else do we know?"

Ornell's face became serious. "In many cases, it appears subjects have traded memories. I get yours, you get mine."

"With no loss," Adam added. "I have yet to hear of any memory loss. Speaking personally, I now have two complete sets of memories."

"That's the case with everybody I talked to." Susan nodded. "Has anyone encountered, or heard of someone who did not experience a memory event tonight?"

The doctors shook their heads. Susan looked back at Joe, who shook his head as well.

"I have not spoken with a large number of people tonight," Ornell said.

"Me, neither," Susan agreed. "That gives us our first question. Joe, put this up: Pervasiveness."

"Or perversiveness." Larry snickered. "That might be more apropos."

"Severity should be next," Susan continued. "Was everyone affected to the same degree?"

"I'll tell you one thing." Larry snickered again. "Tonight is really going to screw up that 'Six Degrees of Kevin Bacon' game."

"I wish I shared your humor," Susan said. "I haven't been able to make a joke since the secretary said the president was waiting for us."

"Au contraire, Dr. Grove." Larry's face darkened. "Trying to bring order to this chaos is the biggest joke of all. There is no way in hell this group is going to find any answers. We're pushing rocks up a hill. Each of us. That's all were doing. I'm here because a couple of marines brought me, not because I thought I was going to do anything productive tonight. We should call this Project Sisyphus."

"We all help the sun cross the sky," Susan said. "It is not our place to know how or why."

She hadn't wanted that to get out. It wasn't from her. It did, however, shut up everyone in the room.

CHAPTER 13

SULTAN

Sultan lived with his family in a villa at Al-Maqtah Bridge. It was a big, solid house from a big solid family, descended from one of the sixteen original tribes of the Bani Yas that came out of the Liwa Oasis. He would be a fool to leave the house before he had to, and so he had developed his own semi-private suite within the complex. If asked how he liked to spend his time, Sultan would say 'getting together with friends, sharing a meal, and talking about the way of the world.' Given a choice, however, on any given day, Sultan would place himself before his 42-inch LED screen and play his Playstation.

Today, none of that was working. He had no interest in friends or video games. He sat outside on a teak lounge chair, in the shade of an enormous palm tree, trying to feel through what was inside him. He had received something early this morning, but it was not a full catalog of recollections like everyone yammered about on the news.

His sister Anisah rounded the corner of the patio and stopped. Two years his junior, she was of such a build, with hair of such a length, and possessing a wit so keen that he had never allowed her to meet even one of his many friends. And never would, if he could manage it.

"I'm surprised to see you." Anisah approached.

"I'm surprised to see you." Sultan rolled onto his side to face her. "Out pondering new memories?"

"I want a cigarette so bad I could kill." Anisah sliced the air with an imaginary sword.

Sultan's eyes opened to their full amount, for the first time that day.

She stood, tapping one foot. "I share memories with a truck driver named Umberto who smokes about 45 cigarettes a day. Every second I feel I'm forgetting something. I look for the cigarette that should be burning in my hand or the truck's ashtray. It is insane. I want a smoke just to even out. To get back to normal. They keep pulling at my brain."

"You know how to drive a truck now." Sultan kept a straight face. "That could be helpful someday."

"I know all the roads from Rome to Bilbao, too. It's not worth it. I need a cigarette."

"I wonder if Umberto got a healthy dose of your *hadith*? I wonder if right now he is not pulled over to the side of a mountain road cursing you for the guilt you've given him. He cries because he knows paradise will be denied him."

Anisah shook her head. "He's Catholic with three girlfriends in two countries. Tobacco is the least of his problems."

"I see."

"I thought walking might take my mind off the cigarettes, but here I am talking about them even more. Did I tell you I was going insane?"

"You didn't need to."

"I am now fluent in Spanish and Italian, though I suspect they are not the dialects that might land me a job in foreign service."

"You learned these languages from a truck driver?"

"Yes."

"Then you are probably right." Sultan smirked. "Still, it does open up new vacation possibilities for you. I imagine you now know good places to eat."

"Not quite," Anisah said. "Umberto can't go two days without eating some form of pork. He picks his restaurants accordingly."

"Not a good match for you."

"No." Anisah reclined and crossed her legs. "What about you? How is your match?"

He's hot, hungry, thirsty, numb. He doesn't want to think. He spends his days desperately struggling to keep his short-term memory separate from his long. Remember nothing. Think nothing. Just tie. Keep tying.

"Are you all right?" Anisah asked. She moved toward Sultan, arms out like she thought she might have to catch him.

"The right question," he mumbled. "Some memories came with the right question. How is he?"

"You don't look well."

"It's him. I remembered being him. He's weak."

Sultan stood. He jumped around and stretched his arms. He needed his blood to flow. He needed to feel all his muscles stretch and squeeze. His body remembered being cramped, tight, yearning to spring and run. It was the big memory, stronger than his name or age or location.

Remembering how to live was the most important thought in his head. The boy with whom he shared memories wanted to live, but he didn't think it possible for much longer.

CHAPTER 14

SUSAN

Adam's phone buzzed. Everyone jumped. It buzzed twice more before he thought of answering it.

"Hello...I guess it's finally working...Yes...Of course. I'm sitting at the table right now with the best and brightest... Heading the president's task force investigating the event."

Adam turned away from the group. He listened to his phone, got up, and walked to the door. "Certainly. Put me on. It's the least I can do."

Susan, Larry, and Ornell looked at each other.

"Adam," Susan said.

Adam turned, saying nothing.

"May I ask to whom you're speaking?"

Adam looked at Susan and held up one index finger. "Mmmm."

"I don't mean to be rude." Susan used her stern voice.

"Excuse me," Adam said into the phone. He pressed it to his chest. "It's MSNBC. They want to do a phone interview."

"Hang up," Susan said.

Adam looked insulted. "I'll only be a few minutes."

"Please, Adam. Hang up."

"This won't take long."

"It's not about the time. Hang up."

Adam put the phone back to his ear. "I'm sorry. Just a moment more."

"This is non-negotiable." Susan tried to keep her voice even. She was tired. They were all tired. 'Fried,' her younger staff members always said. She had always liked the truth in that phrase.

Adam again put the phone to his chest. "With all due respect, Susan, I think this is my business."

"Lieutenant Scott," Susan said. "I hate to put you in the middle of this, but could you confiscate the doctor's phone."

Joe stood. He didn't walk over right away.

"You're kidding me, right?" Adam's lip curled on the left side.

"As I said before, the humor's gone out of me."

Adam stared into Susan's eyes. She could see the muscles in his jaw pulsating, like he was trying to bite through a rubber band.

She had taken a shortcut once, near the village. Antonio had never taken this path before, but it was a sunny day at the height of the rainy season. A day when everyone smiled. The two men with machetes were not smiling. They had come out of the brush so quietly that, at first, Antonio thought they were from some other world. The man before him had sweat under his nose. The one behind him shifted his weight from foot to foot, as though the ground were too hot. They were nervous like men, not spirits.

"Your sack and your money," the first one said.

"Your grandfather's watch," Antonio said.

They stared each other in the eyes.

Adam returned the phone to his ear.

"I cannot talk right now. Sorry for the inconvenience." He pressed the 'end' button.

Susan titled her head just a little, like a reasonably proud third-grade teacher. "MSNBC?"

"Does it matter?" Adam barely moved his mouth.

"We talk to the president first. That's our duty."

"I don't recall signing anything."

"It wasn't necessary," Susan said. "Not for any of us. You work for the institutes. It's a given."

"I hope you're enjoying your moment at the top."

Susan smiled slightly. "Do you know why the secretary asked me to head up this auspicious group?"

Adam gave her a quick scan. "Because you look so...
correct."

Susan smiled fully. That hadn't taken long. Sometimes
it took years for reverse discrimination resentments to
surface. Sometimes they never did. Adam's must have been
bubbling up from before to get to the top so quickly. She
was glad. Now that the trouble was at the top, it could be
popped.

"No," Susan said. "The secretary picked me because I'm
an asshole. He needs recommendations—now! I don't mind
getting—or giving—a few black eyes to see things done.
Your one of the smartest people I know, Adam. I hope you
can sit down and work with us."

CHAPTER 15

NIVEN

Niven Burgess gave himself the name. Israel Goldstein simply wasn't what he wanted. Izzy, they called him growing up, like he was one of Captain Kangaroo's puppets. It was not a name for a prince of New York, a jet-setting trendsetter, an ad man. He picked his favorite actor and his favorite writer and forged a new life from the names they donated.

Niven was tall, and fit, with a slightly feminine chin and cheekbone combo that a certain kind of woman (and man for that matter, though of lesser interest to him) found irresistible. He'd let the gray hair and crow's-feet flourish. They, too, seemed to be a hit with a specific kind of woman he had no trouble bumping into at the various shoots, openings, and outings at which he found himself. And if the attention waned in any way, if he felt the chill of someone cooler than him within 25 feet, he adjusted: clothes, hair color, lip size. After changing your identity, everything else was giving candy to a baby. He changed his look, his locale, his body (when and where possible), and his friends. He was 59 and there was no changing that.

Being an art director at a major international advertising agency was the best thing Niven could imagine being. Sure, people admired astronauts and threw themselves at rock stars, but when it came to power, glory, and sex, without the security risks of fame, his job was the greatest in the world. That meant holding onto it was a second job all in itself. When asked what kind of work he did, he often joked that he worked at keeping his job. Every two months brought someone fresher, brighter, and intolerably younger snapping up behind him, biting, clawing, and kissing whatever it took to knock him off his perch. Niven remembered cutting Rubylith and layering color separations. He remembered running copy to typesetters, trimming boarder tape with an X-ACTO knife, and calling for stats "stat!" He had no idea what a podcast was and didn't really want to learn. But if he didn't learn, if he didn't force his attentions down into the nascent gunk forever brewing in the clubs, schools, and street corners of the world, he'd be slid to the side, into the realm of 'new responsibilities', more of a 'management role', keeping the agency on the 'right course' that no longer involved choosing models, scouting locations, and stating that this was the right shade of blue because he said it was the right shade of blue.

On May 5 he was still ahead of the yips and yaps of youth, working late to secure his berth and fare. Sometimes ideas flew in, ephemeral butterflies, vibrant, weightless, suddenly there tickling your brain. Other times, ideas came like wine gushing from rocks. On May 5, tumblers in his head crushed together, grinding out a trickle of nothing. If this went on too long, a day or three, it became dangerous. The young guys could do it all night. They still had dreams to mine. Worry, worn to panic, made the rocks of Niven's thoughts seize, and yield nothing.

His plan was seasoned cunning over kiddy zest. He had simply decided to conceal the fact that Eden/FCJ was purchasing Biobrex. He knew he could keep it a secret for three full days, giving him plenty of time to get out front, have a few ideas in the hopper before the babies had scratched the sleepy-sand from their eyes. Getting the jump on the juniors. It was a good plan, too, provided he actually came up with a couple of innovative, viable approaches to market their premier drug.

For three days now the stones in his head ground together, craggy on craggy, huffing and coughing, producing...mental dust. This had happened to him many times in the past. It was the way of imagination. Staring at the blank page was always the most terrifying and electrifying part of the job. The nightmare that this block was the final one—that this time no idea would swoosh in at the last minute and swing him to the other side of the chasm—was as real as the night sky. It was getting late, he was getting tired, and this was going to be the deadline he missed.

And then, at 10:23 PM he had an epiphany. A whole new way of looking at the brand and its ties to the market and...and...and....

They were coming out of Tuoyaozi a few minutes behind schedule. Ming Lin hated being behind schedule. It was a matter of personal pride, and pride in his locomotive. It was old, dirty, and ran on steam, but it was still a loyal workhorse, of great value to the People.

Niven's idea was gone. It had been alighting on the outer edge of his brain. One third of a second more and Niven would have wrapped himself around it and drawn it full into his consciousness. Now, he could not recall it. He could recall that Engine 011 was pulling eight empty wagons to a coal mine 74 kilometers from Huanan, but he had lost that idea that would preserve, for at least another few months, his job.

Huanan, in the People's Republic of China. A memory, recent, with nothing else attached. No, not true. Niven could hear the click-clack of the train wheels skimming the rails. He could hear the puff of the locomotive, smell the oil—lubricant levels were fine—and the burning coal. He could smell the spring air, moist and alive. Ming could tell the approximate date by smell alone, though feeling the temperature and hearing the birds helped. And he could use their help, because his eyes never offered any.

CHAPTER 16

SUSAN

"We need more data," Ornell said. "I haven't seen results from a single test."

"We need more of everything." Larry sat as low in his chair as his spine would allow. "This is the most monumental event in human history. We can't digest it and regurgitate some hypothesis in a couple of hours."

"I'm not so sure." Adam scribbled away on his yellow legal pad. "Who's to say this is the most monumental event in our history? Who's to say it didn't happen before, perhaps thousands of years ago? There are quantum leaps in human evolution for which we've never been able to fully account. We may have just lived through one."

Larry tossed his hands up. "You're right. Who's to say? But that's my point. What are we even doing here? Jumping because the president said jump?"

"Yes." Ornell's voice punched.

Susan heard his voice echo across Lake Atitlan. Legend says that once you taste the water you never want to leave. Antonio was certain this was true, though he had never tested the rule. He never left. He frequently traveled around its perimeter and crisscrossed the surface, visiting every town in the vicinity, but he had, in his whole life, never been more than a day's walk from its shore.

A gringo told Antonio that a volcano had formed the lake. It was a bowl set between three other volcanoes. The ash, lava, and water made the area around Atitlan lush. The mountains made the winds and weather calm. It was, the gringo said, a secret paradise. Antonio laughed. It had not been a secret to him and his father and his father's fathers going back to the beginning of people.

Atitlan was the bellybutton of the world.

"It's difficult, isn't it?" Joe whispered.

"What?" Susan twitched. Her mind came back to the room.

"Staying out of your new memories," Joe went on. "It's like somebody gave me a book I can't put down."

"You're right." Susan sat up. "That is what we should be concentrating on. Our collective lack of concentration." Susan slapped her hand on the table. "Doctors, the country doesn't need speculation. It needs first aid."

"Ha," Larry kicked his head back. "That's the first good idea I've heard all night. Put your feet up and get a blanket. We're all in shock."

Susan nodded, but didn't smile. "You're right. We are. And that's what we need to tell the president: not our unfounded theories about what happened, but good prognosis about what is going to happen."

She got up and stood in front of the dry-erase board. She erased everything on it, then she picked up a pen.

"Distraction," she said. "Impaired ability to focus. Anger. Stress. Fear. What else? What else can we expect from people?"

"They're going to call in sick," Ornell said. "By the millions."

"Good," Larry added. "We don't want anybody operating heavy machinery right now."

Adam said, "We need to set up a study of the phenomenon. The president could order a Manhattan Project-like body to direct and oversee—"

Susan cut in. "Triage, Adam. Right now the nation is hemorrhaging. Hemorrhaging attention. We need to apply a tourniquet. I think we should get out in front of the symptoms, so much as we can anticipate."

Ornell nodded. "Give him our best guess at what tomorrow's going to look like."

"Exactly," Susan said. "Then let him decide if we get a national sick day."

CHAPTER 17

CINDY

Cindy woke in the front seat of her truck. One of those jerk and gasp wake-ups, in that 'where the fuck am I after too many beers and a boy with one thing on his mind' haze. She'd only slept with eight guys in her life, but five of them had no last names that she could remember. Two of them, no names at all. She could remember smiles. That was her thing. Nice teeth, full lips, that curve like the cuts in a good guitar. This morning was one of those clammy-skin, dry-mouth, 'I've got to straighten myself out' mornings, with a bone stiff neck on top.

It came back to her in a bunch of choppy scenes, like a movie preview, except she had just lived through it. Flipping Brad. Training in the Swiss Army. Taking Brad's pick-up and driving to Lorna's. All the lights. Everyone in the freakin' world was awake. Lorna's boyfriend's car sat dark in her driveway. Cindy decided she needed a little peace, to sort things out. She went to the lake, knowing all the good, secluded spots a girl might want to hide a full-size Ford F-150. The radio was busting with special reports. The whole world was buzzing. It was, she decided, the safest night ever to be out. Every lunatic, strangler, and asshole was occupied.

Cindy drove down a twin-rut access road, up and under and between scrub and trees, finally parking with a nice view of still, little Bailey Lake. This was the first time she'd ever seen it without someone trying to put his hand up her shirt. She was all wild inside, pumped up from beating Brad and taking off. Florens filled her mind, his first time with a girl was by a lake a lot like this one, but with mountains on the other side. They had made a parachute jump together a few weeks later. What a rush. She could feel it in her in stomach. She was never getting to sleep. Never...

Now she dug her fingers into her neck muscles, trying to pull them apart, separate the knots, just like you do with long hair all tangled from a crazy night before.

Crazy was right. She needed coffee. And a shower. In that order. There was only one place to go, but it was about the last place she wanted to be.

Cindy's mom lived in a tiny yellow house on big piece of property. It had been in the family for two generations. She loved the sound of the gravel popping under the tires as she rolled up the long eyelash of a driveway. No idea why she liked the popping. She'd driven over miles of stone just like it. This sound sounded different, though. It sounded like coming home from a drive-in, way past bedtime and faking sleep so Daddy had to carry you into the house.

She got out of the truck and walked toward the front door.

"Hold it!"

Cindy followed the voice to the front window. Two inches of a rifle barrel pointed in her general direction.

"Cut the crap, Wendell." Cindy pushed through the front door.

Mom—Eileen, as she preferred to be called in the company of other people, particularly men, single and straight —was not yet 50 and doing her best to look like Cindy's slightly older sister. Most of the time she did a pretty decent job of it, too. Most of the time did not include this morning.

Eileen hung over the scuffed kitchen table, hands locked around a steaming mug, stiff blonde hair ready to fall right out of her head. Her eyes reminded Cindy of catfish mouths: all wet, red, dark, and dead.

"Sweet girl," Eileen said in shaky, funeral voice. "How you doin' sweet girl?"

"Sorry 'bout the greetin'." Wendell had dug himself into an armchair by the window. He'd scooted the TV out, so he could watch both that and the front of the house by turning his head a tad. His old wooden Enfield crossed his lap, the canvas strap drooping around his knees. The rifle didn't look like much, but Cindy knew better. The gun was just like his beat up truck with its perfectly tuned engine, which was just like him. A sleeper. He wanted no one to know what he was like inside.

Somebody knew the real Wendell now, Cindy thought to herself.

"Come over here." Eileen put her arms out. Cindy strolled over and gave her a brief hug, then bee-lined to the Mr. Coffee.

"Rough night?" Cindy asked.

"Isn't this terrible? It's like the world's comin' to a end."

"I wouldn't go that far."

"This ain't right," Wendell said.

"No." Cindy poured herself some coffee. "But I wouldn't go all Chicken Little just yet."

Eileen reached for her coffee mug and pushed it with her fingers. She yelped, started crying, face disappearing under a hay bale of hair.

"There she goes again." Wendell watched the TV.

"What's wrong?" Cindy sat down.

"She swapped with a lefty," Wendell said. "Says she can't use her hands right. Every time she tries to grab something she starts to cry. She can't walk too good, neither."

Cindy reached across the table and placed the mug in her mother's hands. "It's going to be fine. It's memories, is all."

"Oh no, Cin." Eileen's face cut through her hair. "Do you know who you are? *Usted le conoce que usted es? Dos personas. Dos personas!*"

"What's that?" Cindy asked. "At the end there?"

"Spanish," Wendell answered. "She does it from time to time."

Eileen's eyes gasped, taking in air, Cindy thought. Not sights. She was seeing something else, from somewhere else, and not using her eyes to do it. Cindy watched her mother's hands shake the mug to her lips and pinch off milky coffee close to the rim. It was a careful sip, as if she'd never tried it before, or thought it might be too hot, or didn't have the whole idea what she was doing.

Cindy had decided years ago her mother was not the brightest bulb on the string. She never held that against her. She was no rocket surgeon herself. The respect she'd managed to maintain for the woman, through the loud divorce, lack of cash and long line of shitty boyfriends came from her cunning. 'Eileen was crafty,' Cindy always said. You had to give her that. She never knew exactly what she wanted, but she knew how to get it.

Cindy's eyes started to flood. This creature on the other side of the table was not the fox that had raised her. This wasn't her home and Wendell was not any part of her family. Those facts rumbled around under Cindy, like she was building toward her own, personal earthquake. A person quake. She was going to crack in two and crumble to nothing there at the fake-oak dinette. And Mom/Eileen couldn't see it. She wasn't going to hug her together. Cindy was all coming apart.

"Who the fuck is Elmo?" Wendell hollered to Cindy.

Cindy stopped and looked at him. "Elmo?"

"Elmo." He adjusted the rifle on his lap. "Some fuzzy red thing, looks like a bathmat in a whore house."

"You don't know who Elmo is?"

"Would I be askin' if I knew?"

"Why are you askin'?"

"I keep getting these flashes of it. I want to know where it is. It seems though everybody in the world should know about it. But I don't. It some dog toy? Son-of-a-bitch!" Wendell sat up, gripping the gun. "You think I swapped minds with a dog?"

Cindy laughed. Hard. Not keeping her breath.

"What's so funny?" Wendell eased back into the arm-chair. "This ain't funny?"

Eileen sniffled. Cindy realized she was slowly and silently weeping behind the blonde curtain.

"You hear of anybody swappin' with a dog?" Cindy asked.

"Not yet," Wendell went back to watching the TV. "But these bastards don't know shit."

CHAPTER 18

ALISTAIR

Wherever Alistair went he was struck by the blankness of the faces he saw. Everyone looked drugged, like they'd done a big hit of something stupefying and they weren't sure the stuff was any good. Daycare was open. The kids were slow and quiet. It reminded him of the day after daylight savings went into effect, only worse.

Lucy and Rebecca seemed fine. They got up, watched their cartoon, ate waffles, and allowed dressing and brushing. There was not as much gabbing as usual. There was no weeping, either. Alistair and Valerie discussed keeping the girls home, staying home themselves, then they decided striving for typical might be best. Give the girls their routine.

People drove more slowly. They lingered at lights. Allowed others to merge. It wasn't so much that there was less traffic, like on a holiday—it was the lackadaisical maneuvering. No one was in a hurry.

He made it to his desk without exchanging a word with anyone. Crazy. The single biggest communication event in human history and the end result was silence.

Alistair drew up bus routes for a living, creating the most cost- and time-efficient ways of getting between two points. It was, he constantly defended, interesting and challenging. Like a video game. His real love. He had gone to school to learn how to program computers with the goal of authoring video games, but ended up at the transit authority. Not that it mattered today. There was simply no way to pay attention to games, trains or buses. His brain was full of all kinds of new, unsorted information. He had to take some time, fit fragments of memory into their proper holes, and then try to move on with his life.

For as long as he had one. That was the real problem. He felt like there was an invisible, man-eating tiger loose on the floor. He couldn't see it, hear it, or smell it, but he knew it was there, watching him, waiting for the moment when his neck was stretched just far enough to allow the perfect, bone-snapping bite.

Fear was Alistair's new background noise. He had no annoying Wiggles songs repeating in his head. He had no thoughts that he'd forgotten to lock the front door or turn off the back burner. Behind every conscious thought was sparkling black fear.

John McCorely read and wrote in Gaelic. He'd learned it as thoroughly as books would allow—secretly infuriated that he was unsure about some pronunciations. He'd never heard the language. Audio equipment was denied him. He was confident that he knew the language better than any scholar on the planet, though always with the fear that if he actually went to a conference, to fucking blow the minds of the tweed heads, they'd laugh at the way he said everything.

Other chiefs in the Brotherhood had been required to learn Gaelic as well. It was a great code because the Oxford University Press sold the codebooks through any bookstore, and the piles of puss that hired their slabs of bacon brother-in-laws into the Department of Corrections could never read a word of it.

He'd mix up some invisible ink, using mashed potatoes or rice or his own urine if there was nothing starchy in the day's meal. Scrape the wax off his milk carton, write on the paper underneath the wax, and send it back to the kitchen. Kitchen staff knew to collect anything he tossed out and pass it on to other Brotherhood officers. The message would be discovered, translated, and then enacted. Whatever it was, without question.

John now knew everything there was to know about Alistair. Addresses, phone numbers, all that stuff was easy.

How and when he went about his mornings. Where he parked. How to get into his house without a key, where he hung his belts, or kept his kitchen knives and the rusty machete he used to clear wild raspberry bushes from near the swing set. John could provide very specific instructions about the quickest and least risky way to kill Alistair Bache.

Just like he'd done yesterday, for Joshua Parks, the lawyer with the U.S. Department of Justice.

Alistair got a whole new kind of stomachache, like everything inside had been ratcheted tightly. There was a slight chance that John didn't feel the need to have Alistair killed just yet. Contacting Joshua Parks, interfering with John McCorely's orders, would make that chance zero. Alistair was, in fact, no threat to Aryan Brotherhood if he kept his mouth shut and if no one ever discovered he was John McCorely's Other.

Calling the Department of Justice would not be the best step in ensuring the latter. They would absolutely fall in love with Alistair. All the names he knew, the codes, the evidence buried to be used just in case. They couldn't know who he was.

Did he need to warn Joshua Parks? The guy had to know he was in trouble, right? You didn't laugh at an animal like John and expect to keep all your fingers and toes. Joshua Parks, 28 years old, top of the world, top of his game. John was going to have that grin sliced off his face.

Joshua had no idea. Alistair knew that like he knew everything else. The young man was just that. A young man. Smart, but inexperienced. He might actually be dead already.

Probably not. Today, nobody was doing anything they were supposed to do. Not even the Aryan Brotherhood. Today would be titled for history as the great day of distraction.

Distraction and fear.

Pelican Bay was in lockdown. Nobody came out of their cells. That was standard procedure. John knew standard procedure better than the warden.

Alistair stared at his phone. *Call United States Attorney's Office, Northern District of California,* he thought to himself. Then tell Joshua Parks he's about to be killed. Get in the mix. Forget the fact that you've never done anything like this before. That you have no skill base. How far do you get in a game you've never played before? No, how far do you get in a new game, on a new system, with a controller you've never touched before in your life?

Never in his whole life had Alistair been in a fight. John must be sitting in his baby-blue cell, looking back into his new memories, roaring in laughter. To be yoked to a light, passive, almost-invisible man. An opposite in kind. Both white, both from the Rust-Oleum-painted American suburbs of cars and trucks and things that go. And yet so far, far apart.

Alistair was born and grew up outside Chicago. He had dreamed his way through high school and attended the University of Chicago. He was going to make video games. Cool ones, like Mossgarden, about a fantasy city where weapons aren't allowed. Or Captain Some-Color Man, about an alien probe that visits earth, gets confused by the deluge of electromagnetic signals in the air and becomes a superhero.

All he had to do was move out to California and finagle a job at a game company. Move. Away. Alone. Which he was going to do after he made a little money working at the bus company, programming routes for optimal efficiency. Right after he got married, and Valerie finished school and they traveled a little, stopped wasting money on rent and bought a house.

Lucy was so cute. Two sets of grandparents four minutes away. How can you beat that? No one had to stop working. It was all so easy to make way for Rebecca and a bigger house.

Alistair had never given a man a line of uncut cocaine and watched his heart burst, just so he could move up in a gang.

John must be having the time of his life in that little cell. Laughing at the wimp he now knew so well. The ducking, the hiding, the shrinking back from every

confrontation, verbal, imagined, but never physical—
Alistair was uncannily able to avoid getting anywhere
near those situations. John created them.

The phone was black plastic, dull from palm prints,
coated with fluorescent light. The phone number for the
U.S. Attorney's Office hovered on his computer monitor.
He knew it would stay there as long as the machine had
power, but it so obviously gleamed of electrons that it
couldn't look permanent. It wanted to go. The whole
website looked uncomfortable on his screen.

The Internet ran slowly today. Too much traffic. The
phone lines were taking a beating. Any form of communication was being stretched and plucked, the way they
make fiber optics, oddly enough. Alistair snickered.
Stretched and plucked.

He zoomed around the Internet, finding an anonymous
mail service that was still working and signing up for an
account with a fake name. He used John McCorely's
information. If anyone had the ability to trace the account,
it would all go back to him. He used the account to e-mail
Joshua Parks, hoping the guy wasn't already lying against
his steering wheel with his head in a freezer bag.

"Joshua," Alistair typed. "The Aryan Brotherhood has
decided you should die. The order has been sent. John
McCorely does not like to be laughed at."

Send.

Chapter 19

SUSAN

The secretary wanted the bullet. The most concise list of simple facts Susan could muster. After hours of wrangling the men, wrestling questions, and throwing down a prognosis, the call lasted under two minutes. Exhaustion followed. She had an office with a couch. She didn't care much about Adam. Larry and Ornell she left to Joe. He seemed to want something important to do. Finding them someplace to nap was quickly becoming one of the most important things any of them could possibly do.

She had only been this tired twice before. Once, pulling an ER rotation at Montefiore Medical Center in the Bronx. 36 hours of broken limbs, gunshot wounds, stabbings, and general lack of respect for one's own or anyone else's body. Susan could have stopped after 24 hours. It was inhumane to ask her to go another 12. Two shifts were nothing, though. All the boys racked up two shifts without a groan. Three, it was said, separated the men from the boys. Susan was not one of the boys.

The second time was a cleansing ritual at the entrance to the underworld. Dusk 'till dawn. The only time Antonio stopped singing his prayers was to take a sip of *aquieltine*. It was painful near the end. The spirits try hardest to stay, just before they go. The worst of them can spin your brain like a top. Only the song keeps your own spirit from spiraling off to another world.

Antonio had been a fisherman first. Then his stomach became twisted. Everything he ate gave him great pain as it tried to find a path through his body. The right path had been turned and turned again. The shaman said he had been chosen by the *nuwals*—the spirits of their ancestors—to the keep the holy days. The pain in his gut was their calling. Only by becoming an *aja ij* would the paths be set right.

The Maya have two calendars. One is 365 days. The world shares that calendar. The other is 260 days. This calendar the world does not share. Antonio had known some of the days. As an *aja ij*, he had to learn them all. Not just the names, but the meanings and the things that must be done on those days. This was taught to him by another *aja ij*.

Antonio knew he had learned well, because the pain went away.

Susan sat up on her couch. The gray tweed covering grabbed at her jogging pants and bunched the fabric in odd places.

"Gastro enteritis," she said. The man had changed his life because of a little tummy bug. A snippet of food poisoning that everyone on the planet's probably gotten at least twice. What a waste.

It didn't feel like a waste. None of Antonio's memories were flavored by frustration or helplessness or regret. They seemed...Susan searched for the right word...happy? Three sets of clothes. A house no bigger than her garage. A dead wife. A dead dog. Happy? Happy with all that mumbo-jumbo?

She needed sleep. Sleep wanted nothing to do with her.

She needed answers much more. Data, hypotheses, findings, new tests—she wasn't going to get any of those things making static electricity on her crummy couch.

The president had something to think about, and more importantly, something to do. In a crisis, people liked having things to do. Grammie always cooked. Susan made lists. She was going to start a mental one right now.

Susan's new first concern was getting beyond the moment. The president was doing a morning press conference. He was going to say he had the best minds in the country working on this, referring to her. That was a whole new kind of pressure. What she felt in school, being the only woman of color in her class; what she felt at those department meetings with all the gray-haired golfers thinking they'd have her place at the head of the table if the board of directors didn't value diversity over merit; what she felt when she took her job knowing she'd have to take money from a project that might save the lives of 100 babies, to save the lives of 102 others. All of that was in her drawer. Just tools for using. A new set of eyes was upon her and she figured this time it was made up of a couple billion.

To say she was used to that kind of pressure would have been a bold lie. No one was used to this. She was fairly certain she could not handle it. She had thought once— foolishly, she now realized—that she been through it all. She had reached her plateau. As tough as the job at the institutes could be sometimes, she had made it. She didn't want to make anything new.

Of course, she could hear Grammie in the back of her head saying, 'What them bowls in the cupboard for if you ain't gonna make somethin' good? The good Lord gave you a big ol' head, you better keep it up.'

Nuwals, Antonio called them. The spirits of your ancestors. They came and spoke to you when you needed them. They offered guidance when the path twisted or grew thick with fog. Susan didn't believe in any spirits. She knew Grammie so well, her memory could construct a reasonable interior dialogue. No ghosts.

Antonio didn't know any better. He didn't know enough science not to believe in the supernatural. Sure, it seemed like Grammie had been here, scolding Susan's tired, muddled head. That was the immense power of the human brain, not the queer tendrils of the netherworld.

"Gets you the same thing anyway," Susan made a quick half-laugh.

The president—the whole world—wanted to know what had happened last night. The guesses were already leaking onto the airwaves. As the president asked for calm, Susan decided to stir things up.

At 7:06 in the morning, Susan fired all the members of her task force. They'd given her a good six hours, but it was time to move on.

CHAPTER 20

NIVEN

New Yorkers were interesting people. A global event occurs unlike any other in the records of mankind, and they show up for work the next day, acting like they'd all hit the same traffic. Blinding mind swaps were not enough to keep Niven's creative team from showing up and getting down to work. This did not surprise him. They'd all been through plane-plunges, blackouts, anthrax scares, and, more ominous but less newsworthy, daily life in an over-populated, towering metropolis. New memories left you with all your limbs, senses, and family. This incident was then, by that bar, no big deal.

Not all New Yorkers plowed through their Friday morning as usual. Niven noticed significantly fewer people on the subway and on the street. Fridays tended to get a little light, especially as the weather got nicer. Today's bright blue sky and warm draft would have been enough to make some play hooky. This crowd was thinner still. More than likely, people had stayed up all night watching the news. This was great for his clients on CNN, as long as they were running spots. In the hours after 9/11 the networks had suspended advertising, pushing Niven out of what was, prior to last night, the biggest event in recent memory.

Recent memory took on a new meaning this morning. Coal trains. Small gauge. Someone named Ming worked on the little things—the locomotives themselves didn't' feel much bigger than a stretch limo—as an inspector. He inspected parts, rails, footings, and ballast, all carefully and efficiently, using his touch, hearing, smell, and, on rare occasion, taste. Niven received no memories of what anything looked like. Impressions. Mental models. Intricate touch maps and audio samples of the way objects should sound when stuck with a small steel bar. He had no memory of what any item associated with a Chinese railway looked like.

Ming was 48, in great shape, and blind. He worked on the Huanan Coal Railway without the use of sight. Amazing and irritating. Niven found his memories distracting. Every change in grade was a sweet challenge. Every trip brought in on time was a reason to celebrate, quietly, to himself. The damn subway ride triggered annoying comparisons with every step.

None of the memories were the one he wanted. The Idea—the big juicy one he'd had for establishing dominion over the Biobrex campaign. He'd fumbled great ideas in the past. Usually, it was a matter of rethinking your steps. Work the brain down the same avenues and you'd find the lost idea, just like a dropped glove. Not this time. The map of his brain had changed. *It was*, Niven thought, *like returning to your hometown after a massive development boom*. The place was now twice as large as you remembered. The old streets were there, along with all kinds of new ones. The simple act of searching his own brain became grueling.

There should have been a natural benefit. It was sounding on the news like people around the world were pairing up. Unexplainable mental yokes, clamping two people together. If this was true, if Ming had all his memories, he should have gotten the big Idea. Niven wanted to call him, but the man had no phone. He was nowhere near a phone. Later today Niven could call the coal station and get a message to him, but he was several hours, or days, from being able to have a decent, two-way exchange. And that was if the phones started working again.

Niven was the first into the conference room. That would freak everyone out. He always came in last, making an entrance that would assure attention. The others—three girls, two boys, ranging in age from 25 to 35—appeared, sporting open mouths, fists full of coffee and electronics, with bags under their eyes. They all wore black and some other loud pink, purple, or lime.

"Niven," Nicholas said. "What the fuck?"

"Seriously." Niven rotated back and forth in the black leather chair at the head of the table.

Nicholas, at 30, was the brightest of the lot. The partners touched him—on the shoulders, elbow, hands—more than any other person in the room, including Niven. Nicholas still had a goatee, like this was the 90s. Niven was tempted to leave a disposable razor on his desk, as a little prank, but he didn't actually want the boy shaving. He wanted him to look a step behind.

Niven waited until they'd all been seated and silent and focused on him. Then he said, "Biobrex", letting the word sail around the room, touching each person. "The makers of the new wonder drug, Evelan."

"Humpf."

"Really?"

"Ours," Nicholas asked, "or ours to chase?"

"The game is afoot," Niven lied. "We have the inside track and a slight head start. The dolts who have them now don't even know the rug is going to be tugged."

"Cool."

"We will split into teams, tackle the groundwork and get back together Tuesday. Julie's with me."

Nicholas stopped mid-sip.

Niven paused to make sure Nicholas knew he saw his reaction and chosen to ignore it. "We'll push everything else to edge for the moment and concentrate on this. The way the world is today, it's left us with an advantage. If we stay focused and work through this craziness, we'll be way ahead of any other agency they may have contacted."

"So you think last night works to our advantage?" Nicholas exaggerated his confused look.

"The clever can work anything to their advantage," Niven returned. "It's all judo, grasshopper."

The room snickered.

"You and Julie are a team?"

"We're all a team. Julie and I will be a 'teamlet,' if you will. We'll pound out some ideas separately—all three teamlets—and then mush them around together four days from now."

"The parameters?"

"Being e-mailed from the tower as we speak."

"You know that?" Nicholas sat up. "You knew the partners were putting out specs? How long have you known about this?"

"Moments," Niven said. *Stolen moments*, echoed in his head. It made him think of the song, by Oliver Nelson he thought. The New York Voices covered it. Niven started humming it.

One of the others asked if Niven wanted an update on other projects.

"Not necessary," he said. "We've been given a great excuse to keep everyone else waiting. If there's a real problem, let me know. Otherwise, give yourselves the rare luxury of solid concentration. It's going to be a quiet day."

"Quiet on the outside, anyway," Julie said. Her voice was flat, nasally, with overtones of irony no matter what the actual words were. If you asked her the time, Niven once joked, her answer would make you feel the whole concept was cruel.

Julie was not yet thirty, with oodles of brownish hair that fell about without any organization. She wore thick-rimmed black glasses Niven doubted she needed. As far as he could tell, she owned four pairs of black trousers and one black skirt, although this did not set her apart from any other woman in the office, or the city, or any other woman that Niven knew personally.

"Come to my office in, say..." Niven pinched his nose, "one hour."

"By your command," Julie returned and left the room.

Niven followed. An hour should be enough to get the rest of his life in order. Check e-mails or phone messages from anyone important—make sure nothing rude had come in the mail—and then focus on the best idea he'd ever had, the elusive scheme, the one that got away.

He'd been thinking about what? Setting Evelan above the audience, at a higher level, making the drug more of an award or achievement, positioning it like Prada or Mercedes. He had boiled this down to an approach. A useable idea. It was right there, in the darkness, just beyond his senses. The darkness was Ming's world. The closer he got, the more of that world he discovered. *The subtle tones of a train leaning left. The distant scream of a locked break. The taste of rust.*

This was not helping. If Niven could sit, quietly for a moment. *Stolen moments,* he sang in his head. *If I told you I loved you...*

Jack Levy was sitting on the edge of Niven's desk, arms crossed. Niven blinked. His mouth formed the start of a W. He hadn't seen Levy in months. The man never came to the building, let alone Niven's office. Portly, khaki pants, boat shoes with no socks. A madras shirt. His gray hair in tight, plastered curls.

Levy showed up in person for two reasons. Sadly, Niven did not have an intern that looked like Grace Kelly.

CHAPTER 21

SUSAN

This was big. Susan was not yet sure how big, but it seemed to be global, the ultimate pandemic. She needed an epidemiologist. Was there such a thing as a pandemiologist? There would be now. She needed clinicians in the field. People to run the data. And theorists. Think tankers. A bevy of neurologists sitting in a room could only think in a few directions. To get answers quickly, she needed people thinking in every direction.

Susan wondered if, when the secretary of Health and Human Services decided he needed a hard-nosed bitch, he thought he might be her first target.

"Mr. Secretary," she said into the phone.

"Go ahead," he returned.

"We need the help of the armed services."

"OK." He sounded impatient already. Susan didn't care.

"Only the military can order people—its people—to answer personal questions. We need to mobilize the medical corps of each branch to collect data. We need to know how widespread the phenomenon is and how deep the new memories go. The military won't give us a respectable sample size given the population in question, but it's a start."

"OK."

"It might be a little outside the normal purview—"

"OK, Susan. Consider it done."

"Oh."

"Anything else?"

"I've disbanded my team."

"Fine."

"That's all."

"Call anytime."

Her mouth hung open for a little while. When she had rehearsed the conversation, the secretary's part went much differently.

I really am in control. The thought was live and bare, like a nerve stripped of myelin, laid out before her in mystery and consequence. It was intimidating. It was always intimidating. Everything. Board exams, reviews, interviews, publishing, always with those eyes looking for proof that you don't belong.

Missy Armstrong. The whole country's another Missy Armstrong, bleeding from the brain, and it was time to get pissed off.

Susan called her assistant, Angela. She was still at home, hedging that she might stay there all day. Susan cut through the hedge and told her to be in the office in 40 minutes. This was one of the days that made up for all the easy ones she got. There was no argument.

Then Susan made a few more calls. Old friends, friend-of-friends and some just, plain cold. Her new task force would comprise people outside her usual circles. She snickered at that thought. If she were to draw Venn diagrams of this group, her set would be one that had never before intersected.

Finally, she called Joe into her office. She wanted to see exactly how far she could stretch her new authority.

"Lieutenant?" she asked. "How many helicopters are at my disposal?"

Chapter 22

NIVEN

"Have you had your rice yet?" Niven swept past Jack Levy—one of the three partners who owned Eden/FCJ, one of his boss's bosses. He positioned himself behind his desk.

"Pardon me?" Levy remained against the edge of the desk, like this was his office, which Niven knew was the point. It was his office, along with the rest of the place.

"Something the man I share memories with says. I like it. Friendly, don't you think?" Niven put his hands on his hips.

Levy turned. "I spoke with Nicholas last night, before all this nonsense. He knew nothing about the Biobrex purchase."

"I just told him now," Niven said. "More or less."

"What does that mean?"

"I told him we'd be pitching Evelan," Niven said. "I have different ways of motivating my people. It's not all carrots and sticks with creatives. Especially this new breed, with no mortgages and no kids."

"Wasting time is motivating?"

"The best rice is cooked with pressure."

"Another snippet from your partner?"

Niven shook his head. "May I ask why you talked to Nicholas about this, and not me?"

"We were discussing another matter," Levy tossed off. "You burned two full days. Not cool, Niven, not cool at all. Now your team is all screwed up because of this brain

business. You may have burned all the time we had. Do
you realize that? The drug is going to be released. We don't
get to choose that time."

"I realize it's the end that matters," Niven said. "You
will be so impressed with the results, you won't even
remember this conversation."

"I remember everything." Levy planted his fist on the
desktop, leaned forward, and lowered his voice. "We don't
go for internal games. Do I make myself clear?"

"As crystal."

"Good." Levy gave the desk a little twin punch and left.

Niven stood smiling, gazing at the cream wall Levy had
been blocking. It all had to be worth it. The machinations,
the deceit, the pushing and shoving. They all had to say
'Wow' on Wednesday morning or he was out. Levy had
probably been looking for a reason already, a crack he could
pry into a 'just cause.' With this project he had his best
chance in years. Normally, it was all about the youth.
Everyone, everywhere wanted 18- to 24-year-olds. Phones,
shoes, cola, socks. Advertisers were under the impression
that young people didn't have enough stuff yet, that they
were just starting their capitalist pigginess, so they were
the ones to go after. As if old people never ate candy bars
or bought a Coke. The closer your creative team was to the
target market, the more effective it would be. Wisdom was
valued about as much as honesty in the advertising world.

The weight of this fact pushed on Niven every day, a
bar across his shoulders, with buckets at each end. Every
day the buckets got heavier. Something cold and heavy
went in. Nothing ever came out.

Ming Lin had no comparable memories.

Niven thought about his job. He found himself on two
tracks, parallel, but not at all the same. Niven's was gummy;
Ming's steely, swift, and steady. Niven could look back at
each length of rail that made him feel that way: the time
Nicholas was awarded the Donavan contract; flown off to
Fiji for a shoot; praised in the quarterly meeting all on his
own, not as part of Niven's team, under Niven's tutelage
and direction.

Ming loved young people. His favorite pastime was riding the rails with new workers, having them close their eyes and listen for pinned brakes, loose ties, clanking couplers—so many problems could be heard and felt long before they could be seen. New hires hung on each word, making notes on little cards, gushing thanks as if the guy was a prophet.

Niven sat down. He cleared his head and called for that idea he'd lost. It was still in his brain. He knew it. Once, back in the early nineties, he'd actually thought about going to a hypnotist to retrieve a missing idea. He'd heard that everything remained in the brain. He'd read about some girl who'd repressed awful memories of her father, completely sealed them off, until put under. He actually phoned one, to make an appointment, though it proved unnecessary. The therapist had told him to relax. Come back to it. Memories were like logs floating down a river. The act of trying to pull one past the others could cause a jam. Relaxing, letting the memories flow freely again, might loosen everything up. It did. Niven saved 80 bucks.

The technique lost its touch. Niven slowed his breathing, calmed his muscles, and lowered his eyelids. Darkness was a new world. The office formed in the black, outlined by his breathing echoing off the walls, the erumpent lumbar support of his chair, the antiseptic sting of the cleaner used last night on his desk. It was all new, and new was dangerous. Not scary. This was a safe place. But his body did not yet know the shape of it all.

Niven opened his eyes. Niven's relaxed state was Ming's most active.

"Well doesn't that just suck," he said out loud.

CHAPTER 23

SULTAN

Friday nights were not Sultan's favorite for going out. He actually liked to calm down before the start of a new workweek. The majority of his friends did not share this affectation. For most of the day, the phones did not work properly. His friends soon figured out text messaging had a much higher percentage chance of functioning, and arrangements for the evening's get-together were sent all over Abu Dhabi. They would meet at a particular coffee house downtown. The last prayer of the day was at 8:40 PM. He left right after.

Sultan drove his Mercedes with the stereo off. Music didn't feel right, and the news was stale. No one knew anything new. It was mostly guessing now, or worse—blaming. No matter what bizarre thing happened in the world, there was always someone pointing the blame westward. Tonight, he preferred the sound of his air conditioner.

Four of his friends were already ensconced in a red leather booth, two hookahs puffing on a low table in the center. He knew without asking that one had fruity *maassel*, the other mint. After greetings, Sultan plopped down and picked up a hose. He didn't bother to ask which pipe put out which. He didn't care enough to waste the breath.

"It is the great exportation of Islam." Saif was snake thin, with too much black hair encroaching on his eyes and ears. He needed a trim, always. Just leaving the salon he needed a trim. And a tailor.

"Where did you hear that?" Zayed replied, ready to laugh.

"Some mullah, I don't know who. His claim was interesting. All of us who have memorized vast quantities of the Qu'ran have been honored with a doubling of that knowledge. We helped carry it deeper into the world."

"Doubling is a bit strong." Sultan drew from the nearest hose and held the smoke for a bit. He exhaled and nodded to Zayed. "Michelin here did not help the cause any. All his great knowledge went to the cemetery."

"It was most likely flawed," Rashid said. Another of Sultan's retinue. He had the body of a soccer player, with the cut and crafted face of a statue. His close beard and fat eyebrows made everything he said sound like a serious accusation. From Rashid, 'hello' sounded like the start of a fight. The man was incapable of telling a joke. Sultan found this quite funny.

"It was not in the great plan to export tainted knowledge," Rashid continued. "So Zayed got a dead guy."

Sultan laughed and it felt good. It felt like he hadn't laughed in two years, since he'd been taken from his parents. *His bottom lip twitched. His mother grabbed for him with clawing hands, his father holding her back. He would work off their debt. They could eat if he worked. That was two years ago. I will forget everything after that. I will remember my parents' faces, even if they are crying faces, and remember nothing else.*

"A dead man?" Saif asked. "So Zayed, you get the bill tonight."

"What?" Zayed sat up.

"Your Other is dead," Saif said. "You didn't have to close out your accounts today or cancel your credit cards."

"You did?" Zayed asked. "You have no money?"

"Right."

"But you came out anyway."

"You wouldn't want me to miss this, would you?" Saif pretended like he was going to cry. "After the day I've had, canceling my cards and shoring up my accounts. The man I share memories with is not to be trusted."

"I wonder how he spent his day." Rashid drew from a hose.

"Canceling his credit cards and shoring up his accounts," Zayed huffed.

Sultan wanted to laugh again, but it hurt too much. The laughter and the pain of not laughing spun together, like cardamom and coffee, like tobacco and mint. Dissimilar and inseparable.

He took another drag from the hose. Warm minty smoke filled his mouth. The base of this hookah was dark green glass, the stalk etched silver, undulating and curvy, feminine in effect. At the top a bowl holding the flavored tobacco, in this one heated by an electric coil.

The Master carried an iron, just like that coil. If you cut yourself with the knife, he pressed the cuts to the iron, burning them so bad you couldn't cry loud enough. You wanted to leave yourself, the pain was so big. You wouldn't bleed on the carpet, though. That was the all he cared about—no blood on the carpet.

Sultan looked at the fingers of his left hand. He could smell his own flesh burning. Clear and disgusting. He could smell it like he it was burning right now.

"Who am I?" Sultan mumbled to himself, staring at his soft, pure, uncharred, never-scarred fingers.

Raja. His memory was sluggish. Muddy. And shallow. As if there just wasn't much of it.

"How old am I?" he whispered. The answer wasn't ready. He was 25. Raja was six when he had been pulled from his mother's side and thrown in the back of a hard, filthy truck.

Two rainy seasons ago.

CHAPTER 24

ALISTAIR

"Who are you and what are you talking about?" Joshua's return e-mail was crisp. Alistair hated to ascribe tone to other people's e-mails. It was not a great medium for nuance. Still, he couldn't help but see a little panic in the short sentences.

"Who do you think?" he typed. "I'm John McCorely's Other. On Monday you interviewed John with regard to an opium seizure in San Francisco. I believe he said it was 'recumbent' upon the defense not to lay down. Which made you laugh. It was, as I think back, more of a nervous laugh than anything. John wanted to kill you on the spot, but that was difficult from behind an inch of safety glass. So he told his brothers to have it done. Disappear. They will find you and kill you. That's all they are good at."

Send.

"Daddy." Lucy walked into the little home office next to the kitchen. "What are you doing?"

"Checking my e-mail." Alistair helped her onto his lap.

"Can we see pictures of the Great Wall?"

"Of China?"

"Yes." She snuggled in and stared at the monitor. "My friend Chu knows about the Internet but he's never used it. He has a farm near part of one of the sections of the Wall, but he's never seen any other parts. Just a few pictures years ago in school."

"I see." Alistair let the creepiness pass through him. This was normal now, for his little girl. He had to maintain that. This was the world now. "Let's see if we can find some pictures of the Great Wall of China."

"Chu has ducks and chickens and cows and pigs," Lucy said. Alistair was thrilled she was talking about her Other. He wanted to know everything.

"One of his chickens might be sick, so he's watching it. I want to know if she's all right. Chu has no phone. He makes calls from a store in town. Maybe I'll go there someday. Not today."

They found photos of the Wall. Lucy watched as Alistair paged through them, waiting for his mail program to chime.

"That looks like a bridge," Lucy said.

"The wall is so big it looks like a bridge," Alistair offered.

"Chu's wall looks like a hill. It's got grass and rocks."

"Some parts of the Wall are so old they look like they belong there."

Lucy hoped off Alistair lap. "Thanks." She ran away.

He heard her shout to her mother in Mandarin. Valerie shouted back in Mandarin. This was going to get pretty annoying. He already felt like he didn't know what was going on most of the time.

The mail program bounced and beeped. He opened another from Joshua.

"We need to meet," the message said.

Alistair typed, "As my four-year-old says: Are you joking me?" Then he deleted the line. Joshua didn't need to know he had a four-year-old. He didn't need to know anything about him, other than he was telling the truth and trying to save Joshua's life.

"You're funny," he typed. "We will never meet. Now go. It is your only chance. It is my only chance, too." Send.

The Internet was painfully slow. So much traffic, so much information pumping through the phone lines and fiber optics and anything else that carried a signal. He wasn't waiting. He had told Joshua everything he needed to know. There shouldn't be a debate. Alistair didn't need to read the next e-mail. There shouldn't even be another e-mail. He should have called him. He could have yelled in his ear. Used his 'Dad' voice. What did it matter, right? So the Feds learned all about him. Was John McCorely really going to let him live? Fantasy. It was all fantasy. It was asinine to believe in saving Joshua and himself, and keeping his little girls from believing the world had not, last night, taken a turn so violently it was skidding out of control.

It was time to be very, even cruelly, realistic. John did not live in a world where the high tide lifted every boat. There was no sense anywhere in his head that to get a bigger piece, everyone needed to bake a bigger pie. His games were zero sum. *Us or them. You only get by taking. You only survive by killing.*

The mail chimed. Alistair looked at the little icon, a cartoon of a mailbox that belonged next to a white picket fence, on an oak covered street in a town whose sheriff kept his gun locked in his trunk.

He opened the message.

"What you know can save a lot of lives. We can protect you. Your family, if you have one. We do it all the time. Let us help you."

The Department of Justice could offer him witness protection. They had done it for seven different men John knew, defecting from the Brotherhood. They got new names, new numbers and vanished into the Pacific Northwest, or, John often thought, right up into Canada. That's what he would do, anyway.

Alistair did not want to uproot Valerie and the girls and tuck them away in Saskatchewan. They hadn't done anything. They didn't know anything. He couldn't ask them to leave their home, their grandparents, aunts, uncles and their friends for nothing. It was so bleak.

Growing up without a father wasn't the best, either, but they'd have everything else they'd come to know.

There was one other alternative. The one that occurs to every snake in a corner, facing the point of a shovel.

CHAPTER 25

SUSAN

Susan's inclination was to treat this gathering like a conference: make everyone feel warm and welcome. She actually thought about sending Angela for stick-on name-tags and a Sharpie, maybe some folders and spare pens.

Then Casper showed up. With one big, gleaming smile she was reminded that her job was herding cats. Bright, highly independent, overachieving cats. She didn't need name tags, she needed leashes.

Casper was famous for once telling the current vice president to "screw the wall instead," the story went. "Everybody will be happier. Except for the wall." Captain Casper Yan had not been fired from his job because he was, as usual, quite right.

Casper. A friendly, Asian ghost in a short-sleeved shirt, with a loaded pocket protector. He had a broad chest and broader smile. Looking back at 50, and quite charming. *Like the Devil,* she reminded herself. He was attached to the Defense Advanced Research Projects Agency. DARPA was the only place in the U.S. government where breaking rules was not only allowed, but mandated. In the time they had spent together, Susan never figured out exactly what 'attached to' meant. He repelled any kind of string, tie, or simple promise.

"I didn't rate a helicopter?" he asked as he approached.

"You are much more the handcuffs, back-of-the-car type," Susan replied.

"No one has to drag me in irons to see you, Dr. Grove."

The corners of his lips curled into a smile. Susan's lips mimicked them, all on their own. They wanted to play along. She caught herself and forced her lips back straight.

"What are you doing here?"

"I was in the neighborhood," Casper said. "I knew you would have invited me if our history wasn't so awkward. Thought I'd save you from the back and forth you were surely having in your mind."

"There was nothi—"

Dr. Michelle Bell, epidemiologist, rolled into the room. She was short. Susan didn't like to fixate on prominent physical characteristics, but the woman could not have been five feet tall. The blast of tight gray and white curls gave her another six inches. Wet, she probably looked like a doll. Round, energetic, mid-sixties. Susan admired her lack of make-up and hair coloring. She wished she could do that. The freedom.

"Grove, yes," she ran over, her hand extended in front of her the whole way, like she was jousting. "As in coconut. Got it."

Their hands met and bounced in eight rapid pumps.

Susan bowed slightly at the waist. "It's nice to finally meet you."

"Likewise. Yes. Wish it were under better circumstances." She stopped and looked off to her left. "No. This isn't at all like a funeral. This is fine." She looked back at Susan. "We certainly have lots to talk about. Is the news I'm hearing correct? Global pandemic? Epic pandemic is more like it. Anything coming in from the field? Anything trustworthy I should say."

Breathe, Susan wanted to say. "Let's get around the table."

Casper touched her arm. "Do I get to sit next to you?"

Adam returned to the conference room. She wasn't expecting him, either. Cruel as the thought was, she knew he was familiar with signals of rejection. She was annoyed that they didn't take.

"I have something you might find interesting," he said as he passed her. Adam stopped at the room's computer terminal and started punching keys.

A few more people arrived. That might be everyone. Susan would have to figure out who was who later. The Adam situation wasn't going away.

"A colleague of mine at Johns Hopkins sent these over." Adam fired up the LCD projector. A glowing blue square appeared on the far wall. He moved the mouse and an image took its place.

The room hushed up. The image was an fMRI, or Functional Magnetic Resonance Image. *A clean one*, Susan decided quickly. A healthy human brain, two clearly discernable hemispheres, no anomalies.

"He was running a test last night as part of a sleep study he's involved with. As you can see, there's nothing unusual at 10:22 PM"

Adam clicked the mouse, and the image changed. The dull, gray lobes of the brain exploded white. All twelve people in the room gasped.

"This is 10:23. As far was he can tell, every part of the brain is being stimulated. The subject was asleep. Nothing else in the environment changed. The phenomenon lasted for one-point-five seconds and..." Adam clicked the mouse once more. The image of the brain showed gray with several white highlights. "The image is what we would expect from a fully awake adult."

"Go back," three or four people yelped. Adam brought up the bright white scan.

"Full stimulation," Susan mumbled.

"Remote transmission of stimulation?" Casper said close to her ear. "And you said it couldn't be done."

She broke from her trance to look Casper in the eyes. She hadn't brought him here precisely because he might bring that up. Their history. Short and not-so-sweet. She glanced at Adam, who watched them. Fascinated she was sure. How much had he heard?

"Michelle," Susan said. "To answer your question, yes. We now have something from the field. Just what it is, I can't say."

"Or won't say?" Adam whispered.

Chapter 26

ALISTAIR

"You're insane," Valerie hissed. Her mouth coiled into a sneer Alistair had never seen before.

"You have to trust me," he said as evenly as he could.

"You think leaving your family right now is the best thing you can do?"

"Yes."

"And that's it?"

"Yes."

The girls were playing in the other room. Fish school. Alistair's favorite game. They lined stuffed fish up like students and taught them things; he wasn't sure what. It was his favorite game because it occupied them so thoroughly and had a connection to education.

"You can't leave us." Valerie's face was locked onto serious nastiness. This was a statement of fact.

"You think I want to?"

"Well you are. What else should I think?"

"There is a gun to my head," Alistair said. "I don't want to dramatize this. But this is a matter of life and death."

"Stop with the bullshit."

"I am not telling you any more."

"If you tell me, you'll have to kill me."

"Not me. Someone else."

"This isn't funny. Are we in danger?"

"I don't know. I don't think so, yet. I'll call you from the road and let you know if I think you should get out of here."

"You're kidding me."

"I'm not."

"I want to know what you're doing. No offense, Al, but you're not Indiana Jones. You're not a guy that just goes off—"

"I'm not *the* guy," he stopped her. "Like everyone else in the world now, I'm two guys, although I appreciate you reminding me of my shortcomings."

"They are not shortcomings. You are a type of person."

"I don't know what happened last night, but there was a change."

"You didn't change. You're still you. You just have someone else's memories." Valerie flipped her hair over her shoulder and changed to her 'Mom' voice. "Just memories. You've got to calm down."

Alistair cleared his throat. "If I'm going to die, it's going to be while trying not to."

"I don't understand." Valerie looked at him, hard in the eyes. He knew she was trying to see if he was nuts.

Alistair was done with the conversation. Spinning his wheels. He needed traction; he needed to be going forward. Rocketing forward. The only thing he had on his side was freedom, not time. He had to maximize the use of his freedom, in his finite amount of time.

Arcade games always gave you a clock. You only had so much time to accomplish some goal. Most of the time, you never knew how much time you had. Just like now—real life—except you only got one life. There would be no starting over.

Valerie spread a tear across her cheek. "How long?"

"How much cash do we have on hand?" Alistair peeked around the corner. Lucy and Rebecca were arranging stuffed fish in the living room.

"None of the cards work."

"I'm going to take as much nonperishable stuff as we've got."

"What will I tell the girls?"

"That I love them," Alistair whispered. "That I have always loved them very much."

He couldn't say anything after that. His voice wouldn't work right. He couldn't get any closer to the girls. He was afraid all the fear and sadness would come squirting out. They'd start crying just looking at his scrunched and glistening face.

CHAPTER 27

SULTAN

Sultan worked for the Zakum Development Company, or Zadco, as everyone called it, in the information technologies division, or IT, as everyone called that. There was nothing the business world loved more than the chance to abbreviate or create an acronym or, better yet, a whole language that only they understood, standing as one more moat around their castles.

Our castles, Sultan reminded himself as he entered the immaculate marble foyer and rode the brass elevator. He was one of them. He did not fight it. He had a comfortable office-like area in the department, with all the bandwidth he could stand. His actual job was deliciously simple: hand out Blackberries and intermittently answer questions with regard to same. Nine out of ten times the answer was to turn it off and turn it on again. Sultan had spent four successful years at UAE University in Al Ain. He could completely reprogram the little text-messenger, phone-things if he set his mind to it.

His mind was usually set to other things. There were e-mails from friends and co-workers to read (where to lunch, where to meet after dinner), websites to visit (cars, car accessories, video games, video game accessories, cheats, blogs regarding all of the above), and wandering to perform. It was time consuming and mentally challenging, to stay on top of the early twenty-first century world.

May 7 was a wonderful day to be in the communications field—nothing worked. It never occurred to Sultan

that this might cause an upswing of activity in his department. Not until he arrived at his office-like area to see a
set of nine Blackberries on his desk, each with a yellow
sticky note bearing the owner's name and in some cases,
a relevant password.

"Can you believe it?" Ahmed asked. The young man
sharing Sultan's area was roughly his age and disposition.
Ahmed didn't stop reading whatever was on his monitor.
Sultan poked one of the black, plastic gadgets.

"Believe this many crashed at the same time?" Sultan
asked back.

"No," Ahmed said. "Can you believe nine guys showed
up this morning wanting these things to work."

Sultan sat down, staring at the Blackberries. "The oil
must flow."

"Sure. Absolutely. What did they all do before wireless
telecommunications? What? I am really asking."

"They used boys like you to run messages around.
They'd give you an envelope with a wax seal and tell you
run it out to the oil fields or down to the docks. How would
you like to do that today? Run in the sun."

Ahmed went back to quietly reading whatever website
he had up. Sultan couldn't tell what it was and didn't care
enough to try. He flicked another Blackberry as if it were
a big bug.

"How do you find a place if you don't know where it
is?" Sultan asked. He wasn't sure if he was asking Ahmed,
or himself. Out loud, outside the strangeness of his
muddled brain, the question sounded more personal.

Ahmed hushed his voice. "The ancients had a way and
it was so effective some still use it today. It's called a map."

"I've heard of them. They won't help me. The place I
need has been kept off maps."

"Does this place have a name?"

"Not exactly," Sultan said. "The vicinity does. After that,
all I've got are visual memories."

Ahmed spun around at the word. It was, after all, as
much the devil today as it was yesterday. He had not
shaved his V-shaped face in several days.

"Your new memories?" Ahmed asked. "You want to find a place you can see in your new memories?"

"You are very clever, my friend. Perhaps too clever." Sultan pointed at Ahmed, as he liked to do, arm fully extended. "No one should have been able to guess that from my pathetic clues. Have you been in my mind too?"

"Yes," Ahmed said without expression. "It is the new thing to do around here. We all peek into your mind and then laugh about what we see. Most frequently it is what we didn't see. There is, as they say, excess capacity in that region."

Sultan let a tiny smirk cross his mouth. He dropped his hands to his lap. "I see India. My Other...he has heard the name Allahabad. But he knows he is...some time from there. On a bumpy road."

"That is all? Your Other is X miles in Y direction from Allahabad? You don't have enough to solve for that."

"No," Sultan said. "I supposed not. It is impossible."

Ahmed rubbed his sprouting beard. His nose crinkled, like it was pumping blood into his frontal lobe. Sultan sat quietly, watching the nose wriggle. A slug scaling a cliff edged in black moss, attempting to escape the fuzziness.

"Not impossible," Ahmed said. Sultan raised his eyebrows, pretending to be surprised. "You have exhausted input for inductive reasoning. You could gather more data and deduce."

"I was up half the night," Sultan said, "mining my memories for more. I do not believe there is anything left."

"There is, just not in your active memory." Ahmed whirled back to his monitor and slapped his computer's mouse. "There could be images of the region. Satellite photos of the area in and around Allahabad. You may not find what you need, but you may be able to eliminate certain directions."

Sultan smiled without showing his teeth.

CHAPTER 28

NIVEN

As Niven was between wives at the moment, he had his apartment all to himself. His thoughts, too, like a reminiscence of growing up in the country, but with color splotches his only visual recollections. To Ming, the world had looked like a painter's rag. Watercolor bleeding on feathery shadows. That changed to black by the time he was four. He fell in love with the clatter and toot of the coal trains the first time he heard them.

Little boys love trains, Niven thought, *even when they can't see them*. Niven had had a black Lionel set when he was young. It had little drops you put in the smoke stack to make faint wisps rise and stream as the engine ran around the triple tracks. Toot and clatter. He hadn't thought about that train in half a century.

None of his friends called. Niven never worried for something to do. In the city—The City—there was ever an opening, debut, get-together, or parting shot to make. This afternoon was unusually quiet. He should have expected it. The world had been knocked in the head. Everyone who could was nursing their noggin in front of CNN or, God help them, Fox News. This day had the potential of becoming one of those icy, alone days he spent most of his money and waking hours working to prevent. There is nothing as lonely as living in the center of eight million people. Stationed in a hut in Antarctica, reporting on the weather, would be less lonely. There was no chance you could do something. You were not being actively ignored, shunned, or forgotten. Alone in an orbiting space capsule would be a result of your choice. Alone in New York meant you'd done something wrong.

Niven paged through his organizer and found the number. It wasn't even close to what he'd guessed. He picked up the phone, heard the dial tone, and sighed. It was working, and nobody had called. It *was* working, though. He dialed the number.

"Hello?" the young male voice answered.

"Pierce? It's Dad."

"I'll be."

"How are you?"

"Usual. Is everything all right?"

"Yes, just checking."

"The last time you called it was because Uncle Ari died."

"Starting a new tradition. I'm going to start calling whenever I feel like it. Saturday morning. Middle of the night. Whatever fits my fancy."

"Cool."

"So everything's...fine? Annabelle?" Niven asked.

"Scott free. We're both, you know. Like everybody this morning. Dazed and confused. No trauma, though. Neither one of us got paired with a serial killer or drug lord or something scary like that. Anna got an oil executive in France. That is pretty scary, but we don't have to go into hiding."

"And you?"

"Oh, nothing special. Why don't you come by tonight. I'll tell you all about it."

"I've got a couple of things going on."

"There'll be room. Crowd was light last night. I'm expecting more of the same."

"I'll see."

"Yeah..."

"If I can move a couple of things."

"Yeah..."

"I'm glad everything's all right."

"Thanks for checking."

Checking was the most important part of Ming's life. At 18 he had applied for a job at the Huanan Coal Railway. At first, they were dismissive. He was already receiving a stipend from the state. He did not have to work. They politely told him to go away. He did not. Ming insisted that he could be of use to the People. He had skills that could help the railroad. The dismissiveness turned to laughter. A blind boy working on the railroad. What was he going to do? Take over driving when they were in tunnels? Ming asked the manager of the yards to do him the final honor of following him outside.

Exiting the main office, Ming took the thin iron rod he'd left leaning on the wall of the building. He walked, swinging it in a narrow arch before him. He didn't want to stumble over a discarded tie or trash, not at this point. The manager and one of his assistants followed him. Ming figured it was out of pity, or perhaps a source for some other joke. Ming tapped the rails until he could place himself in the network. Then he moved quickly, heading up a side track at just under a run. The two men behind him had to hurry to catch up.

Clink. Clink. Clang. He found the spot he'd discovered earlier. A crack. He spun and planted his rod on the rail, cupping his hands over top.

"The rail is cracked," Ming proclaimed. "The crack will spread if not tended soon."

The men shuffled around him. They stopped shuffling. The source of their breathing lowered. They were, he presumed, on their knees, getting their eyes close to the long strip of steel.

"He is right," the assistant said. "Here, near the tie down."

"Humpf." The manger stood. He was half an arm's length away. "You heard this? No one else showed you this?"

"I have been walking between your rails since I could walk. For 15 years I have listened."

"Are there any more bad rails in this yard?" the manager asked.

"I will check," Ming had replied, 30 years ago.

CHAPTER 29

ALISTAIR

Keep your nose to the grindstone. Like all clichés, Alistair hated this one. *Except,* he thought, *maybe today it had new and more significant meaning.* If you pour flour into the mill too quickly, the stones jam or fail to fully grind your grain. If you pour too slowly, the stones will rub each other, build up friction, and start cooking your goods, giving rise to a burning scent. Hence the bit about where to keep your nose.

Most people used the phrase as a call for diligence. Alistair decided—as he drove through the flat fields of Kansas, alone, hungry, physically tired but mentally racing—that the cliché was also about timing. You've got to be smooth and even. Not too fast, not too slow.

Lowbrow, philosophical road-thoughts were a pleasant distraction. The deeper he thought about mills and grinding and grain, the less he had to think about everything else that lay ahead.

John McCorely was in lockdown. He was sure of that. Anything weird happens at Pelican Bay and the first thing they do is seal the place like a diving sub. There is usually, by John's estimate, three days' supply of food. Nine meals is how long they can go before they have to let the kitchen crew move about.

Alistair had two days. John could do nothing but sit and think. He had no way to communicate until the lockdown was over. It was not, by Alistair's estimate, nearly enough time.

He had to call James "Ivory" Cunningham at exactly the right moment. Too late, and Alistair wouldn't have time to pull off his plan, too soon and Ivory would have the chance to figure out Alistair was full of shit. 'Just a body waiting for bullets,' John would say. Oh, would they fill Alistair with bullets.

In 1996 a group affiliated with the Nuestra Familiar, another prison gang extending its influence into the world, decided that drug trade in a Latino section of South-Central L.A. really should be left to the NF. The Aryan Brotherhood would need to move across the street, so to speak.

John had ordered Ivory to put together a little shock force. They hit the gang military style, capturing the leader alive. Ivory chained the kid—what was he? 24?—to a warehouse wall and shot at him, trying to see how many bullets he could get into him before he kicked. You had to be careful, directing fire to the hands and feet, arms and legs, hoping you didn't get any major blood vessels.

He eventually sent John a message that said simply, "42."

Ivory was in prison, but had a cell phone. Go figure. If you needed a gun, any kind of gun, he was the man to call.

Near the Kansas-Colorado border, Alistair got a hotel room. The place was dark, quiet, cleaner than he expected, but retaining that feeling that none of the guests ever stayed longer than two hours. He sat on the edge of the bed, dialed, and waited.

"Yeah," came the voice, Ivory's, just like Alistair remembered it sounding. His spine froze. His sphincter clenched like a camera shutter.

"*Dia dhuit.*" Hello, in Gaelic. It would signal several things to Ivory, some of them a little confusing.

"*Cad atá uait?*" he asked.

"*Ord. Stáisiún busanna.* Salt Lake City." Alistair snarled as he said it. Having to break protocol and use an English name for the city, he wanted to sound extra mean and angry.

The pause on the other end was unnerving. Ivory wasn't jumping to action like a good little soldier. John would have expected him to, but Alistair wasn't John. Ivory knew that. John couldn't call him on the phone. Some of the captains could, on John's order maybe, but not with an order like this. But the Gaelic was right. The number was right. Alistair could almost hear the slow, greasy gears turning in the asshole's head.

"I... me..." he started to say.

Alistair stopped him. "*Práinneach.*" The word 'urgent' should be enough. The penalty for ignoring this kind of call was death. Alistair's heart pumped hard. He could feel the blood running next to his throat. The penalty for just talking to these people was death. No one who came in contact with them could go on to lead normal lives. The only real defense was distance, and he was actively trying to close that. He was lowering himself into Hell and his body didn't seem to like it. He stood.

"Fine," Ivory said. "Two days."

"One." Alistair crushed the phone into its cradle. He wanted to keep crushing the cradle through the desk and make black powder on the floor.

Slowly and evenly, he wanted to grind up everything in the room.

CHAPTER 30

SULTAN

"May I help you?" The man was burly, and a full six inches taller that Sultan. He spoke Arabic with an accent. Canadian? Australian? Sultan had never been good at distinguishing between the two. The man wasn't American, you could tell by the walk and where he put his hands. He wasn't British. They moved their heads differently. The man wasn't an Arab. He wore blue pants and a white polo shirt with a blue crest—a vaguely human-shaped swoop, reaching for a what? A cloud of angry bees?

"Selling a lot of phones today?" Sultan looked around the showroom. Halogen projector lamps beamed posters of people in photogenic locations—snowy mountains, dripping rain forests, the bow of the cleanest cargo ship ever—all talking on chunky black phones.

"I am sure it will be a good day," the salesman said.

"I will make sure of it." Sultan walked to the large yellow, chrome, and black podium holding one of the phones from the photos. "I have developed a need for one of these. How is your service running?

"Wonderfully, sir."

"You're covered in Northern India?"

"Into the Himalayas. We have professional guides using them."

"They are GPS capable?"

"Better than that. They can be used as actual GPS devices, should you wish. Mountaineers like them because they can broadcast their location. The phone can tell us where you are. In the event of an emergency, for example."

"That is all I needed to know. If these are good enough for the Sherpas, they are good enough for me. Let us discuss a price."

CHAPTER 31

NIVEN

Ming was punctual. Niven could feel the bumps on his brail pocket watch. Ming ran his fingers over it constantly, believing that the clock was the most important machine on the railway. He had little fascination with timepieces—they did not clink and clatter, fill his nose with grease and oil, or blow his hair back. It was the clock that measured the rail's success, and his personal worth. Ming helped ensure things ran on time. The clock watched him.

Six o'clock in the evening, New York. Seven in the morning, T'o-yao-tzu, Heilongjiang Province, China. Ming only came to the office every few days. Niven had to place his phone call precisely, working his way through the bureaucracy quickly enough to catch the man. Niven's *putonghua*, or common language, was slow. He understood that Ming had a lot of *Hakka* influence in his personal dialect, but that wasn't the problem. Niven's mouth didn't seem to get in to the right position fast enough. The language made his tongue feel heavy. The receptionist, then the clerk, understood him. Barely. They knew this wasn't business or family related. Niven wasn't calling from farther up the hierarchy or on Party business. He certainly wasn't a doctor. Luckily, 'Other' was quickly becoming as important as 'husband' or 'wife.'

"Ming," Niven said with force. "This is Niven."

"Ah," came the voice Niven had only heard in his memories. His neck tingled. Your voice. His voice. *Our voice.*

"I know you do not have much time," Niven said.

"For you, none," Ming stated. "You are an asshole."

The line went dead.

CHAPTER 32

ALISTAIR

Alistair could drive about as fast as his Honda Accord would let him. There were no cops hiding on the highways. They all had better things to do—something he thoroughly understood. Those that weren't home, dealing with whatever new memories needling their brains, were probably working at protecting people like himself. How many people suddenly knew something terrible? Serial killers, rapists, drug lords, assassins, terrorist cells. There could be millions of people in the world that suddenly knew something they shouldn't. A world with no secrets was not, at first, a safer place.

It was a faster place. In Colorado he got in with a pack of cars doing over 100 miles per hour. His car wasn't entirely happy at this speed for prolonged periods of time. He laughed at himself for being worried, even for an instant.

"That's right, Al," he said out loud. "You're gonna need an oil change after this."

What a sheep. What a fucking sheep. 'You have not earned your right to live,' John would have said. Fix this, clean that. Don't be late. Change your oil. If you don't know how to live, you forfeit your right to live.

To John McCorely, justifiable homicide was killing anyone who couldn't stop you. If you were too stupid, too slow, too unaware—you lost. He won. That was all there was to it.

John made every member swear oaths of fealty to the Brotherhood. The gang was more important than your life. He did this, Alistair knew, not because he believed it, but because it served him.

He had personally, with his own hands, killed two brothers. Both murders lead to his advancement in the organization. There was no well of guilt anywhere in John's memory. Alistair looked deeply as he drove, coming up with nothing. The guy just didn't seem to have it anywhere in him. If John wanted something, he took it. The only force that ever stopped him was physical. You had to have more muscle, more guns, or glass and bars to dissuade him. He was, at once, the type of man to move on to something easier and the type to lose all judgment, to pound his fists bloody on crackling safety glass because his wants had taken over his brain.

Alistair could see both types in his memory. At John's first parole hearing when his request was denied. All he could think of was squeezing the judge's fat neck until his eyes popped out. He leapt over the table, sprang at the man, and actually got within inches before the guards pulled him away. He'd been expecting parole. As a favor, the Brotherhood had killed the only witness planning to speak against him, the nigger wife of a boy he'd killed with the cement block. She didn't have any real sway with the parole board. Still, the Brotherhood was like that. Any little thing to help. That was power, and the power should have been enough. John lost his mind when his hopes were crushed.

In the summer of 1997 a black man named Clive Thompson had asked John if his mother was a bitch—you know, an actual garbage-eating dog—because he couldn't imagine a human giving birth to him. He *could* imagine John's old man getting drunk and fucking his dog and nine months later seeing John crap out.

They were in the yard. John's one hour a day. Six other blacks hovered around, looking this way and that, listening and waiting. John had no one. Clive was trying to make him start something, who knew why. Boredom? Initiation into one of their tribes? If they wanted him dead, they should have done it already. He didn't know what they wanted, but he wasn't going to give them this. He had smiled and swallowed and moved on like they'd been discussing the weather.

John never forgot. He thought about that incident every day, puzzling over the motive. Wondering when he'd figure it out so he could finally have Clive killed.

Maybe they wanted a distraction? Lure some of John's soldiers to that area, so they could peel off someone else?

Alistair needed to start thinking about something else. He wasn't in a cell 23 hours a day with no one to talk to.

"No," he said, "you're in an even smaller space for 24 hours with no one to talk to."

He laughed. That was cool. *Laugh more, go nuts less.*

He had laughed the first time he killed someone. *John. The first time John killed someone.* That black boy. He couldn't believe he'd done it. It wasn't a funny laugh, more a steady cough with a smile. The fucker had looked at his girl, so he followed him outside and jumped him. The boy had a move. He knocked John back, which was his big mistake. He should've let John smack him around a little. He'd still be alive if he did. If he'd stayed in his place. When John fell back, he landed next to a cinder block. The boy came over. He was going at him. John swung the block into his face, putting the piece-of-shit flat on his back. A woman screamed "No!" as John dropped the block on his piece-of-shit head. John waited for a second, then he lifted the block off, holding it in case he had to drop it again. The look on that boy's face...the big eyes saying "What the fuck?" That had cracked John up.

Alistair could see the misshapen mouth, the gape of surprise, the smear of blood. Some memories were so strong you couldn't get rid of them. You could try to push them down, like apples floating in a washtub. You could hold some near the bottom, but then others bobbed up to the top.

Alistair had to pick some others. He needed to swish around and bite something better for his brain.

Lucy was two when they told her there was a brother or sister on the way. She had looked at Alistair and Valerie and said, "Oh, great." Flatly sarcastic, with a squint that

said 'What were you morons thinking? We have it good.'
It was so freaking funny to see that look on a two-year-
old.

He laughed again. Alistair laughed every time he
thought of that moment. He kept it up top, a moving picture
on the edge of his mental desk.

He wondered if he'd laugh the first time he killed someone. Would it even feel like the first time? John's memories
felt no different than his. They sat in his brain alongside
his first date with Valerie, the time he crashed his Toyota
sophomore year, and the lyrics to "Stairway to Heaven."

"You're not him," Alistair said, looking out at the blue
and gold of Nebraska. *You'll feel it when you kill someone.
And you'll know soon enough.*

CHAPTER 33

SUSAN

"Hypotheses?" Susan panned the whole table, making eye contact with each of the eleven people she had called in. Or kidnapped, was more like it. She could not think of one person, herself included, that did not have something better to do than sit at a *faux*-oak conference table as the world shuddered.

No one said anything. She understood. Each of them knew just how little they knew. They had very little data about what had occurred the previous night. What data they had were not the kind scientists, medical professionals, and engineers liked. Hearsay, anecdotes from the media, highly subjective personal experience—any one of these sources was flawed enough to keep it out of mainstream science. The fact that these were the only sources had a chilling effect on conversation.

But it was another issue freezing conversation solid. Susan guessed these skilled, educated, intelligent people were not so much concerned about what they did not know. They were, in the deep, outside corners of their consciousness, afraid that everything they knew was wrong. Mind-reading, precognition, remote viewing, out-of-body experiences—all of the paranormal, the superstition, the silly stuff they worked to debunk now and again—it was no longer out-of-bounds. Nature had pulled the fringes of science a whole lot closer to the center. It had, for lack of a better analogy, yanked the rug out from under everyone.

Antonio was probably better suited to receive Susan's memories than she was to receive his. He expected the world to play jokes, perform impossibilities, and pluck logic apart. He believed in the tree of life, growing through this reality and others. Roots entwined in the underworld, branches holding up the heavens. Time running like sap.

Getting someone else's memories? She wanted to sit down with Antonio and hear what he thought. He'd be more forthcoming than this group. She could not recall any story about shifting memories. Susan wanted to curl up with a cup of green tea and look back through her memories and make sure. These recollections were so foreign and familiar, so irrational and right. She knew Antonio was not, right now, bothering with the 'how' of leaping memories. His concern was for why. A message from the spirits? An omen? The morning stretch of a new world waking? Or winds from an approaching storm?

Make my guilt vanish, Susan recited in her head. *Heart of Sky, Heart of Earth, do me a favor, give me strength, give me courage in my heart and in my head, since you are my mountain and my plain; may there be no falsehood and no stain.*

She—Antonio—said this prayer before beginning something holy. It felt right to say it now.

'Only a fool jabbers on about what he don't know,' Grammie said to her once. 'You want to jabber, you best know something.' Susan could hear that alto singsong clear as how many years ago? 30? 35? Funny to think of it now.

'Not funny at all,' Antonio would scold. 'Never ignore the voice of a *nuwal*. They bring wisdom and warnings.'

Garbage. Bunk. Crap. The last thing Susan needed was yet another voice in her head dealing out lazy super-stitions. No one else runs this world. We do. People. Throwing your hands up to God or the Heart of the Sky or the ghost of your Grandmother was surrender. She didn't get where she was by giving up.

"The joke's on us," Susan said. The mumbling stopped. Everyone at the table turned to her. "I think it's reasonable to say that nobody's model predicted what happened last night. There is obviously a huge gap in what we thought we knew about brain function and this new reality."

"And physics," Casper cut in.

"And who knows how many other disciplines," Susan continued. "So let's start by discussing that. Gaps. Let's list the deficiencies we already knew we had at ten o'clock last night."

The group continued to stare, iced over. Susan had to break it, which she did not count as one of her specialties. "I'll start." She pulled her mouth into what she hoped might look like a smile. She had little confidence in it. "There are billions of neurons in the human brain. We do not know exactly how any one of them works. Although they transmit and receive electromagnetic pulses, they are not computer circuits, set to one or zero. Do they accumulate charges? Average charges? Multiply them or react to sudden changes? In light of last night's phenomenon, I'm wondering if the electromagnetic activity we have measured recently accounts for all of the stimulation a neuron may or may not receive."

"You mean quantum activity?" Adam asked.

"Or external broadcasts," someone else said. "Can a neuron act like an antenna?"

The group rumbled. Words, huffs, nips of discussion.

Susan's fake smile turned real. "I've got a couple of ground rules. We all have different areas of expertise. To work best, we need to communicate and that means clear language. If you use a word or, even worse, an acronym I don't understand, you give me a dollar. The same deal goes for everyone. Speak up if you don't catch something. You might learn something and get a free coffee out of the deal. If you cuss, I get five dollars. Otherwise, say anything you want. Nothing leaves the room. You talk outside the room, I get fifty thousand dollars. OK? Who wants to start?"

Chapter 34

ALISTAIR

The bus station—the *stáisiún busanna*—in Salt Lake City was much nicer than Alistair had anticipated. He wanted something beat and dirty. He got something clean and well lit. The tangle in his gut clenched a little tighter as he walked in. He wouldn't have thought it possible. After a while, he figured the 'I'm scared' muscles must get tired.

He walked slowly, without looking around too much. He tooled around the outskirts, found the ARRIVALS sign. Stared at it a bit, then made for the men's room.

He entered the first stall, sat down and waited for the room to be free. He fished around behind him and felt nothing. Someone else came in, so he waited till he left. Then Alistair moved to the next stall. Behind that toilet was a fat slab of duct tape. His heart rate picked up. He peeled it back and pinched off the key.

The Aryan Brotherhood was exceptionally good at carrying out arcane orders. Alistair's almost nonexistent commands, in an old Celtic language, had led someone to tape a key to this toilet. Amazing. Did the FBI have that combination of communication and devotion? He stopped short of admiring it. As a process, it was cool. Its purposes, he reminded himself, were never for the betterment of mankind.

Gangkind. Each individual in the group saw that as an honorable goal. The gang was made better by such simple things as taping a locker key to a toilet in a bus station. They didn't have to think beyond that fact. And that was one of the great benefits of membership: letting someone else do your thinking.

Alistair shoved the key in his pocket, washed his hands, and left the men's room.

Ivory Cunningham was as good a gang member as you could ever hope to have. He was smart enough to carry off nearly any task tossed to him—drug distribution, money laundering, secret communication—but not so smart that he'd scheme to be any higher in the hierarchy of the Brotherhood. Oddly enough, he was the type of man Alistair usually respected. Ivory knew how smart he was. He had no idea who wrote *Othello*, but he did know the world wasn't quite right at the moment. The way things usually worked might not be the best way at the moment. Alistair knew Ivory would be careful.

Alistair walked around the terminal one more time. He found the locker to which he had a key without having to stop and stare. Then he checked his watch, like he was waiting for someone, and sat down.

There were probably 40 people in the terminal, 20 of whom seemed settled in for a long wait. Only five of those had an unobstructed view of the locker. Two men, three women.

One of the women wasn't bad looking. Mid-twenties, her blonde hair was too long and chemical-fried, but she had a decent figure, from what he could tell. She was bored, but alert. A basic shirt, vest, and jeans that had been through the wash more than once. She could have been a girlfriend of nearly anyone in the Brotherhood.

She never let her eyes roam too far from the locker. She noticed everyone that moved around the bus station. Alistair saw none of this behavior in the others.

He walked over and sat down next to her. She didn't bother to look. She'd been sat down next to by strange men before and knew the routine.

"I'm your potty break," Alistair said.

She spun, looking completely disgusted.

"Ease up," Alistair smiled. "I'll watch the locker while you do whatever it is you gals do in there."

"They didn't tell me," the woman said.

"You get what you need." Alistair took his smile away. He was playing his part and it wasn't supposed to be too friendly. "You got five minutes."

The woman must have had to go, Alistair thought, because she jumped up and scooted to the ladies room fast as she could walk.

Once out of sight, Alistair darted for the locker. He plunged the key in, pulled out the brown-paper bag, and snapped the metal door shut. It was a struggle to walk, not to break into a run, bag in hand. He made it through the exit, looking back only when he thought the glare of the glass might hide him. The woman wasn't back yet.

He walked around the outside of the building, weaving in and out of big, silver Greyhound buses, breathing in the diesel fumes. He paused by the edge of the lot, near the dumpsters. He didn't want to go near the dumpsters. It looked like the perfect place to jam someone up.

There was no one around. He walked the long way to the parking lot and got in his Honda. Only then did he peek into the bag.

A Glock. 9mm. Loaded. He'd never held a handgun before in his life. Strangely enough, John McCorely hadn't, either. The big, tough leader of the Aryan Brotherhood had never shot a gun. He'd spent almost his whole life in prison and never had the chance. They knew about guns, both John and Alistair. John read a lot. Alistair played a lot of first-person shooters.

"Point and shoot," Alistair said. You didn't need to know a whole lot more than that.

He got back on the 15, headed for Reno.

CHAPTER 35

SUSAN

Day two of Susan's conference was noisy. She liked it better that way. She had crammed the disparate and the disassociated together in the hopes that there would be lots of noise, and from that noise there might come some sense.

She had $14 in front of her.

The neuroinformatics specialist from Cornell argued with the neurophysiologists from MIT. *Like fencers*, she thought. Thrust, repost, parry, thrust, thrust. They were not building a consensus, but if they ever agreed on anything, it would have to be the truth.

Others listened, not including Michelle and Adam. They discussed the data now dribbling in. Susan could not join them. It was like watching titration. Drip. Drip. She did not know much about the workings of the military. The troops certainly seemed eager to line up and answer weird questions. Medical personnel from around the world posted answers to a database at the institutes. Two new entries every second.

"Lunch?" From Casper it sounded like a date.

Susan's eyes slid to see him and his tiny, one-lip smile. "Should we pass around a menu?"

"I thought a little fresh air might do us both some good. Increase our intake of oxygen."

"I can't believe you. I've got to be here."

"There are matters we cannot discuss here."

"This is hardly the time to worry about security clearances."

"My superiors would strongly disagree with you. They are scrambling around Arlington as we speak, putting plywood on the windows and duct tape on the door seams."

"I wasn't aware you had any superiors."

Casper laughed through his nose. "The people who sign my paychecks. Reluctantly sign my paychecks. They have already demanded to know who my Other is and how they can contact her. They will not take kindly to any other leaks at the moment."

"The president himself wanted this group."

"There is an old joke at DARPA," Casper said. "What other society in the history of the world, with the power and resources of the United States of America, puts a temp in charge?"

Susan snickered. It took a special kind of elitist to look down on the office of the president.

"We'll talk..."

The door opened. The secretary of Health and Human Services walked in. He was back in a blue suit with a tight yellow tie.

"Hello, everyone." He moved around the table, headed toward Susan. Some of the group started to get up, others looked around. No one was quite sure of the protocol. Susan stayed in her seat.

"Lesley," she said.

"Wanted to meet the best and the brightest."

Casper got up and offered the secretary his chair, which he took. The secretary clasped his hands on the table and ran his smile up and down the table like a spotlight.

"So," he stopped at Susan. "What have we got?"

She glanced at Casper. He folded his arms and leaned back against the wall, like he couldn't wait for her next sentence.

Susan swallowed, then said, "There is not a lot to go on."

"There is no need to hedge."

"Reliable field reports have come in from several points around the country. Military bases from Northern Main, to Alaska to Hawaii. We have reports from England,

Germany, Japan, South Korea, and five testimonials from Antarctica."

"Nice."

"This fascinoma covers the globe, going on the assumption that the military would be no more or less affected than the rest of the population. Every collection point registers 100 percent penetration. There is no way to underemphasize this point. The early numbers point to 6,379,157,361 spontaneous cases. The majority of the subjects report memory sharing. Subject A gets B's memories, and B gets memories from A. In the portion of cases in which sharing is not reported, subjects still detail an event. Flashes, sounds and general feelings like happiness, contentment, hunger, or fear have been common."

"Something happened to everyone."

"Something. There is no known trigger...there is simply nothing that can do this. Any type of biological agent is, of course, incapable of instant global span. A solar flare reaches 40 percent of the planet at best. A nuclear event, considerably less."

"What about..." Lesley paused and wiggled his mouth. "Any other man-made causes? Do you have the ability to vet those?"

"Yes," Susan said. "I've got no way of knowing for sure what the Chinese or Russians play with when we're not watching. I can say that a device capable of reaching six billion targets at the same moment would be visible. A hundred and twenty International Space Stations visible. No one's got a chain of secret satellites like that, let alone the method of drawing the energy needed."

Lesley raised his left eyebrow. "No one?"

"Not even us." Susan squelched the urge to glance at Casper. "I can say that with even more certainty."

"This...what did you call it, fascinating rhythm?"

"Fascinoma. An interesting abnormality."

"This fascinoma is as big as everyone thinks, has no known cause, and operates with no known mechanism."

"Yes."

"Where does that leave us?"

"Scratching our heads," Susan said.

The secretary didn't smile. He moved his thumbs around each other, watching them like pets.

"One last question," he said. "Is it going to happen again?"

She had been at it for 39 hours. Even in sleep, which was minimal and sporadic, her mind probed and prodded the problem. During that time she had never once addressed the issue of reoccurrence. She didn't need to. The question had only one answer.

"I have no idea."

The secretary pressed his lips together. He rose, unlocking his hands, standing as if for a photo.

"The president, the country, and quite possibly the entire world thanks you all for what you are doing right now. It is not easy. The absolutely necessary rarely is. Whatever you need is just outside the door. I have confidence that everything we need is on this side. Thank you all again."

The secretary left. As the door closed all eyes returned to Susan. Silence was not the default state with this group. It took more energy for them not to talk. Who was going to fall first?

"Susan." Gary Peabody, MIT. "We could probably do it with six satellites."

Susan rolled her eyes. "It was probably done with none, whatever 'it' is."

CHAPTER 36

ALISTAIR

The shame of the thing was that Alistair had so much goddamn time to think. Flying his car through the desert, there was virtually nothing to do but think. He couldn't take the radio. It was either music for which he had no taste or idiots talking and talking about what might have happened, about how meaningful this event was, and about how the market would open again soon, as if the New York Stock Exchange was the arbiter of all life in this country. He turned the radio off when he heard, for the tenth time that morning, that people certainly would remember where they were the night of May 5. That sentiment was not informative to Alistair. It was so far from being informative as to be sickening.

He wondered if he'd get sick committing his first murder. *You never know 'till you try.*

He loved video games in which you plowed through no-name after no-name, killing digital people left and right to achieve some silly objective. He never stopped to wonder if any secret CIA operative really had to shoot 417 people before reaching a vault with smallpox in desperate need of incineration. Shoot, run, shoot, run, hide, shoot, shoot.

It was a guilty pleasure. In the back of his brain, he was never entirely comfortable reveling in wanton destruction. He never wanted to make a game based on busting things up. He liked solving puzzles. In most of the good games, though, there was a mixture of both. You had to kill things to get to the puzzles. Blood and riddles.

It would seem his life was now like that.

He wanted to call Valerie again. Their last three phone calls had been filled with whirling gaps of silence. They both had so much to say that nothing came out. Each conversation hovered like a fly you just missed swatting. Afraid to go forward, afraid to go back, waiting for the air to stop moving. He lived for hearing about the girls. That was easy enough. Avoiding any discussion about what he was doing was getting really hard.

And it was hard to think of anything else.

John had about 12 hours left in lockdown, if Alistair was lucky. He did not feel too lucky. There were tons of other variables, but John had been sitting, cross-legged on the floor, pondering the predicament. John was a fan of Sun Tzu's *Art of War*. He'd studied Machiavelli, Patton, and—Alistair found this hard to believe, but it was right there in his memory—a lot of Tony Roberts. John would carefully consider every option before doing a single thing. He would wade into his new memories and, as Sun Tzu advised, know his enemy.

Alistair banked on his past. Let John look at Alistair's placid life, free of violence and confrontation, void of nearly any conflict not involving his wife and money. Alistair battled the union at work, if that counted. It was Alistair's job to make bus routes as efficient as possible, which did not translate into easy work or long breaks for bus drivers. But even those conflicts were orderly and across a table. No matter where John looked in his new memories he wasn't going to find someone to fear.

That might give him a little time. John would come to the conclusion that Alistair had to die. But when? Would the order go out after his first meal?

Twelve hours was not enough time. Alistair pushed the pedal down a wee bit farther. The Honda edged up over 90. He had to make the time. He had to get to Granny's.

CHAPTER 37

SULTAN

The trip from the airport to Allahabad gave Sultan his first glimpse of India, and what he was up against. The terrain was fairly flat and grassy, dotted with trees and lined with electric cables. Towers and polls suspended lengthy stacks of wires across the horizon, on either side of him. He didn't know if he'd ever seen wires hung from towers, he probably had somewhere, but nowhere were they this prominent or prodigious.

His cab was some small, white compact of a make he couldn't identify, which was intriguing. He thought he knew every car and light truck and motorcycle on the market. India had its own things and was big enough not to worry about exporting them. Very intriguing.

The main highway between the airport and Allahabad was bland. He'd been on roads just like it, crossing the Middle East, Europe, and America. Black, wide, and oily. His glances off the road were far more rewarding. Thin skins of shoulderless pavement, undulating and winding between crazy, patchwork buildings. Wood, stone, canvas, brick all on the same corner, no structure more than three or four stories, nothing reaching for the clouds.

The River Ganges lay wide and rich. *More a soup than a waterway*, he thought. It lacked the clarity of the Gulf water he looked out on every day. But the Ganges was full, thick with color and alive with tiny, mingling ripples. The surface, especially around the shores, was alive. Crossing the bridge, he couldn't count the number of small, palm-shaped boats, many with arched canopies, each adding more reds and yellows and oranges to the seascape.

After five minutes in Allahabad he had seen more bicycles than he had in his whole life prior. Multi-colored rickshaws with bicycle front ends, wide delivery bikes and hundred and hundreds of standard bikes. Most were ancient looking black and brown beasts, though every tenth one or so was painted wild, with yellow and orange stripes, festooned like dancers.

Women were everywhere. Old, young, in long loose saris or European business attire. Nice, fitted suits. Long black hair. Deep creamy skin. Walking in wide, confident strides, fussing with a storefront, reading an open newspaper.

He studied the terrain between the airport and city, assiduously searching for anything that might register in his memory—his new memory. Raja's memory. The last time the boy had been outside his compound he was six years old. He didn't think in terms of street signs or landmarks. Sultan recognized nothing. The boy's memories were vibrant, but few.

The hotel was low, bone white, with arched balconies. It was not as kept or modern as Sultan was used to. Of course, he wasn't in the habit of traveling to places back from the cutting edge of everything. When he left the comforts of Abu Dhabi, it was usually for the comforts of New York, London, Paris, or Singapore. He had never been any place like Allahabad.

Once in his room, Sultan laid out his atlas and visually spiraled out from the location of his hotel. He wanted to work while the sights were fresh in his mind. Allahabad sat at the point where the Ganges, Yamuna and Saraswati rivers met. It was, more or less, surrounded by water on three sides. Sultan closed his eyes and tried to reach back to the day he was taken. The back of the truck, hard, rusty, hot. The ridges of the truck bed hurt his bottom with every bump. *Where?* Little Raja kept thinking. *Where am I going? Why am I going? I don't want to miss dinner.*

Sultan tried to visualize the route. Raja had not seen much. He was small and stayed low so he wouldn't bounce out of the truck bed. There were few trees when he started out. The place where his family lived had few trees. Then the road took them through a place that had more. The sky was blue, filled with puffy clouds. The two men driving the truck never said a word. Once in a while they looked back to make sure he was still on board. The back glass of the pick-up truck slid. They had it open. They could have talked to him, but they didn't.

They drove on pavement for a while. Raja couldn't remember how long. He had little sense of time. The ride was boring and scary, so it took forever. Years, he would have said, but it was still sunny when they arrived. The sun was not high. How long was that?

Sultan stood straight. He took a bottle of water, went to the patio and looked out over the Ganges. Glittering brown, like gold just out of the ground. Boats roamed close. Open, purposeful wooden shells, packed with parcels or people. There were people everywhere. Down by the shore, crouched, washing or working. Up near the hotel, walking or talking. Nooks where there should have been no one, he saw two people. Paths where he expected to see pairs, he saw groups of four. Patches of ground where five friends might have gathered held ten or twelve or more. The most—the only—peaceful place he could see was the middle of the river.

No bridges. No big bridges, anyway. Raja did not recall crossing any large feat of engineering. The truck had stayed away from the enormous population and the waterways. Sultan rushed back to the map. That was significant. The boy traveled a couple hundred kilometers at the most and never crossed a large body of water. This could narrow down his search by a few thousand square kilometers...if he knew where to start.

"Where are you from, Raja? Because you can't tell me where you went."

He checked his watch, a brilliant, chunky, overly complicated Breitling. It was just about time for 'asr, the third salah of the day. He dug his compass out of his duffle bag, found north, and adjusted himself until he was facing Mecca.

Allahabad could be translated as 'City of God,' using the Arabic word for Great Creator—Allah. Sultan was not given to talking about signs, but he noticed that one. An Indian city with Arabic roots. A swirl of history. Cardamom and coffee. Allahabad was also known as Sangam, or 'the Confluence.' Three holy rivers met in a whirl strong enough to take the dead from the ethereal cycle of birth and rebirth. He had no idea what that meant. Sultan had spent the balance of his conscious life studying Islam, leaving little room for any other faith, the mysteries of Hinduism very much included. He'd read this morsel on the plane and it had stayed with him. Another sign. That made two.

This salah was not for divination. It was communal. To send and to receive from Allah. He refocused his concentration. This was Allah's time. Not Raja's. Not Shiva's or Vishnu's or the other deities now polluting his mind. Devotion was not the word for Raja's faith. He was too young for that. What he had was pure. Any cleric would envy the certainty of his beliefs in this assortment of gods and goddesses. They were as real to him as tigers and trees. It was a pity that Raja had not been introduced to the true faith. As it was a pity, Sultan realized, he no longer had an eight-year-old's conviction. Every day the devil was doubt. It was only natural. The world threw questions, the mullahs blocked with verses. The world hurled temptations, you shielded yourself with faith. More verses, stronger faith, service to Allah.

His new memories were not in service to Allah. They were impure. He wanted nothing to do with Raja's beliefs. Raja certainty made them feel appealing, like a soft bed in a sturdy house. These characters were so vivid in Raja's mind.

Because they competed with nothing else. They were all he knew. He had learned little in life beyond his religion. He loved Ganesh, the god with the elephant head, and loved his trips to his shrine.

Sultan sat up on his knees. A charge rushed through his body. The Shrine of Ganesh. The enormous rock shaped like an elephant. Standing with mother and father and his little sister. It was at the edge of their village, a few minutes' walk from home. His true home. His family's home. Sultan could see it, faded and distorted by thirst, hunger, and time. The boy tried to keep the memory fed. He drew it over and over in his mind, the things he loved. The shrine. His sister. His father. His mother. Day and night, while he sat, knees aching, he brought their images into his head. But there was nothing with which to compare them. Raja could never check his work against the real things. In his mind he tried to weave a carpet to match one he'd not seen in two years and he knew, despite his age and his ignorance, that his image was drifting from the original. He was no longer sure of the truth. No longer sure of anything.

Except that, on the happiest days of his little life, he'd visited the Shrine of Ganesh.

CHAPTER 38

ALISTAIR

Alistair had, of course, never been to Granny's. John had only been there once, in the sliver of time he was not incarcerated, late in the 80s. More than twenty-five years ago.

"This is not a good plan," Alistair said to himself at least once every hour, as he cycled through the details.

He knew Granny's was still there. The Brotherhood used it now more than ever. In this part of the country, things hadn't changed much in 25 years. The desert was dry; Granny's sat in the middle of nowhere. Neither sprawl nor landslide had moved the place. Still, 25-year-old memories from another person were not always your best traveling guides.

The closer he got to the turn off, the queasier he became. It was 9 PM. Not the time he would have picked for this chore. During the day, Granny could see the dust cloud of someone approaching for three or four miles. At night, cars were crazy noisy. In the twilight, Alistair was both loud and visible. Granny probably knew he was on his way before he did.

He pulled over half a mile from her house.

Alistair checked the Glock, pulling back the slide, making sure there was a round in the chamber, feeling his index finger along the safety in the trigger. He slipped it into the waist of his pants, against the small of his back. He opened his trunk and took out his black carry-on bag. It had toothpaste, underwear, and an electric razor inside.

Granny's was a pale blue ranch house about the size of two trailer homes. There were no trees or bushes or barns anywhere around it. A new Chevy Suburban and a huge satellite dish were the only other lumps on the landscape. Besides clean windows all the way around, Alistair had no idea what kind of other traps or alarms might be in place. There was no menu-screen to help him. No cheat-site to visit and get clues. If he messed up, he was not going back to the first level to start over. His mouth had no moisture. He could feel his blood rush through his body.

He went straight up to the house. Hesitation would kill him now. He looked through the first window, into a living room. A couch, an enormous flat-screen TV, a Lazy Boy chair. A woman in her mid-sixties sat on the chair, holding out a remote control. She was pipe-cleaner thin, with gold, spotted skin and what might be bright blonde hair. It was tough to tell in the glow of the plasma. Fully reclined on the couch was a guy about twice Alistair's size and half his age. He wore jeans. That was it. His skin was prison white.

As quietly as he could, he moved to the next window, which was painted white on the inside of the glass. Stylish. The room after had curtains. He could just make out the lace and shades of a single woman's bedroom. He rounded the whole house, seeing only two people. Granny and the boy.

"Fuck it," he said.

He rapped on the door. "Granny," he called out. "You up?"

He leaned back. He saw the boy roll off the couch.

He rapped again. "Granny. Emergency."

Alistair waited. He saw shadows adjust inside and then Granny peek through the window.

"What you want?" she asked.

"What you think? I wanna come in. I'm one a Ivory's."

The pause made Alistair want to puke. His stomach couldn't take any more twisting. His pores ached from constant sweating. His ears burned from too much blood.

The knob turned and the door opened. Alistair breezed in, smiling, bag over his shoulder

The boy stood in the middle of the room with a short shotgun pointed at his chest. His face was gnarled, Alistair thought, like he'd just fired up every brain cell he had.

"Stand down, little fucker." Alistair kept smiling. "I'm just here to make a little deposit in the bank of Granny."

Granny stood to the side. She knew enough to stay wide of the shotgun barrel. "No one said nothin'."

"No one could. The whole fucking world's freaked out. We've got all kinds of security concerns." Alistair looked at the boy with the gun. "You keep that thing on me if you want. I just don't want you getting jittery. I don't know you."

"I don't know you," he said in voice higher than his body suggested.

Alistair dropped his smile. "You don't need to know shit, junior. You just need to listen. I'm going to take this bag to the back room. Then I'm going to leave. If you could keep from shooting me during this time, I'd appreciate it."

The man lowered the gun, but kept his hands on it. He stared Alistair in the face, looking for a reason to bring it back up and squeeze.

"Granny," Alistair said, trying to pretend the guy was no longer in the room. "If you would lead the way."

Granny looked Alistair up and down. Her face was sour. Alistair knew he wasn't sitting right with her. She'd been around men like John, Ivory, and this confused side of muscle her whole life. Alistair wasn't in their club. He couldn't even pretend with a woman like her.

Alistair put his hands on his hips and rolled his eyes. Granny held out an arm. "I'll take it."

"Even easier." Alistair smiled again. He almost started laughing. He didn't know how much longer he could control his face. He wanted to start howling and stomping.

He bounced his shoulder and let the bag slide off and down his arm, catching it all cocky in his hand. He held it out and Granny stepped into the middle of the living room to get it.

Alistair smirked, out of pity, but for whom he didn't exactly know. He yanked the gun out of his pants and brought it around. It took the boy a second. Granny was in the way. Alistair's first bullet entered through the boy's left eye and blew out the back of his skull. His next shot hit the wall. He couldn't believe how much kick the weapon had. His hand shook and his ears rang.

Granny dropped to the floor and rolled. She was terrified. He could see it on her face—stark panic. But she was no potato bug. No curling up for her. She grabbed the shotgun.

"NO!" Alistair shouted. "Come on..."

She whipped it around. Alistair shot her twice in the chest. She jerked back to the floor, like she'd been stapled down.

"Really," Alistair said. "Come on now! What did you think you were doing?"

Granny lay next to the boy, eyes and mouth stuck open. No wriggling, no last minutes epithets. He felt chilled and shaken. He shoved the pistol back into his pants, suddenly afraid he was going to drop it and knock out another round or two.

Granny's was two things: the first being a safe house. Granny had been the wife of the Brotherhood's founder, who went to prison in 1970. She'd been his contact on the outside since the mid-seventies, slowly growing into the nickname. Alistair couldn't remember much more about her, other than she was off-limits, a kind of Queen of the Brotherhood. No on said 'boo' to her, not in this gang or any other. The rule had been effective for the last 40 years, protecting her from drug-dealers, rapists, murderers, and seriously imbalanced psychotics.

Not from Alistair, though. *Beware the suburban father of two.* He pushed that thought aside and walked down the hall of her little ranch house to the two back rooms, the ones with the windows painted white on the inside. Those had to be the ones he wanted. They were locked. Stupid. He had to go back and pry the shotgun from that kid's hands. He wondered if the boy had a bumper sticker declaring that this was, in fact, the only way you'd ever get his gun.

Alistair didn't want to start his ears ringing again. He thought about jamming things into his ears to deaden the sound, but decided it would take too long. He blasted the knob clear off the door and kicked it in.

The room was lined with gray metal shelves, each stacked with banker boxes. *Appropriate*, he thought. *In addition to being a safe house, Granny's was also kind of a safe.*

Discharge from the shotgun tussled a few of the boxes, leaving them looking like mice had attacked. He dropped the gun, then knocked a box to the floor. Stacks of 100-dollar bills fell out.

Alistair stepped over his mess and began searching the room for a small vault. He knew the combination, though he did not know the vault itself. It didn't take long to find it: a small fire-safe in the first closet he opened. The combination took him a couple of tries. He couldn't remember whether to start turning the dial left or right. Once it opened he reached inside and found the leather case he needed.

It was brown. The type of case you see every year in May, when kids start graduating. Alistair snapped it open and looked at the plain, plastic pen. A fake Mont Blanc. Next it to was a needle and a small vial.

Alistair started to snicker. Tears filled both eyes and his mouth filled with acid. He looked at his watch. 9:18. He laughed, out loud, softly. He was ahead of schedule. Killing people was the easiest thing he'd done in two days.

CHAPTER 39

SUSAN

Susan lay in bed, unable to sleep. Her body too spent to pull up the sheets. Her brain too fidgety to let her nod off. Her mind leafed through memories, each one both old and fresh.

Antonio knew a story from the ancient Mayans, about two brothers who play ball and disturb the gods below. The brothers are killed by the gods. One comes back as a gourd, hanging on the Tree of Life. He spits in the hand of a beautiful princess and she becomes pregnant with twins. These two new brothers avenge the deaths of the originals and go on to become the sun and moon.

Susan loved the story and this realization was disconcerting. She normally hated that crap. Personification, anthropomorphizing, and anything forcing the majesty of nature into human guise repelled her. Quaint tales born of ignorance. Far too frequently, magic filling gaps of understanding fought off the real answers.

This one, though...this story had resonance. She did not believe the myth. She was not certain Antonio believed it. It did not matter. Devout belief added nothing. The story was not meant to be early science. It was tradition. Simply telling it made you part of the tradition, in the long line of tellers and listeners, going back to the birth of language. The story itself was the thread, tied round the waist of the first teller, weaving through everyone after, leading to you. You hear this story and you know you have a place, you hold together yesterday and tomorrow.

You help the sun move across the sky.

Susan sat up in bed. Sometimes it was easy to hate an idea, even a good one, if it made you get out of bed to find paper and a pen.

CHAPTER 40

ALISTAIR

"I've got a deal for you," Alistair said into the cell phone, a tiny silver flipper he'd taken from the shirtless young man he shot to death back an Granny's. He didn't care if this one got traced or not. He didn't care about much, anymore, other than the girls. Valerie, Lucy, Rebecca. Everything else was in another room, a different part of his brain.

"I'm not in a position to make deals." On the other end of the call was Joshua Parks, U.S. Department of Justice.

"Sure you are, Josh," Alistair returned. "Everyone is. That's how we live."

"I've only got so much leeway."

"This is between you and me. It's got nothing to do with a case or prosecuting or any de facto Ave Maria corpus crap. You and me. First, let me congratulate you on still being alive."

"Thanks. The department is good at that."

"Second, let me lay out the plan. You make a call to Pelican Bay and say you're sending someone to see John McCorely tomorrow morning. First thing. As soon as lockdown is lifted, before he eats, shits, or showers."

"I can't do that. I could lose my job, or worse."

"Yeah," Alistair said. "Worse. That's what I'm talking about. If I get into the system, I can call off the hit on you. I don't care if Justice has got a SWAT team watching you day and night, tell me you wouldn't sleep better if the whole damn thing was called off?"

Silence followed. Too much silence. These cell phones cut off everything, no white noise like landlines. Alistair liked the white noise, he liked hearing the connection.

"What am I going to see him about?" Joshua asked.

"You're not," Alistair answered.

Another pause. Alistair assumed this guy wasn't stupid. He'd made it through law school and into a decent job.

"What are you going to do?"

"Take care of things," Alistair said.

"It'll come back to me. I can't. Whatever you do will come back to me."

"Figure it out. Suck it up. Blame your Other. Lie. I don't care—you shouldn't either. If you want to live, make the call."

Silence again. Was he losing him? Was Alistair giving him too much time to think? Too much time to talk himself out of this?

"Who?" Joshua asked.

Alistair smiled. "Alistair Bache. Tell them to accept his driver's license only. He has important papers for McCorely to sign."

CHAPTER 41

NIVEN

Niven's Chinese got better during the second hour of interrogation. The more he spoke, the more his facial and tongue muscles caught on with his memory's program. Hearing the language helped him adjust his tone and inflection. Then, of course, there was the panic. He really wanted to impress these officials—he still wasn't sure if they were police, customs, or what—that he was trying to visit his Other and that was all. No side trips to naval ship yards, munitions factories, or launch pads. He hoped that fluent putonghua, with Hakka influence, would convince them his story was true.

So far, it hadn't. It seemed, against logic, to make matters worse. After 12 hours on a pair of airplanes, he'd made it as far as the Beijing airport. Routine questions from immigration officials had landed him in an eight by eight, windowless room. The walls were the color of pistachio ice cream. At first they made him hungry. Now he was fighting an empty nausea.

"You are headed to the North Korean border?" Number 34 asked again. He was tiny, impish, with hair like black ink dripping down from a well on the top of his head. He had done most of the talking so far. Number 107, the slightly older, heavier agent next to him did most of the staring.

"No," Niven answered. He was pretty sure this was the third time this question had been asked. "I plan to go no farther than Huanan."

"Then ride the train to the border."

"That train doesn't go to the border. It is a narrow gauge coal train serving the Honggang mine. The consist is only eight hoppers."

"Who sent you?" 34 asked as if reading from a card. Niven drummed his thumbs on the wooden table, clubbing his frustration. *I am good at this*, he reminded himself. Idiot clients. Full-of-themselves partners. If he couldn't manage two twenty-something government drubs, he deserved to be thrown in jail.

"I sent myself," Niven said.

"To whom do you report?"

"I report to myself."

"To whom will you be speaking upon your return to America?"

"My friends, my family. I don't know. No one about my trip."

"Why must you keep your trip here a secret?"

"I don't," Niven said. His tone went up a few notes, so he brought it back down. "No one cares. I may tell some friends about it, but nobody will care. Nobody cares at all that I'm over here."

"We care." 34 locked eyes with Niven. Niven refused to look away. The boy's eyes were small, black in the poor light. To Niven, they did not look entirely real. The scene didn't feel real, either, which was the only fact keeping Niven from sweating to death.

Agent 107 opened his arms, palms up. "You paid thousands of dollars to fly here to speak with your Other?"

"Yes."

"To talk?"

"Yes."

"Nothing else?"

"No."

"Do you understand why it is difficult for us to believe this?"

"Yes," Niven pushed against the table, getting as close as he could to the young men. "It is difficult for me to believe. This man knows me better than anyone else ever has or ever will. I can't call him on the phone. He doesn't have e-mail. There are things I want to remember and the only way I am going to learn them is to sit with him. Do you know the phrase, 'One soldier blocks the entrance, ten thousand cannot open it'? Ming Lin uses it as if everyone knows it. I am...unsure. Ming has my secrets and I must be in the right location to get them back."

34 and 107 looked at each other. It was the first time Niven had seen them acknowledge each other. He didn't know what to make of the pause in conversation. He wanted to think he'd been convincing enough to get out, but Ming knew better. The automatic sounds of their voices, their lack of shifting or fidgeting. There was no sense of urgency. Ming's experience shadowed Niven's, pulling Niven's hope thin, askew, and well out of the light.

34 swallowed, then looked again into Niven's eyes. "You have secrets to protect. You have come here to kill Ming Lin."

CHAPTER 42

SULTAN

Landmines lay everywhere. That was, pretty much, Sultan's philosophy of travel. The whole world was a big minefield and the best way to avoid blowing up—or a place's particular equivalent, like getting robbed, bitten, or arrested—was to follow a native.

"I want to go to the Shrine of Ganesh," he told the concierge at his hotel.

He was thoroughly thin, with skin a shade darker than Sultan's. He wore a plain white suit that had not, in Sultan's opinion, seen a tailor.

The man lowered his chin and looked Sultan in the eyes. Sultan understood that his knowledge of Hindi came from an uneducated eight-year-old, but it was not a complex sentence. He stared back.

"If I may, sir," the concierge finally said. "Which one?"

"I do not know. That is why I need your assistance."

"There are, perhaps, more than a thousand."

"This one is a giant rock that looks like an elephant."

"I am sorry to say I am not familiar with that one."

"Your knowledge of geography is not my concern. Getting there is my concern."

The concierge moved his head in a small circle. It was not an affectation Sultan had seen before, but he understood the unspoken message. The man was summoning patience.

"I would like to assist you—"

"Then please do so," Sultan said. "If you do not know where the temple is, find me someone who does. This is

a fine hotel and I do not believe it would employee anyone..." Sultan did not have the right word in his lexicon.
He was forced to pull back. "Anyone who was not fine.
I will wait here." Sultan pointed at the chairs in the center
of the lobby.

The concierge slid sideways to his computer and began
typing, as if it was what he had wanted to do all along.
Sultan sat down, squeaking in a curvy white wicker chair,
and picked up a newspaper. While he could speak Hindi,
reading was beyond him. Raja had never been taught. He
had never attended any kind of school, not even religious.
And his religion seemed so...big.

If there was ever a faith in need of its own school, Sultan
thought, *it was Hinduism.*

Just from what he'd received from Raja he had decided
Hinduism was monstrously complex. All of these gods and
goddesses, who are aspects of the same one god everyone
else in the world worships. Raja couldn't be right. He
misunderstood. Christians and Muslims were not Hindu.
The characters themselves seemed like something out of
a video game. Ganesh, with the elephant head, was Raja's
favorite. He granted success and happiness, two things
so foreign to Raja that Sultan believed the boy scarcely knew
their meanings. Success was not being hungry. Happiness
was sleeping in the same house as your family. That was
as far as the boy's imagination could go.

"There is an elephant-shaped rock," the concierge said.
"The Shrine of Devarajaswamy in Chennai was built on
a large rock called Hastagiri."

"How far away is it?" Sultan asked.

"Several hundred kilometers to the south."

That seemed too far. Sultan put down the paper. "How
big is this rock?"

"It is the base of a building."

Sultan slumped in his chair. "That can't be right. I am
searching for one that is no bigger than a car."

"Sir." The concierge took on a teacher's tone. "There are
probably thousands and thousands of small shrines, as you
describe. It is common for Hindu families to keep their own
such shrines right in or behind their homes. If you look

just in this region, you will need to peer into more than a million homes."

It was like being popped with a pin. Sultan refused to let it show, but the elation he'd experienced before in his room rushed out, leaving him sagging and empty.

India was big—a billion people—and uncoordinated. He could see chaos around every corner, creeping in every alley. He could feel it pushing, even in this clean, highly insulated hotel. The mass of India. Sultan's country would fit nicely into the area immediately surrounding Allahabad, and would not be noticed by the rest of the populace.

He turned the page of the newspaper, revealing another spread of words he couldn't read.

Coming here had not been his best idea to date. He was not used to bad ideas. Sultan was not used to laying out plans. In the rare case that he did, he was equally un-used to their failure.

I must have been terrible in my last life, Sultan said in his head. *That is why this life is so bad.*

Pollution! Sultan slapped the newspaper to the table. This child believes he—no, we—are punished for things we did before? In some other body? Lunacy. The fact that the idea entered his mind, coloring his failure, was even more infuriating. Accepting defeat was worse than defeat.

Sultan stood and walked back to the front desk. The concierge smiled at him, as if they were meeting for the first time.

"I am looking for a boy," Sultan stated. "He is being forced to make carpets sun-up to sun-down, every day of his life. I believe this...carpet place is a few miles north of your beautiful city."

The concierge's face grew long. Sultan could not tell if he was surprised, horrified, or offended. He hoped it was all three.

"There are authorities—"

Sultan hit the table with a soft, but audible thud, depositing a small roll of Euros.

CHAPTER 43

CINDY

This was not Cindy's first time at the sheriff's station. She'd been brought in once, along with four others who shouldn't have been riding in the back of a pick-up. In the middle of the night. On a golf course. She came another time to get Brad, as his blood alcohol level was just shy of embalming him before the undertaker got the chance. This was Cindy's first time at the sheriff's station, and actually wanting to be there.

The foyer was smooth nothing. Walls, a few old chrome and leatherette chairs, and a half-wall of safety glass at the end of it all. In the middle of the glass was an opening made up of lots of little holes. You had to shout through them to get any attention.

"We're a little busy now, hon," the woman behind the glass said. She was pushing 60, with yellow hair poofed up on top her head. She wore silver glasses and the fluorescent lights smeared purple and green across them so you couldn't see her eyes well enough to know if she was being sassy or cute or right on the cusp of mean.

"That's why I'm here," Cindy said. "'Cuz of the business. I'm figuring you could use a little help."

"Awe, that's nice of you. You want to bake somethin', or somethin'?"

Cindy held on to her smile. "I want to be deputized."

"Wooh," the woman howled. "A little slipper of a thing like you. What you want to be a deputy for?"

Cindy didn't have an answer. She stared into the woman's color-washed glasses, letting the question echo

in her head. Her two heads, as she was starting to think
of the mess.

"I can," slipped out of Cindy's mouth. "Because I can."

"Just 'cuz you can don't always mean you should. I
imagine a Twinkie like you can be doin' a lot of things
she shouldn't."

"I'll be the best deputy sheriff Attala County has ever
had."

"I'm sure you would, hon."

"OK, that's enough of that. I don't want to be rude,
but my name is Cynthia Benning and I want to see the
sheriff."

"Well." The woman pumped her shoulders. "Like I
said, Miss—"

"Mrs."

"Mrs. Benning. Like I said, the sheriff is very busy."

This was supposed to be the start of her new life. God
had delivered to her a head full of fresh knowledge with
a tutor on top. This Florens guy could look at a fork in
an old back road and know which way to go. He wanted
to be the best at something, and then freakin' went and
actually did it. He was smart and determined. He didn't
use his looks to make people look the other way. He did,
however, use his body to get on the police force in the
first place. He was lusciously big and strong. He used
what the good Lord had given him. It's a sin if you don't,
right?

Cindy flipped her hair like a blonde, silk bedsheet,
cocked her hip, and smiled without showing her teeth.

"Let's try this again. I'm gonna wait here all day today,
tomorrow, and till the cows fly home. How happy is the
sheriff gonna be when he finds out how long you kept
a Twinkie like me waiting?"

CHAPTER 44

SUSAN

"Again," Susan said from the head of the table. "Your Hypotheses."

The team was crumpled. Most of them had not slept the night before, and it showed. The haggard, pink, raccoon look people got after a few days at a conference was already on these people. It might be on the whole world. Susan didn't know. She hadn't seen any of the world in the last two and a half days. She'd gone home the previous night. She showered and tried to sleep. By the time she was back, it felt like she'd never been any place else.

"Fine." Susan flapped a stack of bills on the table. She wanted into the game. "My take from yesterday. I am going to try very hard to keep it all. Which should not be terribly difficult. I have a hypothesis and it is not terribly technical. I call it String Theory."

Casper smirked. "Not to be confused with String Theory."

"No," Susan huffed. "Confuse away. Connect, inter-twine...weave, I don't mind. That's what it's for." She paused and made sure she had everyone's attention. "What if we are all threads, not the distinct, people-size particles we want to believe we are. We are, instead, strings bound in a big cable, running through time/space. And what if the cable twisted, breaking those strings and all of our ends re-attached to the next available string. We now see pasts that we didn't live through, but we are still ourselves, with the memories that make us...us."

They stared at her like she had just grown a second head. Susan was not surprised. It was the way she would have looked at a neurologist from an Ivy League school that had just said the same thing. It was the effect she was trying to achieve.

Adam's nose wrinkled. Something didn't smell right. "That's more of an analogy than a practicable hypothesis, wouldn't you say?"

"What are memories? Our recollections of moments in time. Easy enough. But what is time? Is there such a thing at all? Nothing else in nature feels the forward current of time. Is it a completely human construct? A method for us to sort and categorize events in our environment? Because if it is a human construct it can be changed. We can change it. That means memories, a by-product of time, could be changed as well."

"Very fanciful," Adam said. "But is it practicable? I can say this whole universe is an opera someone else is watching, but does that make any difference?"

"Yes and no. Your theory—opera theory—is a dead-end. We get watched. Big deal. My theory purposes that memories are as malleable as time."

"First of all, what you're proposing is a hypothesis, not a theory." Adam looked around the table. "Second, it's not helping."

"It's not testable," Casper said.

Susan said, "The first inklings of big ideas rarely are."

"Time is not a given," Gary Peabody spoke up. Susan smiled. A defender. That meant conversation, argument, thoughts, and ideas and it wasn't going to be about the lack of data and the impossibility of what was, as of Thursday, demonstratively possible.

Susan did not know Gary. He had come on recommendation. She remembered his name by picturing his small, round, balding head on the body of that cartoon dog that had a time machine. He stood next to Sherman, Rocky, and Bullwinkle. There was no need to incorporate MIT into her memory device. That was indisputable.

Gary continued in a soft voice, like he didn't want to start a fight. "There is no proof that time as we know it exists outside the mind. All moments can exist simultaneously and time may very well be our way of organizing the data."

"And all of us together just happen to have the same perception?" Casper asked as if he knew the answer.

"No."

Casper turned toward Gary.

"Time is relative," Gary continued. "I'm sure you've heard that."

Susan snickered. She didn't think he'd meant it to sound so cutting.

Casper's eyes narrowed. "So you're saying that the whole population stepped to the left, into their neighbor's time stream. The world is doing a cosmic electric slide?"

Gary suddenly looked confused. Susan figured the dance reference threw him.

"Gary is saying," Susan said, "that our notions of time are not the reason to throw out my hypothesis. He's not arguing for the whole idea, just reminding us that time is relative, plastic, and not a rock on which to build a foundation. I do like 'electric slide' better than 'string theory'. I think I'll call it that from now on."

The rest of the room laughed. Susan knew it wasn't because she was all that funny. They wanted the tension to snap. She, however, wanted the opposite. She wanted to pit intellects.

She cozied up to Casper. "You got a better idea?"

"I'm working on it."

"I do," Michelle Bell said. "I've got a completely different premise."

CHAPTER 45

ALISTAIR

Pelican Bay was actually near a bay. The countryside was pretty, though not as nice as the other parts of California he'd just driven through. He'd taken Route 101 through Redwood National Park, with its big, bold trees. The whole landscape looked cool, like Clint Eastwood. Unrushed. The knowing kind of cool. The trees and weeds and warblers had seen people stumble in and fumble about, and learned long ago not to pay too much attention to the silliness. Northern California was the perfect place for a supermax because it was long done being nervous.

Alistair's body was through being nervous, too. *It must be like that in war*, he thought. *After being terrified for two days and three nights, the brain knew to set the fear on the back burner. Let it simmer and bubble and threaten to boil over any second, but behind everything else.*

There were no other cars in the visitor's lot. It was early and the place was still in lockdown. He put on his suit by rolling around on the backseat of his Honda.

He took out the pen case he'd taken from Granny's. His hands started shaking, so he set it down on the center console and took a couple of deep breaths. He wiped his hands off on his pants and shook them like mad.

His plan depended on ludicrously exact timing. Both his vocation and avocation insisted on skill with the clock. Video games hinged on split-second decisions, movement without thought. His job was demanding in a different way. Drawing out bus routes, making them match with others for easy transfers, potty breaks, lunches, traffic.

He was good at it all. He was ready for this. He should have felt confident, but his years spent carving time had taught him that no matter how good you were, the real world was always better.

This was ridiculous. He couldn't come all this way, murder two people, and then chicken out because of a cheap pen. No way. This all had to matter. Living was never supposed to be easy. You were supposed to have to do all kinds of hard crap just to eat and stay warm and procreate. Opening this pen case was easier than running down a wooly mammoth. Entering the prison was easier than crossing the Bering Strait. Ending this will be easier than starting a fire with flint and steel and straw. Way easier.

Alistair lifted the lid, removed the pen, and unscrewed the back. He picked up the needle. He opened the vial, dipped in the needle, and slid it into the back of the pen. He closed the vial and the case and put the pen in his breast pocket, right over his heart.

CHAPTER 46

SUSAN

Susan nodded to—gray-haired munchkin in a church tower—Michelle Bell. "Thank goodness you've got an idea. I thought they'd spend the whole morning shredding mine. Dr. Bell is an epidemiologist. I'm sure you all understand her discipline. Michelle, just as a reminder, not everyone here has an extensive medical background. There is even an engineer in the room. If you didn't bring cash, speak carefully."

"Oh, sorry, no," Michelle started. "An engineer? Wicked. No need to worry about that. Gave up speaking Latin long ago. Let me tell you, it doesn't help you in Nigeria and it doesn't help you in Queens. In my line of work you learn to ask and answer as simply as possible. Ha. Sometimes it's more charades than anything. But I'm losing track here. Sorry. No. OK. This theory I'll call the Tipping Point, thank you Mr. Gladwell. Charming book. Could have been more about my field as we see tipping points all the time.

"We all fight sickness continuously. Every body at this table has foreign invaders in it that our immune systems fight off. We are marvelous little machines packed with marvelous little machines. Once in a while, the numbers get too much. A virus reaches a strength in numbers that makes us sick. A tipping point.

"Inside the body, as out, I always say. Nature repeats itself. Example: one or two people contract Hanta virus in New Mexico and it is contained, treated, and eliminated. A whole village in Durango gets sick, and people begin to die. The disease outpaces our ability to contain it. OK? Tipping point. We've all got that now."

Susan took inventory. Most gave Michelle some kind of affirmation. Casper looked bored. Adam annoyed. She hoped Michelle didn't notice.

"Personally, I've always been intrigued with the idea that our minds may not be bound by our brains. I won't bore you with the history of this quibble, at least more than saying everyone loves a good ghost story, yes? Yes. Some years ago a physicist took off on a similar idea."

"Roger Penrose," Gary offered. "He pondered whether or not the brain functions at a quantum level. If so, it may react to subatomic particles that fly freely about, through skulls and across time. Very ignorable stuff if it didn't come from a Nobel Laureate."

"Ah, yes," Michelle said. "Particles flying between brains. That is where we're going. Given what happened, we must lean even closer to the fact that brains are exchanging something. So maybe it was happening all along. Penny—"

"Penrose," Casper corrected.

"Penrose," Michelle repeated. "What a sweet name. You'd think I'd remember it, yes? OK, Penrose was right. Our brains have been catching quantum bits, exchanging thoughts and memories. A snippet of déjà vu here, a little ESP there. Then boom. The tipping point. We each get a big, whopping dose."

The group paused. *They're either not sure Michelle is done,* Susan thought, *or not sure what to do with her idea.*

It was on the fringe. Susan had said she wanted fringe. Right? With all the ESP and voodoo that walked the edge of it. Ideas in the shadows of the tree line. That was where they all had to go, because the wide-open center of science had nothing like Thursday night in its sights.

"ESP?" Adam said, looking at Susan.

Dr. Maria Serrano cleared her throat. It was the first sound she'd made since arriving. Susan had never met her before yesterday. Susan remembered her name by picturing her face—45 years old but wrinkle-free, with its dark Latin features and flow of black hair—on Natalie Wood. She held a big ear of corn up to herself, singing 'I Feel Pretty'. Maria, in *West Side Story*. Corn stood in for Cornell and her career cross-pollinating sciences.

Maria headed up the fairly new science of Neuro-informatics, a subset of neuroscience, dealing with information collection and management. It combined computer science, physics, biology, medicine, and other interests. Maria had coined the term 'salsa science' in an interview with *Discover* magazine. She had regretted the slip ever since, thinking it slightly racist, and made a habit of denouncing it in every subsequent interview. Susan had the habit of chuckling every time she heard an attempted retraction. She found it ironic that an information organization specialist fought one of mankind's basic organizing techniques. Stereotypes could be good, as long as you used them as Band-Aids and not sutures.

"While still a resident," Maria started, "I was called in to evaluate brain damage to an eight-year-old girl who had hit her head in a community pool. She'd had no heartbeat for 12 minutes. Dead for more than 12 minutes when the ER docs revived her. As part of the evaluation, she told me how she had left her body and looked down at the people trying to save her. A story I dismissed as pure imagination. She drew a picture of the event with remarkable detail. One of the doctors had red hair. I asked her about it and she told me the doctor with red hair had saved her life. If I ever saw him, I should tell him thank you for her. If I ever saw him. She never had, outside her death dream."

Maria swallowed. Her voice took on a tiny shake. "I would have dismissed the drawing, too, if I had not left through the ER that night. Passed a doctor with red hair. I asked him about the girl and, no—they had never met. Never while she was conscious."

"Oooo," Casper said. "Spooky."

"You would know." Maria bounced her eyebrows. "I've never told that story before."

Again the group paused. Susan figured they didn't know what to make of her. As a rule, she thought, neurologists should refrain from discussing the supernatural.

"I bet we all have a story or two," Michelle said. "Don't we, yes. Some little unexplainable tale? I think the difference is now, we all have a big one, too."

Casper leaned forward. "Recent events aside, I think we should try to keep this conversation within the boundaries of good science. I'm not discounting Electric Slide Theory or the Tipping Point—there's nothing to discount. Because there's nothing."

"We're in the realm of ideas," Susan said. "On Cinco de Mayo we left one world and entered another. One in which mind reading is possible. That is not a comfortable fact, but it is a fact nonetheless. We are out on a new branch of the Tree of Life. Like it or not."

Casper opened his mouth. For moment, nothing came out. Then he found his voice, "Not what I expected to hear from you."

"This is not how I was expecting to spend my weekend."

"Because we are out on a new branch, as you say, I think we need to get back as close to the roots as possible."

Susan titled her head. "I agree. To figure out where we are, there is as much sense in looking backward as there is in looking ahead. What does hard science have to offer us? Anything?"

"Method," Gary said. "Science offers us a way of going about the question. Observe, hypothesize, predict, and test. It's time honored and proven."

"We are still observing," Adam said. "We need more data before we can move on in any responsible manner."

This brought noise from the group. *General agreement*, Susan thought. Everyone wanted to see more data, more fMRIs or other tests being done at the time of the fascinoma, more interviews from around the globe.

Susan did, too. She had the nagging thought, though, that they weren't looking in all the right places.

Daykeepers help bring white clarity to the dark world.

Antonio was taught that with more conviction than she had leaned the scientific method. Observing holy days was ancient when science was born, and proven to every generation.

'Oh, child,' Susan could hear her Grammie say. 'You gonna burn up that head of yours.'

Chapter 47

CINDY

Sheriff Michael Lowe had a goatee and eyebrows that pointed up on the outsides, like a devil in old cartoons. Despite that, he looked happy. Not like he'd snuck a few cookies from the jar, but springtime happy. He was younger than Cindy expected. Over 50, but shy of a crisis.

Cindy sat down on the edge of the hard brown chair in front of his wide paper-covered desk.

"I want to be a deputy," she blurted.

"So I've heard," he said back. "You know there's applications and tests and we send a class to the police academy."

"I understand all that, sir. I've known boys that did it."

"Ah, good. So you understand it can be kind of a lengthy process. This ain't like learning the Slurpee machine at the 7-11."

"No. It's..." Cindy paused. This wasn't the sheriff she was expecting. She didn't catch him once sneaking a peek at her boobs. "I know you're busy, and all. It's the reason I'm here. I figured you could use some help."

"You got that right." The sheriff waved his hands over the desk, like it was the lady he was about to cut in half. "Calls are up about 400-percent. That's my conservative guess. We haven't had time for any actual accounting. There's suddenly a new witness to every crime in the county and a whole lot a people willing to do the right thing."

"So you could use another deputy."

"I could use 20 more deputies. I'm runnin' my guys ragged."

Cindy swallowed, took a deep breath, then spoke. "My Other is a Swiss Air Tiger, one of the most elite law enforcement divisions in Europe. He was trained as a patrolman for the cantonal police—cantons are kinda like counties—and was quickly snatched up by the Swiss Federal Office of Police, because he's the best of the best. He is master of armed and unarmed defense. More importantly, he's been trained to read people and situations. He's like a freakin' mind-reader when it comes to preventing crime.

"And all this..." Cindy lowed her head just a smidge. "All this skill and knowledge. I got it all. I can speak Swiss German, French, and English. I'm trained in three forms of martial arts. I can take apart and reassemble a SIG A75 blindfolded."

"Tried that yet?" the Sheriff asked.

"Don't have to," Cindy continued. "It'd be like washing my hair."

"Wow." The sheriff nodded his head. "That is amazing. You made out well with all this crazy mind swapping. You're gonna make an excellent candidate."

Cindy's shoulders sloped. "Candidate."

"I am sorry, but I'm sure your Other will tell you, not all that training carries over. You've got to learn the laws of the State of Mississippi and Attala County. Those are the laws a deputy sheriff will be enforcing."

"Oh," Cindy breathed. "I do appreciate your time."

"Any time," the sheriff said. "I like to encourage people to consider the career."

"How come?" Cindy raised an eyebrow. "How come you became a cop?"

The sheriff's eyes refocused. Cindy saw his lids lower and head tilt to the right. Maybe his left eye was stronger than his right. He ran his tongue across his front teeth. A tick, she knew. An outward sign that his brain was taking it up a notch.

"You do what you know." The sheriff leaned back. "I wasn't a bad kid, but I'd been in the system a couple or four times. Once I smartened up I realized I could do some good on the other side of the desk. Like a bank hiring an old safecracker as a security consultant. Know what I mean?"

"Yes, sir." Cindy sat back. "I certainly do. I want the same thing, to do what I know. To do some good."

The sheriff smiled wide, creasing and sharpening all the points of his face and brows and beard. "You playin' me, girl? You using some interviewing techniques on me? Getting me on your side."

"Yes, sir."

"Not bad."

"Thank you, sir."

The sheriff scrubbed his head with his fingers, his eyes shut tight. Cindy didn't say a word. The subject can't talk if you're talking, they taught you. Keep your mouth shut and listen. Neither really being Cindy's thing. She was learning, though. She was learning technique and determination. She bit her bottom lip to hold it in place. That she taught herself.

"Crazy," the sheriff said. "The world was crazy before. I got to see a good helpin' of it. Now everyone's seeing even more. The good, the bad, and the ugly."

"That's the truth." Cindy bit her lip again.

"I share memories with a woman in the Darfur region of Sudan. Know anything about the place?"

"No," Cindy didn't want to stop him.

"She's about your age. Her mind's occupied by a nasty memory. It comes up all the time, all day. She hates it and keeps calling it up because the pain is the last thing she's got of her son. She's in her village and these men tear through on horses. *Janjaweed*. Lynch mobs, we would call 'em. Hootin' and hollerin'. They come from the direction of the village well. Her intuition goes off and she tears toward the well. The screams start before she gets there. Other women. Other mothers. There's..."

The sheriff runs his tongue over his teeth. *Different this time*, Cindy thinks. *Harder. More hurtful.*

"There's heads," he continued. "Boys' heads circling the well, carefully arranged. The faces are stuck in shock.

I can see them as easily as you. Eight years old. Ten years old. All young. My Other never finds her son's body. Just the head. They come to learn the well's all packed with the rest of the boys, making it pretty useless."

Cindy didn't have to bite her lip any longer. She sat with her mouth closed, feeling her breath come down that area between your nose and your lips. The sheriff's body was still on the other side of desk, but she thought maybe he'd lost his head for a second.

"I...ah..." The sheriff shivered, like he'd walked through a cobweb. "We got it good, here, huh? Worst thing to happen to me this morning was my coffee went cold before I finished. So what did you say about French?"

"That I speak it."

"I can hire consultants, just like a bank. I don't need no safecracker, but I could use someone who speaks French."

"Really?" Cindy said. She hadn't expected that to be her biggest selling point.

"There's just one other problem. I've got a warrant for your arrest. You know anything about that?"

CHAPTER 48

ALISTAIR

Due to the peculiarities of the modern world, Alistair remembered the interview room, never having been there before. The walls were white, but not pure. The fluorescent lighting was overdone. The table sat big and immovable. His aluminum chair was half as heavy as it looked, designed to be incapable of even smudging the Plexiglas running down the middle of the table, exactly as expected. The tanks at Seaworld were not as thick. The mouth-high nest of holes drilled to let sound waves through did not seem up to the task. Or any task. That part bothered him.

The guards looked like two stacks of tires. They opened the door, did a little, well-rehearsed dance around the prisoner. A meeting this early, and after the mess of the last three days, had them wired hot. They were fully expecting this to be an assault on their lives.

John McCorely lacked expression. Alistair had been hoping for some wink of surprise or some snicker of self-satisfaction, acknowledgement that he knew this get-to-gether was coming. He got nothing.

John was much pastier than Alistair remembered. Do we remember ourselves right? It's not like the guy even had a mirror. John's build jibed with his memories, bridge-cable muscles. You could see them right through his orange overalls. His face was the only relaxed part of his body, and even that seemed forced.

His face was frightening. The deep lines around his mouth made it like a marionette's, like John's mouth could open wide enough to bite a four-inch hole in your skull.

The guards sat him down, adjusted his shackles so he could put his hands up on the table, and stepped back. "We're cool," Alistair said to them. They did nothing. "Privacy," Alistair said like an order. "You can wait outside the door." The guards glanced at each other, saying 'It's his funeral,' without using the words, and ambled out the steel door.

"Your voice sounds different than I remember," John said.

"Yours, too."

"You got more balls than I thought."

"Whatever," Alistair said with a lazy blink. It was fake tough and John had to know it. "We have things to discuss."

"I got all day." John smiled. Alistair's skin prickled. It was a smile directed not for him or because of him, but at him.

"I've written down everything I know." Alistair leaned forward. "If anything happens to me or my family, Joshua Parks gets everything. All the names, places, people, and shit I could remember. Stream of consciousness. I went all Joycean on my computer. You know Joyce, right? The writer?"

John's eyes stopped on Alistair's. "I know everything you know, partner. How Valerie likes it. Where Lucy should be tickled. Rebecca's favorite books. I could step right in and take over for you, if you wanted. You might not want that, as I think I may improve on a few things. Like actually doing something. Going somewhere. You wasted your life on your little games. For what? Shit, you've wasted more time out there than I've wasted in here. I sat for the last three days and looked back through you like a picture book and saw the whole pathetic mess. Now what were you saying?"

"Leave us alone," Alistair said. "For your own good and the good of the Brotherhood."

John sat back. "That's a good one. The Brotherhood. I ain't going to kill you. You don't have to try some fucking

Hollywood deal with them fucking ice-cream men. You don't need no deal 'cause you're not worth it. You think you know shit, but you don't. You wouldn't if it was shoved down your throat. But that's not the point, either."

This wasn't working. John was leaning back, relaxed. How could Alistair know so much and get everything so wrong?

"What's the point, John?"

"I love your family." John's face changed. The arrogant smirk vanished. He sat upright. "I love them like they're my own. I never had anything like them. Not in my whole life. That feeling when Rebecca was born. Twenty-three hours of labor, then BOOM, a new person. Squeezing your finger. A little critter holding your finger 'cause you're everything. You're her whole world. And then Lucy, her pain-in-the-ass little buddy. That time she swatted big sister Becca with a curtain rod and scurried up on your lap. Lucy the loon.

"I never got anything like that in here, Al. I never got anything like that out there, either. None of those feelings. Then Thursday night I got 'em all at once. Christ, was that a drug. Thirty-nine years of your happiness. Your peaceful happiness. So peaceful you don't even notice it most of the time. You've gotten so used to sitting in a tub of happiness you expect it."

John leaned forward, hands folded neatly between their shiny chains, eyes on Alistair's. "You're an ignorant son of bitch, but I won't kill you. I love you."

Alistair ripped the pen from his breast pocket and jammed it against the middlemost hole in the glass. He took a deep breath, kissed the pen, and blew with every piece of power he had.

"Ow." John lurched back, hand on his face. He pulled the needle from tender skin just under his left eye. "What the fuck?"

Alistair put the pen back in his pocket and sat back. His body trembled. Too many endorphins or something.

"You..." John finally showed emotion: surprise, whirling into horror. "My plan. A blow gun with curare."

"Crazy, huh?" Alistair said. "Now you'll know if it will actually work."

"You better hope it works, fucker." John looked at the door and screamed. "Door! Door!"

Death from curare was courtesy of asphyxiation. The poison relaxed muscles, so much so that after a few minutes the ones in charge of bringing oxygen in and out of the lungs simply didn't bother. On a respirator, John knew he could ride out the poison.

"Door!" he roared as his life depended on it.

Alistair knew the batch was highly concentrated. It would work in minutes.

The lock made an icy hiss and one of the guards looked in.

"We're not done," Alistair shouted.

John swung his head around, eyes so wide they might have plopped out. His head hung to the left. He couldn't straighten it.

"Give us a minute," Alistair said and the guards looked at John, who said nothing. They backed out of the room.

"It was a good plan," Alistair said. "I'm sorry if all that stuff about my family was true. I guess I'm sorry, anyway. There are a lot of people who would prefer you died never knowing a minute of happiness. Even someone else's."

It would be a good five or ten minutes before John actually died. Maybe longer. The guy was in good shape. His ears and brain would work right up to the end, shutting down after his lungs gave up.

"That black boy—young man, really—was offering you a hand, John. He was helping you up and you cracked the life out of him with a cement block. That's the kind of guy you were up until Thursday. Maybe you do love Rebecca and Lucy. Maybe you got enough of me not to be you any-more. I don't know. I'll never know. Couldn't risk it. I'm sure you understand. I never took an oath or anything—never had to—but I always put my little gang first."

Alistair stood. John's eyes didn't move, but Alistair thought he could see the life raging behind them. They weren't closing at all, probably starting to burn from lack of blinking. His mouth wouldn't close all the way either. A trickle of spit oozed out the left corner.

"Not a great way to go, I know. They'll treat you as dead a good five minutes before you are. That's cruel, but you wouldn't have thought twice about doing it to someone else. So I can live with it. I can. Live."

He picked up his briefcase. "Door!" Alistair shouted. This time the bolt of the door slid.

He walked quickly down the hall, through the first set of doors. Two more sets to go. This would take eight minutes. They'd take John for dead, as opposed to just obstinate, in about six.

CHAPTER 49

SUSAN

A pale, delicate woman with fire for hair, standing between an Abby and a Port-a-Potty.

Susan held her upturned palm out across the conference table. She moved it like a gauge until it pointed at the redheaded psychologist, Abigail DiLoro, from Johns Hopkins. Susan had had her snatched up and delivered to the institutes because of a study the woman had started in grad school, and continued in her professional career, regarding the nature of memory. She'd become somewhat famous testifying on the veracity of repressed memories. Abigail believed, after years of clinical study, that memories were mercurial, recreated when recalled, with little on which to base reliability.

At 29, Abigail was the youngest in the room by several years. Susan knew her brain was racing. She also knew this group must be intimidating. Susan felt it, and she was the one who'd put the group together.

"What are you thinking?" Susan asked with a smile.

Abigail looked like a fifth grader caught daydreaming. Her mouth fell open and she glanced right and left.

"My thoughts," Abigail said, "are still...raw. I mean, like, they're not done yet, not ready for talking. Out loud."

"That's OK," Susan said. "We want them raw. This isn't a peer review. Nobody expects a publishable statement."

"Yeah, I can...it's just that everything's so disturbing. I'm still in my hole, you know?"

Susan did know. She nodded and gave a reassuring smile. "I don't know what the socio-protocol is going to

be, but I think I should share this with you. My Other—
the man I share my memories with—is a daykeeper. He
practices a form of Mayan religion that I thought had died
out thousands of years ago. On certain days of the year,
he prays for four hours before entering a cave he firmly
believes is a kind of lobby or parlor for dead ancestors and
living spirits. There is not a person on the planet more
unlike me. Funny, isn't it?"

"As a head wound." Abigail caught herself. "I'm not
sure I should talk about my Other. These memories aren't
mine. I mean, they are, but not. The real bite here is that
maybe they are. Maybe these memories are yours, too. All
of ours. You asked what I was thinking and just when you
asked I was wondering: what if Carl Jung was right?"

"Mmmm." Susan sat back and folded her arms. "Go on."

Casper said, "Got any singles on you?"

"I'll pretend this is an intro course." Abigail clasped her
hands and leaned over the table, looking like she was about
to deliver terrible news. "Jung was a protégé of Sigmund
Freud. His main thrust, if you will, was psychology, but
he studied all kinds of cultures around the world and was
fascinated by the similarities he saw. Pyramids in Egypt
and Mexico, for instance. He developed this theory called
the collective unconsciousness, which sort of states that
there is this big sea of ideas floating around that we tap
into. We learn that pyramids are worthy of building because
of some archetype in the ether. OK?"

Abigail waited until a few people grunted or whiffed
or tilted his or her head.

"A lot of his stuff has been disproved, like our supposed
innate fear of snakes. It turns out babies don't fear them
out of hand. Heights and loud noises, however, every little
rug-rat loathes those. From Siam to San Diego. Does that
mean there's a collective unconsciousness? Not really. But
that's never been the point. Jung still gets taught because
the metaphor is useful. As humans, with similar brains,
in similar circumstances, we all run the chance of having
the same ideas once in a while. We are not completely
unique or completely alone on this planet. Got it?"

The same set humphed and nodded.

"My disturbing thought for today is, what if Jung was right all along? What if there is a sea of metaphysical thoughts and we're all throwing in and fishing out ideas all the time?"

"How?" Larry snipped. He stared at Abigail, daring her to answer.

"Not my forte, doctor. Ask one of these physics guys. They're always finding new particles and new planets."

"'Always' is a bit of a stretch," Gary said.

"I'm just saying, it's not like you all are done, right? All of the physicists in the world didn't pack up and go home. There are still a few unknowns out there."

"There's plenty we don't know," Gary said. "Having questions with no answers is the very nature of science. I'm quite proud of the continuous—"

"Yeah," Abigail cut across his sentence. "We've all got questions. In my neck of the woods, you're not going to find a decent theory of how we learn. Language, how to skip—nobody knows. All I'm saying is, Jung had this idea that no one accepted because they couldn't see the mechanism. Since Thursday, I'm thinking that just because we couldn't see it, doesn't mean it wasn't there."

"We're back to ESP again." Larry stood up. "I wish we didn't keep coming back to that."

"If wishes were fishes the world would smell pretty bad." Abigail shrank down. "Sorry. Habit. See why I don't like to, you know, shoot from the cuff?"

"You're fine," Casper said toward the ceiling, hands behind his head. "We asked what you were thinking, not whether it made any sense."

"That's the thing, right," Abigail said. "Who's to say it doesn't make sense? The fact is that on May fourth I couldn't speak Cantonese or build a motorcycle from scratch. Now I can. That doesn't make any sense. I took a big download, and gave one up. Massive peer-to-peer filesharing like you wouldn't believe. We all lost our right to call ESP bullshit. Jung thought something else was going on. The mystics of the world thought so. Acceptable science accepted the term 'neurotransmitter' years ago, and the collective subconscious—excuse the pun—was probably

onto something. Neurons transmitting. The sooner we agree
a Jungian mechanism is in here—" Abigail tapped her head,
"—the sooner we get about finding it."

"Wow," Casper said. "Do you want to erase hundreds
of years of natural science?"

"No," Abigail lowered her head. "I want to... expand...
conflate. Is that the word?" She looked around, but no one
answered. "Bring in some people we've kept waiting
outside. Jung studied everything. Literature, anthropology,
theology, anything that caught his eye. He thought that
everyone had something to offer. When Susan asked what
I was thinking, that was pretty much it. What if Jung was
onto something?"

CHAPTER 50

SULTAN

It was Jeep-shaped, but wasn't an actual Jeep. It was some kind of knockoff, like the 'Rolax' watch a kid tried to sell him in Singapore. The lack of doors, padding, and plastic said military surplus, despite the flat red paint. The back had been enclosed in diamond-patterned steel plates, making it not quite a van. The thing was topped with a single flat piece of water-stained khaki canvas. The driver leaned across the passenger seat. He was a few years older than Sultan, with short hair, a mustache, and a large birthmark that looked like mistakes with a marker.

"Get in," he commanded, then quickly smiled as wide as he could. Sultan figured he must have realized how rude he sounded.

Sultan flopped in the Jeep, letting out a small "ow." The seat felt like electrical tape over a toolbox. "Sultan bin Abdul—"

"No full names!" the driver clipped Sultan off. Again, he smiled and put his hand on his chest. "Ashok."

"Is that your real name?" Sultan narrowed his eyes.

"Yes, yes, yes." Ashok looked offended. "Just no full names."

"Perhaps we should use phony first names as well, then."

"You already told me your first name."

"You are so sure?" Sultan's face was stern. So stern, in fact, the man had to catch on to the joke. He had too.

The man smiled broadly again and put the Jeep in first gear. "I'll call you Sultan. You call me whatever you like."

They pulled out into the midday stream of bikes, rick-shaws, scooters, and small vans. The moving mass was crazy, but it was moving. Everyone obeyed a form of rule. In that respect, it was an improvement over home. Abu Dhabi had nicer cars and worse drivers.

The Jeep jerked, slowed, nearly stalled, and zipped ahead.

"This is my nephew's," Ashok said. "My own car would not be right for our tour."

"As long as this one gets us wherever we are going, I have no complaint." Sultan planted his foot in the cut of the door and grabbed the edge of the windshield. "Where are we going?"

"My cousin said you were interested in carpets."

"Not to buy," Sultan said. "He explained that to you?"

Ashok chuckled. "This will be no shopping trip."

The city became grittier the farther they got from the hotel. The intricate buildings of white rococo with taut red roofs began to blend with simple concrete boxes, finally giving way to worn, wooden structures seemingly made from nothing but old shutters. The fronts in this area pressed in on each other to become a continuous market. Huge bowls of spices, set like soccer fans at a small stadium. Bundles of vegetables, hanging meats, and forts of wooden crates punctuated the streets, recurring, paced—but still random. Music Sultan could not follow, but still enjoyed. There was romance in the open street markets that he fully understood.

Overhead were the wires. Crisscrossing, fat and skinny, black and grey, reminding Sultan of a great spider web. The entire city was trapped.

"It is your Other?" Ashok asked.

Sultan glanced at him, through the corners of his eyes. "My Other. Yes."

"My Other is a Yankee. He beats his beautiful wife. She could be on one of those stupid American shows, she is so beautiful. The lifeguard show."

"Baywatch," Sultan said. "Why did I not swap with one of those women?"

"Another disaster of math."

Sultan snickered. "A Yankee. That means you can speak English."

"I could probably get one of those telephone jobs now, if I wanted."

"Would you?"

"I like what I do."

"What is that?" Sultan asked.

"I help people. Like you."

They turned so many times that Sultan expected Ashok to pull up in front of the hotel and laugh. Instead, he snapped the Jeep into a triangular space left by a poor arrangement of olive-colored motor scooters. Ashok leaned back and pointed through the windshield, down the street.

"This is the carpet exchange." His voice had gained weight. It was as if another person had taken over the tour. "Up in these buildings. Hand-tied rugs are brought from the countryside and bought by middlemen who, in turn, ship them all over the world. Many are sent to the Middle East and then resold as authentic."

"They are made out in the country," Sultan said.

"A thousand knots per inch. The process is painful and deadens the mind. The poor, who can't find other work, will do this. There are also carpet slaves. Children are forced to tie knots for 12 or 14 hours a day, sometimes with no food or water until nightfall, when the light is too bad for working. These children have been sold into slavery by desperate parents, or kidnapped outright."

"It is disgusting." Sultan could feel knots being tied in his stomach. Hearing about the rugs, the knots, the dwindling light, and the growing thirst was pulling up raw memories—wordless anger and fear and helplessness.

"My government is ashamed of it. There are, maybe, more than 100,000 children working as slaves. Many have been working to eradicate the practice. The difficulty is in finding these places. The men running these slavery operations drop rugs here and then disappear. When we do get a lead, we frequently find an empty set of shacks or a barn. They can move their operations in a moment, like snakes down a hole."

"What hunts snakes?" Sultan asked. "A mongoose? Is that right?"

"You read Kipling before visiting India?"

"I like animal shows on television." Sultan stared down the line of shaky, patchwork warehouses. Dark green wood, against gray concrete. The few windows he saw were boarded or curtained, set between black pipes with no beginning or end. The streets were lined with crushed boxes, sealed plastic barrels, and trucks, some new, some held together with bailing wire and nylon cord.

"Changed my mind." Sultan swung out of the Jeep. "We *are* going shopping. Come on."

CHAPTER 51

NIVEN

The cell was nicer than Niven had expected. His imagination—now a montage of his and Ming's expectations and experiences—had drawn a dank, rotting cage-cave as his Chinese prison. The reality was a spotless, hospital blue cube with one glass wall. He had an aluminum chair, making the whole thing rather stylish. Like a severely austere Danish hotel room. He could maintain that fantasy if he avoided looking down. They'd taken his belt and shoelaces. As far as he knew, they didn't do that in Danish hotels.

"*Shi wai tao yuan,*" he said to himself. The peach land outside the world. He wasn't fully sure what the phrase meant. Ming used it when he hoped someone—or a couple—would end up in a world of their making. It slid across Niven's mind from a more sardonic cubby. He preferred peach worlds—the ones of his making—like his imagined minimalist hotel room. He called it his coping mechanism. The part of his brain that belonged to Ming called it something else. And it wasn't peachy.

Niven still did not like to close his eyes. Closing his eyes opened a door to Ming's world, which was far from relaxing. With the surfacing of each new memory his brain re-sorted the sounds and smells. Rice Krispies snapping and popping in his head. The echo of his breathing measuring the room, warning him that he was shut in, between hard, smooth walls. New air, from above and to the left. New, not fresh. Not from outside. He was deep in a maze.

Sound shows depth. Scent reveals detail. Niven's mind tried to tie laces already in knots. Their brains were different. Square pegs looking for round holes. His—Ming's—memories were relational. The locomotive was a barrel of dark sound rolling on six bright sounds. Thin sounds sometimes snaking out the side or top. It was an entity of grease smell, coal powder, steely cold, and boiling hot. Niven could not see the engine. He could relate the touch of cold, pizza sized wheels to whirling round noise. The tank curved, boiled, rode on the noises. Men stood behind it all, quiet in comparison. That was as close as he could get to the object of Ming's affections.

Niven tapped his gold ring on the side of the chair. *Ping. Ping.* Ming would know it was a small metal circle—soft metal, probably gold, on an edge of rolled metal, unpainted, probably aluminum. He just would.

Ming's first job was as a rail inspector. He and two others rode out to a span of track, carted in empty hoppers like huge chunks of coal. The hoppers had short sides, maybe a yard up. More like long pick-up truck beds than the rectangular funnel cars Niven had seen carting coal, back in the old days. In New Jersey. Once dropped off, Ming and the others checked the tracks and ties, walking for miles, until another train came back from the mines. On the way back they rode on top of the coal, sitting cross-legged, or lying flat, continuously adjusting for comfort or just to stay on board.

The others inspected rails by walking and looking. Ming used his iron rod. He tapped. A good rail made a good sound. A broken or rusty rail made a broken or rusty sound. Loose tracks or rotten ties made other sounds all together. Ming's specialty became seating. Crumpled ballast beneath the tracks, or cracked spikes—these were impossible to see. Not until they were trouble. Ming heard them before they caused a derailment. It only took a few months for the crew to proclaim Ming an asset. He not only decreased derailments and slowdowns, he increased the efficiency of repairs.

Walking and tapping. Walking and tapping. Following the tracks as they wound through patches of whispering breeze, around chutes of fast wind and shade and echo, over gurgling water and earthy scent. Tapping and walking. Tapping and walking. In two years he'd personally walked every meter of the Huanan Coal Railway, including the yards, where trains were made, stored, and repaired. He helped coal get to people, to keep them warm and light their lights.

Niven pinged his ring on the chair forever. Eventually, an official approached on the other side of the glass. He pushed a small piece of paper under the door. The top and bottom had Chinese characters, which Niven couldn't read. The middle was English. Plain and curt, under a seal of the U.S. State Department, it apologized that no one had yet been to see him and assured him someone would in the near future. It was, he knew, the type of universal note sent out by someone with no understanding of a particular situation. It was a note from an overworked, under-experienced person. Between the lines he read a different message than they may have intended to send: the world's fucked up. You're on your own for the moment.

This was the way things were done. Niven felt Chinese. The American memo made him feel Chinese. The sticky goo of American bureaucracy was nothing compared to the five-thousand-year tradition of Chinese red tape. The American consulate was not his problem. The problem was the insane amount of work created for the consulate by a chilled Beijing. Millions of Chinese officials snapped straight, like hairs on a neck. The frightened shuttered their windows and bolted their doors. Niven came knocking. He didn't realize how stupid he'd been until this moment. Ignorant. No...Nonintegrated. When he left New York he was Niven, with a jumble of stray thoughts. Now, in this cell, he was Niven Ming.

Zi Zhi Zi Ming. 'Know your own brightness.'

Niven did not. He could hear Ming chuckle because he had so much to learn. And, it looked like he was going to have time to spend on his lessons.

CHAPTER 52

SULTAN

Sultan climbed the outside steps to the second-story door, outside the warehouse. The steps complained all the way to the top, wiggling and screeching. He felt like he was exploiting a living organism to move up in the world. Ashok did not follow right away. Sultan did not ask him twice. He was not in the habit of ever asking twice for anything, and he wasn't going to start now. Certainly not now. He wanted his head in exactly the opposite frame of mind.

The door at the top of the stairs was locked, so he pounded slowly, rhythmically, rapping with the backs of his knuckles. Ashok came up behind him as he did so.

"What are you doing?" he shouted in a whisper.

"Shopping." Sultan continued to knock.

"This is not that kind of market."

"There is only one kind of market," Sultan said.

"Yes?" A voice came from inside.

Sultan smiled at Ashok, showing all his teeth, trying to imitate Ahsok's own grin. "I have a full basket of cash, and an empty basket of patience."

"We are closed," the voice shouted back.

"Fine," Sultan said. "I go next door now." Without hesitation, Sultan turned, urging Ashok to do the same. Ashok took two creaky steps when the door opened the width of an eyeball.

"Let me see your cash," the voice demanded.

Sultan looked into the one steady, green eye he could see. "No."

"Who sent you here?"

'Where is your money?' 'Who sent you?' You have more questions than I have patience." Sultan looked down at Ashok, paused two steps below. "Come in." The man moved from the door, leaving it open.

Sultan waved to Ashok with just his fingers. "I do not want my throat slit." Ashok said it so softly Sultan got most of the message by reading his lips. "It would not be my choice, either," he replied in full voice. They entered the top level of the warehouse.

The inside was plaster and oily corrugated metal, a patchwork, as if the building had been built by accident. The only light came from windows in the ceiling. The middle was half the size of a soccer field, filled with mounds of canvas rolls. Their size and limpness made them look, to Sultan, like bodies. The air had the unmistakable scent of fresh carpets.

The man from the door stood with his hands on his hips. His loose pants and tunic were bone linen, creased and smudged like it had been balled and tossed. He wore a thick black belt, with an enormous, curved steel knife tucked in. A carpet knife, sickle-like, for cutting knots. Sultan could feel it in his hands. He hated it. Clumsy. Painful. The cutting of knots should have been an ending, but it was only the beginning of another rug to tie. The cutting never ended.

Sultan forced himself to walk forward and look around. There were five more men, four similarly disheveled, one who looked fairly crisp. The oldest one, maybe in his late 50s, hands behind his back, stared at Sultan, who refused to stare back. As Sultan was going to play things, he was now in charge. He marched off into the rows of rugs.

"Wait—" the man from the door called out.

"Much to do," Sultan rolled over whatever the doorman was going to say.

The older man meandered, glancing at different bundles. Sultan could tell he was aiming to intercept him near the second stack. The other men moved around. Sultan could see that they were cutting off any means of escape. He snickered. As if he'd walk into a maze, and let them block any escape, if he had fear of trouble. The fools thought they were being so smart, so secure, cornering an unarmed man. Quiet cowards, with their mean little knives.

"Sorry to..." Sultan didn't know the Hindi word for 'intrude.' He smiled and spread his arms. "Surprise. Sorry to surprise you this way."

"Do I know you?" the crisp man asked, smiling back, bereft of any mirth or even politeness.

"You know my money." Sultan checked on Ashok, who hovered near the door. He was attempting to look calm, but had no idea what to do with his hands. Sultan scolded himself. He should have bought him something to eat or drink. Nothing made one look more relaxed than snacking.

"You will have to introduce me again." The man laughed as he approached.

Sultan made himself chuckle and looked at the pile of wrapped rugs next to him. He peeked in at the end. The navy blue was uninteresting.

"All of these, in this stack, are like this one?" he asked, as if he were in a department store.

"I still do not know what you want." The crisp man was close now. "I still do not know who you are. Tell me."

"No." Sultan clasped his hands behind his back, mimicking the older man. "I do not want to know your name and you do not want to know mine. We both want to do business. That is all, right?"

"I do not do business with people I do not know."

"The men I usually use are..." Sultan clamored for the right words. Raja needed to get out more. "Taking a break. This business with the memories has set them back. There are no secrets anymore, it seems. Still, I have orders to fill."

"You work with buyers?" the man asked. "Can I have their names?"

"I don't know what names they use with you." Sultan stepped very close to the man in charge, their noses almost touching. "I will look at your wares. If any fit my needs, I will pay you and be on my way. This may be...not normal for you. These are not normal times."

"You are right about that." The man did not flinch.
"Are the rugs grouped by kind?"

The man looked into Sultan's eyes. He could feel the man trying to reach in and pull something out, a thought, a feeling, a reason to have him sliced and sealed in one of those blue plastic drums sitting at the curb. Sultan slowly brought his wrist up and glanced at his Breitling. He didn't lower it until he was sure this neat, clean man in his late 50s had seen it too. The money. The taste. It was not a watch worn by a tired, underpaid government official tracking down tariff violations.

"How many rugs will you need?" The man asked as if prompting a password, a test more than an inquiry.

"Ten thousand in total," Sultan said. "They may not all come from here."

The man took a deep breath, then stepped to the side, bowing slightly and unfurling his right hand. "I have hope that you will find our merchandise to your liking."

Sultan moved quickly down the row, looking for a trace of crimson. At the fifth pile, he motioned to the nearest man to unroll the top rug. Sultan was impressed with the intricacy of the pattern, the interlocking loops and rectangles, and orderly repetition of grays and blues and greens. It was a pattern with which he had no familiarity, so he moved on.

The men unrolled another eleven rugs, all done with a crimson base color. Sultan had never seen any of them before. He walked back to the door through which he arrived.

"Nothing today?" The man in charge followed. "Certainly there must be something here you can use. These are the finest—"

"Thank you for your kindness." Sultan pushed out the door.

At the bottom of the stairs, Ashok grabbed his shoulder and pulled his mouth next to Sultan's ear.

"That was not wise. We could have been killed."

Sultan turned under Ashok's hand and placed his own on top, pressing it down, hard. "I have never been killed shopping."

Ashok was confused, but quickly shook it off. "This is where we part."

Sultan threw his hand off Ashok's, like he'd been burned. "Turn your back. It is no...surprise to me."

Ashok's mouth dropped at the corners. "I help. All I can, I help. I will continue, as long as I'm alive. The longer I am with you, the less likely I am to stay that way."

"I do not live just to live," Sultan said. "I am part...I am one of the many knots that makes this grand carpet beautiful. All of us, woven together. One tied to the next, using this one's strength to give strength to another. Can you see the beautiful design? You helping me helping a boy who will help another. A knot with thousands of others makes a carpet. A knot by itself is a scrap. You, my friend, are not a scrap. You are one of the honored anchor knots, the strongest and the most important."

Ashok ran his fingers down each side of his mustache. He glanced at his Jeep, at the warehouse they'd just visited, and back at Sultan.

"We must get you a drink," Sultan said. "Before our next warehouse."

CHAPTER 53

SUSAN

"Pull over," Susan said.

Casper got worried. "Everything all right?"

"Right here." Susan pressed her hand to the window of his black BMW.

Casper checked all angles and slipped the car against the curb.

Susan said, "Look at that guy."

The man was clear into his seventies, thin as a set of golf clubs. His black skin shone. The baggy shorts, polo shirt, and cap were regular attire for this area. He looked like Susan's grandpa, and thirty of his friends and all the guys that he jawed with at the barbershop, the grocery, and the bait store.

Except for the skateboard. The old guy jumped, flipped, twirled it, kicked it around, then trapped it back under his feet and kicked off. A bunch of kids stood and cheered.

"There's something you don't see every day." Casper waited for Susan to get her fill before driving on.

The restaurant was one of her favorites. Susan wondered briefly if Casper had traced her credit card transactions to learn this, or any other secrets. The idea was strangely unaffecting. The night Mom dropped her at Grammie's never to be seen again, the blue bike, her first kiss, her first period, the A+ in biology, her acceptance to Columbia, the afternoon she sat in Central Park and realized Gordon was never going to let her have a career—those memories were all out now. Logically, it was only in the head of a man in the highlands of Guatemala, who had no reason to ever tell anybody. Yet, the feeling was, her closet door was open. She no longer had any complete and total secrets. Casper using a supercomputer to figure out what kind of restaurant she liked simply didn't seem all that invasive anymore.

Casper set down the wine list. "Pretty women like to be complimented on their brains, smart woman on their looks. So what in God's name does any man ever say to you?"

"Do you take cream or sugar?" Susan said. "I've always like the sound of that."

Casper laughed. "Ah. You look very powerful tonight. How's that."

Susan laughed back. "You've got my number. Clever."

"That is my stock-in-trade."

"Must be. I was under the impression that no one stayed at DARPA for more than five years."

"Yes." Casper shifted his eyes, readying a secret. "They've found me somewhat indispensable at the moment."

"It's turning into a long moment."

"We miss you over there."

"Wish I could say the same."

"Still?" Casper urged.

Susan thought about it for second. Why shouldn't she miss the secrets, the security, the constant pushing on her Hippocratic oath like it was a Hefty bag they were testing.

"Still," she said, "I'm in the business of making people better."

"So are we, just in a more roundabout way."

"Yours is more chemotherapy. Not my preferred method. Ever."

"We're not as harsh as all that." Casper planted his elbows and laced his fingers. "If you are so disapproving of my life's work, why did you allow me in?"

"First of all," Susan cocked her head, "you have my utmost approval. You know that. I just saw my career steering away from all the boys and toys. Second, even if I did disapprove of your work, it wouldn't mean it wasn't good. You were the first person I thought of after the secretary anointed me."

"And yet you didn't call."

"And yet you showed up. Imagine that."

"I thought of you, too. As I do quite often."

Susan smiled. The sentence sounded sincere, which sent a little wave of warmth down through her. She wasn't prepared for it. Or for Casper, again. She needed a waiter and a glass of wine and something to put in her mouth when she ran out of things she wanted to say. There were always things she didn't want to say. She had plenty of those.

"Did your research continue after I left?" Susan asked.

Casper leaned over the table. "I can't discuss it."

"Let me put it a different way. Have you been up to anything new?"

Casper snorted. "Now that's clever. Ha!" He sat back and crossed his legs. "I've had a hand in several other projects. I've also kept alive one old project, near and dear to my heart."

"Or head?"

"Closer, yes. It still doesn't work."

"How sad."

"We never found a way of producing the...desired effect from a distance. Not more than a couple of centimeters. Even then, the sound of a crying baby generated more havoc for the nervous system than anything we were doing. The 'pocketbooks' have become more enamored of sonic stimulation. They are putting money on hard, oscillating sounds."

"I understand the effect can be devastating."

"Not really. Confusing and incredibly annoying, but not what I would call devastating. The Israelis have a mobile unit. They've yet to release their results. They said things went well. If that were true, they would have shut up and implied failure. I'm sure they are not pleased."

"What would please you?"

Casper's eyes twinkled. Susan was not sure how a man could actually do that.

Susan rolled her eyes. "Why do you want to sleep with me anyway? I'm old."

"You're hot."

"You're not."

"I'm clever and you're not shallow."

CHAPTER 54

SULTAN

The barrel of the gun seemed huge at eye level, like seeing the moon low over the desert. That moon is no closer to the Earth than it is for the rest of the night, its size is an illusion. Just like the dead black hole at the end of the pistol seemed to be as wide as a grave.

Sultan and Ashok had scammed their way through three warehouses. Entering the fourth as if they owned the place, they met a dark, scraggly bearded scarecrow of a man with a long, pewter-hued revolver. The kind from old movies. Sultan had never seen one like it in person. He had not spent any time around firearms. They were not his thing, being incapable of playing music or going fast or sparking the interest of attractive women. What he knew about guns would fit nicely into the barrel into which he was now looking.

"Is this needed?" Sultan asked.

"Quiet," the man spat.

There was shuffling on the right side. Sultan fought the urge to look. He didn't want to divert his attention and he really didn't want to make any sudden movements. He could only assume Ashok was right behind him, the man was so absolutely silent.

"I am looking for rugs."

"I said quiet." The man bared his teeth, a cat caught in an alley.

Sultan decided to wait. The man's arm was going to get tired soon, holding the gun out like that. He took in as much as he could without moving his head. The warehouse had probably not been originally designed for storage. It was darker than the others, with big, square pillars every few feet. Not the optimal configuration for moving goods, but very good for hiding and obscuring.

"No," called a voice from outside Sultan's field of vision.

"Get out." The man with the gun jutted his chin at the door.

"I am looking for rugs."

"No rugs. Get out."

Sultan put his hands on his hips. "My money does not work here?" Sultan looked in the direction of the other voice. A man, in the shadow of a big pillar. "Do you have any rugs for sale?"

"Get out now," the gunman growled. He waved his gun toward the door. Sultan heard Ashok take a step backwards. The man near the pillar said nothing. These men were the most skittish they'd met so far.

They must have the most to hide, Sultan decided. He walked toward the shadow of the pillar.

"Stop," the gunman said.

"That is not how business gets done, my friend."

"I said—"

"I heard you." Sultan continued. The man near the pillar stepped sideways, to block him. He was thin and dark, with shaggy black hair, younger than the other, dressed like everyone else he'd met today: unkempt linens and sandals.

Boom.

Sultan dropped to a crouch, hands over his ears. The man from the shadows ran toward him. Sultan spun on his toes. Ashok and the gunman twirled, arms forming a giant spearhead, aimed at the ceiling, pistol at the point.

"Allah, please," he said in Arabic. He hadn't been in a fight since he was nine, wrestling at school about some stupid affront. His plan was to avoid fighting here, in India, at all costs. Violence was not the last resort—it was failure. It was the sign that things had gone wrong, that he'd lost control. Control was key.

Sultan sprang at the men, climbing them both, stretching for the gun. They all toppled from his weight. He fell on Ashok and the gunman, everyone huffing and grunting.

Sultan found the gun barrel and bent it back, the wrong way out of a hand. The gunman screamed. He cranked harder, wrenching the pistol from the clawing fingers. Someone pulled his legs. The other rug merchant. He spun the gun, spun his body, spun his head—twisting from the man's grip. Sultan sat, knees bent, pointing the revolver at the very scared, very surprised man from the shadows.

"I *never*," he paused, calming his voice, "had this problem at Prada."

The man made no sign that he understood a word Sultan had said. Ashok and the other man uncoiled and jumped to their feet. Ashok positioned himself behind the one who used to be the gunman.

"What has you so...afraid?" Sultan remained sitting.

"We thought you might be someone else," the man's voice was high and shaky.

"I am not, and yet you still shoot at me."

"Please, forgive my friend."

"Who did you think I was?"

"No one."

Sultan rose, keeping the gun aimed in the man's general direction. He glanced at the other man. Ashok was ready to grab him again if he did something rash.

"I am looking for red rugs," Sultan said. "Show me what you have."

The man from the shadows looked at his friend, then back at Sultan.

"Will shooting you in the head make this go faster?" Sultan asked.

"No, no. I will show you what we have."

"That is all I am asking."

The man walked backwards until hitting a box. He then summoned the courage to turn from Sultan and the pistol and walked passed the first line of pillars. Sultan followed. These carpets were not rolled. The were all laid flat, in stacks of 50 or more, each turned a few degrees from the one below, creating tall, dismal flowers with short, floppy petals. They were arranged by size, not by color. The man stopped at the first stack of very large rugs and Sultan urged him on. Medium size, the kind that fit under a table.

The man flipped up a few of the next, revealing a shinny, deep crimson. The light from the dirty side windows was poor, but not destitute. Sultan saw the pattern. The knots. His stomach convulsed and the back of his neck prickled. He shoved the gun in the waistband of his jeans and grabbed the edge of the carpet above the red one. He ripped the top of the stack off and looked down at the red, 6 x 8, white circle, white square, white circle, specks of green and red and blue. A thousand knots per inch. He wanted to vomit. Right onto the rug. Onto all of them.

"Where did this come from?"

"I don't know," the man said.

Sultan pulled out the revolver and held it up, checking the number of bullets. "Where did this rug come from?"

"The makers, they just show up and we buy." The man's voice was tight.

"You have no way of talking to them."

"No way. They simply appear."

"Do you know what I think?" Sultan passed his hand down the barrel of the gun. "I think you are afraid of your Other. I think you are afraid some secret got out, like where these rugs come from or who makes them."

"There is no—"

Boom.

The man from the shadows crumpled to the ground, hands covering his head. Sultan's hand, with the gun, arched over his head. He hadn't expected that kick. He barely held on to the weapon. He looked toward the door. The other man had not budged. Ashok stood behind him. He looked back down at the other, cowering next to the stack of rugs, just realizing he'd not been shot.

"Phone him," Sultan said. "Now. I know he has a cell phone. I am guessing that you know numbers. A number of numbers. Enough to fill you with fear."

Sultan walked the man back to the others. He made them sit down, near the door, with their backs to the wall. Then he turned to Ashok. "Check around for rope or cord. Then go fill the Jeep with gas."

CHAPTER 55

NIVEN

Jet lag was bad enough—Niven had lost track of local and New York time, his body going off and doing its own thing, and the lack of contact with the world meant there was no one, no society, trying to correct him. Not even the sun and moon did their duty. He hadn't seen either one in...he wasn't sure. They'd given him five meals—but the periodic reorganization of his brain fogged him. Every time he peered into some new corner of his mind he seemed to be separating strips of Velcro, painlessly tearing, revealing a new blank.

He had only seen two women in the last five meals. He knew they were around someplace, but rarely in this holding area. Women were always such a nice diversion. At least, when his memories were all his own, they were.

Ming had been with a woman once. A prostitute his buddies provided. She was bone thin, softer than anything he'd ever touched and she smelled heavily, heavenly, of roses and baby powder. The scent rang in Niven's memory, like getting mugged when he was 18 and the day Kennedy was shot. Roses and baby powder. Girl and woman. Sexy and sweet. It whipped Ming up and held him that way— Niven assumed it would—forever. The scent of baby powder or roses was enough to give Ming an erection. Niven could feel his own tingle, recalling the fact. Ming kept baby powder and rose water in his apartment, for use as masturbation aids. Porn.

"Even his porn is nicer than mine," Niven said out loud. A clean, sweet scent. No crude objectification of women.

"What the fuck?" That's what Nicholas had said at the meeting Friday morning. Niven thought at the time it was because he was already at the table. Perhaps it had more meaning. Nicholas knew about the purchase of Biobrex and he knew the creative team hadn't been informed. It was thus a legitimate question. And maybe even more. Why was an ad agency buying a small drug company to begin with? Vertical consolidation was bullshit. Diversification from marketing to medicines was ludicrous. Advertising something that people can't go and buy, something for which they must pester their healthcare providers—who were 50% more likely to give in to a marketing attack— was creepy. Niven provided justification for a great deal in his life, his profession being his leading customer. Advertising provided information that made the market-place work. It was a crucial ingredient for capitalism and, therefore, America. Advertising something a consumer couldn't consume spoiled his broth.

Biobrex was not the first sour patch he'd forded. Niven hated pretending one soft drink was any different than another. Candy bars, aimed at five- to eighteen-year-olds were even worse. Still, people could choose the dalliance. No one hoped the gooiest nugget in the universe was going to cure herpes.

Once, in the rail yard, standing next to engine 090, Ming felt a sound in his ear, too high for him to say he heard it. He groped around, with his hands, prodding with fingertips and yanking them back before the heat took the skin.

"You are out of water," he shouted.

"I know," a young voice called back, accompanied by a clink and the *glug-glug* of pouring liquid.

"What are you doing?" he shouted louder and faster.

"Adding water," came a second, more irritated voice. Two men, atop 090, effecting some sort of repair. Cold water on the super-hot crown sheet in the boiler.

"Jump!" Ming yelled, running backwards.

The top of the firebox burst. The boiler tank blew sky-ward. Ming could hear it roll through the air, getting farther, then closer, then crashing. Hollow metal on dirt. Not on him, he realized and breathed. Not on the two men yelling. They were relieved, not injured. So relieved, in fact, that the two men bought Ming a hooker.

No one at the candy company had ever been grateful enough to buy Niven a hooker. Not even once.

Of course, Niven asked in his head, *what would one whore do with another anyway.*

"The past," Niven said. Again, out loud. He wondered if they had cameras on him. If these Chinese officials thought it odd he occasionally spouted disjointed phrases. Maybe everybody did this after five meals in captivity. "All in the past."

He must have lost his job by now. His whole career. He hoped that big Biobrex idea he chased never occurred to him again. If it was great, he'd blown it. If it wasn't, he was a fool.

Nicholas will make a wonderful new director of creative services and I, Niven decided, *will serve as a wonderful cautionary tale for new hires.*

CHAPTER 56

MRS. ENFIELD'S THIRD GRADE CLASS

Cathy Enfield walked the long way to school as vestiges of morning dew refracted early morning sunlight into tiny rainbows that floated over the trees and grassy fields which lined her walkway. She enjoyed going through the great front doors of Public School 23. They were large enough for elephants, cut from oak older than Christ. Schools didn't get these kinds of doors anymore, and even this one probably wouldn't have them much longer. Someone would find a reason to replace them: lead, asbestos, fire-hazard, brother-in-law's door company needs the work. If it were really snowing or really raining, she'd dash through the back doors like every other teacher in the school. Otherwise, she went up the stone stairs and through the big doors.

The school was a three-storey cement block building, all rectangles. Small rectangular windows were stacked in neat rows between angular buttresses and fluted bulwarks. It was a 1930s WPA project, built during one of the world's last continental upheavals large enough to tussle Lockport, New York, a city quietly notorious for missing most of them, ever since the Erie Canal was relegated from commerce to song. Public School 23 was a bulky, solid box, built to protect kids from weather and abject ignorance. A vault for children. Cathy always thought if more people knew about the school, more movies would be shot here. Spooky movies, about a past that wasn't nearly as safe and secure as everyone remembered.

Remembering would be today's lesson, though she didn't have an approved plan. There would be little use in trying to talk about anything else. Not the first day back. Not all the kids would be back right away. There was no sense in penalizing them with missed lessons, just because their parents were over-protective or slow to adjust. Or, more fairly, because the child needed some time. That was certainly a responsible reason to keep a child out. There were plenty of kids out there with memories they shouldn't have.

Hell, there were plenty of adults out there with memories they ought not to have. She was one of them. When the kids asked her about her Other—and they would, by no later than 8:30—she'd need something to say.

Cathy was small, 28, invisible when she wanted to be, exceptionally noisy otherwise. She kept her hair short and trouble free, as it was a bright enough blonde to still look plenty feminine in a bob. At least she hoped so. It was not like her husband was ever going to tell her. As long as she actually had hair, and it didn't interfere with fantasy baseball or playing golf, all was right with the world. Her husband liked to hold her face in both hands, say "My little doughnut face," and kiss her. She used to take offense at this until she realized that comparing her to a doughnut was deeply affectionate for him.

Teachers hugged in the faculty room, as if there had been a terrible bus crash. The principal gave everyone a pep talk of the kind Cathy herself might give to a group of 8-year-olds. She already knew her duty to the students, how much they looked up to her, and all the responsibility that came with that honor. Cathy had wanted to be a teacher since she was five. The principal was treating this like a first day when, for Cathy, not even her first day was much like a first day. She wasn't destined for administration. She'd always known that.

She didn't know what to expect when the kids arrived. She'd spent the last three days and nights with her husband, jumping from news to news, breaking only for a baseball game on Saturday night. While brain-sharing may have been the single biggest event in human history, it wasn't a rain out. She hadn't talked to too many other people. Her family, her in-laws, everyone was healthy. She hadn't spoken with any kids. Not knowing what to expect proved the best preparation.

The kids came in like they did every Monday. Talking, slugging fatty backpacks, clumping, shouting, giggling, bumping. 'Kids are Nerf balls,' one of her professors had said. Infinitely resilient. They bounce and bounce back. Let them be that way.

The outstanding difference this morning, rising above the shuffling and locker slams and calling of names, was the language being used. *Languages*, Cathy corrected herself. With a capital 's.' A few kids called out in foreign languages, like birds looking for mates. She couldn't identify all of them, sorting only by general class—Romance, Germanic, Slavic, Asian. Lots of Asian, and possibly Hindi. Soon they were all shouting out, seeking someone else who shared their new language. The hall was loud, crazy, but like a festival.

Cathy heard Korean. She walked that way. The accent was poor, though she was sure she'd do no better. She couldn't make all the sounds come out the way they started out in her head. She heard it again. "Does anyone speak Korean?" And there was something about the intonation, something unidentifiable in the soul of the sound, that told Cathy this little girl shared memories of someone from the North.

She doubled her pace. She lived to help children. This one was going to need her.

CHAPTER 57

SULTAN

Sultan and Ashok gobbled curry quickly from bending, aluminum dishes. Sultan was amazed how good it was. Spicy enough to blow his tongue off, but with layers of passing flavors that made it well worth the pain. They drank Coke from glass bottles. *Female-shaped bottles*, Sultan thought. They fit so naturally in the hand he was quite sure it was the bottle alone that had given Coke its prominence. Sitting in the Jeep, eating by streetlight, they both kept their eyes on the side door of the warehouse.

"I am..." Sultan started, then stopped. Raja didn't know the Hindi world for 'dread.' Maybe there wasn't one, but more likely he'd never learned it.

"Yes?" Ashok asked as the pause went on.

"I am tired of waiting and I am in no hurry to go." That was as close as he could come to what he wanted to say.

"Yes," Ashok replied. "I feel like going in two directions."

"Your night would have been easier if you had not saved my life."

"My day would have been easier if I had ignored my cousin's call."

"Why didn't you?"

"I do not know." Ashok slumped in the driver's seat. He continued to stare, but Sultan had the suspicion that he was no longer seeing the side door. His eyes were envisioning another scene. "I practice the four tenets of the Vedas. Did you learn about them? From your Other?"

"Very little," Sultan replied. "They are rules?"

"Suggestions about how to lead your life. 'Dharma' is duty to your family and society. It is important to me. I want to do everything right...that I can."

"There are things you can't do right?"

Ashok rolled his eyes, as if there were a world of things he'd done wrong. He stopped and tapped the olive green dashboard of the Jeep. "Do you like the way this truck looks? It does what we need it to do. If I had a choice, I'd put something soft on these seats and get rid of this ridiculous chest behind us and paint it an opulent, shiny saffron. My nephew needed a truck, he got one even the army didn't want anymore, with terrible seats. He needed a place to lock up his tools, he built this box. He needed paint, he used what he had left over from a store he fixed. Someday, when I have a little extra money, I will buy my nephew some real car paint."

"That is a nice story," Sultan said.

Ashok turned to him. "What is your story?"

"The same," Sultan said. "There is only one story."

Each popped a piece of curry. Ashok did not take his eyes from Sultan, chewing and waiting. Sultan did not take his eyes from the spot on the road he expected to be used soon as a parking place.

"Man tries," Sultan said. "That is the story. Everyone has different...the stories are different a little. Mostly, they are the same: man tries."

They watched the traffic amble past the front of the warehouse. The trucks were more infrequent now, as the evening calmed. In terms of distraction, what the vehicles lost in numbers, they made up for in flash. Strings of lights in every color lining the sides and tops, draped, swagged, or pulled taught. Nightclubs on wheels. It got so annoying, Sultan was happy to see a plain white cube van pull up, with nothing but a few amber teardrops on top.

"What about you?" Ashok asked. "What are you trying to do? Get shot at again?"

The driver of the cube van got out and walked to the side door of the warehouse.

"Everyone needs a little fun, right?" Sultan watched the driver pound on the door, while keeping an eye on the truck he'd just exited. Sultan handed Ashok his dish and got out. "I was going to buy a boogie board and then this came up."

Across the street the driver pounded harder, keeping his back to the door and guarding his truck. Sultan jogged across the street and walked toward the warehouse. He faced forward, pretending to be oblivious to the man knocking on the door. The man rapped again and stepped back, scanning the building's windows. Sultan's heart rate surged. He focused on a signpost ten meters ahead, holding the man from the cube van in his peripheral vision. The man looked at Sultan. Sultan dared a glance.

Stark fear. Terror. Searing pain. Sultan clenched every muscle in his body. The man's eyes twitched. He saw the fear. Sultan tore his face away. Vomit. Everything in his stomach was coming back. *Distract yourself!* He slammed a vision of the orchard near Liwa into his mind. Placid, soothing green. The happiest place he knew. Hold the vomit. He doesn't know you!

The man pounded the door, it sounded to Sultan like he was using both fists. He was out of sight. Sultan ran to the corner, looked back, then crossed the street and hid around the side of a building. His mouth was full of acid and his body shook.

The man beat boys. He slapped them with an open hand if they made a noise. He used an old, rusty piece of rebar if it was more than a noise. When the new boy made a terrible mistake—he made one pattern when it should have been another, working all day on a mistake—he got beaten on the knees with the rebar. Beat and beat and beat until the boy could not longer cry, he lay on his side making a huffing sound. Raja thought it was the sound of the soul trying to leave his body, but getting sucked back in, trying to leave his body, but getting sucked back in. Over and over, until they were all asleep. The new boy was gone in the morning.

The cube van made a wild U-turn and chirped down the street. Sultan came out from the protection of the building and waved to Ashok, who rolled the Jeep forward. Sultan swung in. Ashok clanked the Jeep into first gear and jittered after the van.

"That is the man?" Ashok asked.

"One of them." Sultan tossed the curry plates to the sidewalk.

"Are you sure?"

"The man hung me...my Other...upside down because I was crying. He let me swing until I couldn't get air up into my lungs. I wanted my head to explode just to be rid of the pressure. You don't forget the face that does that."

CHAPTER 58

MRS. ENFIELD'S THIRD GRADE CLASS

Samantha Courtie was not one of Cathy's students, but she knew her by name. She was a poised, pretty, popular girl who tended to win awards and make speeches, earning the attention of teachers other than her own. She stopped shouting in Korean when Cathy caught her eyes. Brown crystal eyes.

"*An-nyung-ha-se-yo,*" Cathy said.

"Your Other is Korean?" Samantha asked back.

"*Ye.*"

"Is it true? Is it all true?"

Cathy placed her hands on the girl's shoulders. "Yes."

The bell rang. It was time for everyone to get to class. Teachers were not going to be too strict this morning, but Samantha wanted to start a conversation it would take days to finish.

"Go to class," Cathy said. "If you need to talk to me, you just tell your teacher. Mrs. Blascek, right?"

"Yes," the girl nodded slowly. Cathy smiled, turned her, and released her like a wind-up toy.

Cathy walked back down the hall, listening to the fading jabbering of the junior United Nations. The Courtie girl was smart. She was going to be all right. Cathy was slightly glad to know there was at least one other person she could talk to about what she'd learned last Thursday. How to cook grass and bark to keep from starving to death. How to ignore your intuition, fold over your sense of right, and bury any fragments of truth you find that don't fit with what you are told. How to live in fear.

Cathy's class of 22 mostly eight- and nine-year-olds lingered around their neat rows of wood and chrome flip-top desks. They were chatty and energetic, acting more like this was the Friday before a holiday than a Monday morning in the middle of May. She was usually in the classroom when they entered, so she wasn't accustomed to this level of disorder. As they noticed her, most moved to their assigned seats. Only three children were absent—no different than any other spring day.

"We certainly have a lot to talk about this morning," she announced with a smile, waving her hands at the few students who had not yet taken their seats. "I'm very glad to see you all here."

The kids kept looking behind her, to her left. She turned and saw Cameron Belleotti in the corner. He looked uncomfortable, too embarrassed to speak, unable to move.

"Go sit down, Cam." Cathy warmed her smile.

"I..."

"It's OK."

"Can I move my seat?" he blurted.

Cathy scanned the room. Five rows of five. Cameron's seat was one of the best in the room, right next to the window, looking at a trio of healthy maple trees. *Soldiers at the ready. Always ready. Never doing. North Korea's military is the biggest in the world, buzzing like bees locked in a hive.*

Cathy wagged her head, shaking loose the stray thoughts.

"You don't like the window?" Cathy asked.

"No," the boy replied. "My Other, where he's from, they never sit near windows. You can't." He bit his lip to stop something—a word, a cry—she didn't know.

"We'll move you over to the wall. Will that do?"

He nodded, but didn't move. Cathy looked down the row. Five girls on the wall, all staring at her. The first four were not pro-change. God knew what the weekend had done to them already.

"Kaitlyn," Cathy said to the last. "Would you mind changing seats with Cameron?"

"Permanently, or on an as-needed basis?"

Cathy stared at her for a second. "For the rest of the year."

"No problem, Mrs. Enfield. If it makes Cameron a more productive student, I'm all for it."

The class went back to chattering during the move. Cathy did not immediately stop them, still slightly stunned by Kaitlyn's diction. The girl was bright, but she'd never spoken like that before. She wanted to ask Kaitlyn about her Other. She wanted to ask them all about their Others. She wanted to know who was going to be screwed up for the next few weeks—or years—and who was going to continue unscathed. Cathy did not know what was appropriate. This was akin to asking about home life or family structure. Private stuff. She could tell already that the kids were volunteering most everything, and she wasn't even sure that was appropriate. She had a few memories she wouldn't want her Other spreading around. Her personal stories were not for the classroom. To be fair, no one else's should be either. Not one of these kids knew how far to go, how much to say, and they'd be looking to her to lead.

'When in doubt,' she always said, 'be honest.' Kids know when you're faking it.

"I don't know what to say," Cathy said. "What happened last Thursday has never happened before."

"As far as we know," Jared said from the second row.

"Yes." Her stunned look was back. She needed to get rid of that right away. "As far as we know."

"What makes you say that?" Alexis was a mouse. In a whole year, Cathy had never heard her speak out.

"We do not know the whole of human history."

"We do so," Alexis said. "Through stories and oral tradition, legend and song. We all know this event was unique."

"How can you be so certain?" Jared asked. "Especially now. Certainty died Thursday night and is yet to be reborn."

"Whoa," Hunter said from the back row. "You pulled that out of your ass."

The class roared.

"Hunter!" Cathy barked.

"Sorry, Mrs. Enfield. My Other speaks different."

"You knew that word before and didn't use it."

"I just..."

"I know. Let's keep control. All of us. OK?" Cathy held out her arms. "OK?" she repeated, this time cupping her hand to her ear.

"Yes, Mrs. Enfield," the class shouted in unison.

CHAPTER 59

SULTAN

"What's a boogie board?" Ashok asked as they sped down the highway, wind pouring through the Jeep's open sides, beating back their voices.

"It is a small surf board," Sultan shouted. "You lie on it, rather than stand."

"Why would you want to do that?"

"I don't."

Ashok stole a peek at Sultan, but the bafflement on his face remained.

"It was a joke," Sultan said. "Everything is a joke."

Ashok scowled. "When my government raids an illegal carpet factory, they use 20 or 30 policemen. They have guns, sometimes gas. That is a joke?"

"Yes," Sultan answered. "It's just not funny."

They had left the highway for a craggy, but still-paved local road. They lagged behind the cube van as far as they could without losing sight of its lone red taillight. The road rose and fell and wound past a constant contingent of one- and two-storey box buildings, and thin strings of trees. *Lots of trees*, Sultan thought. *The collections were not thick, and the trees were not monstrous. Still, there were plenty of them.*

Then there was no pavement. They drove down a strip of dust between lines of thin, short trees. Sultan thought they might bear some kind of fruit. It was too dark to know for sure. The air was sweet. Hot and tasty, like smoke from a hookah. His nerves began to fire again. He altered his breathing, commanding his lungs to make long, full breaths.

"We are there," he said. "I can smell it."

The scent of the trees sent memories spinning in his head. The compound, with its house and barn. The huts for the boys, two per hut, with sleeping mats and looms. The tops were corrugated steel, open during the day unless the sun was right overhead or it was raining. The doors were old fencing, sides of crates, or chicken wire. Raja's hut had a door of chicken wire. His whole hut was like a chicken coop—except they cleaned out chicken coops.

Up ahead, the red light flickered. They were losing sight of the truck. Too many trees and curves. It didn't matter to Sultan. They were close enough now that he no longer needed a guide.

"Slow," he said, his voice a little higher than he would have liked. There were only two more bends before the compound. He let Ashok lumber on, then asked him to pull over before the end. He reached down between the seats, brought up the revolver, and flipped out the carriage. Five rounds. He pushed it back in, listening for the decisive click. He put the pistol back under the seat.

Ashok asked, "Don't you—"

"This is as far as you need to go," Sultan said.

"You sound like the leader," Ashok said. "You always sound that way?"

"It would be easiest for me to go by myself."

Ashok made one of his huge smiles and got out of the Jeep. Sultan followed. They walked down the road, staying close to the trees, attempting to make no sound. Outside their vehicle, at a much slower speed, the trees were spaced farther apart. They offered little protection. In only a few steps Sultan saw the decrepit buildings of his memories: the house, the barn, the huts. Nine of them. Tiny, flimsy, sharp-edged, rust-spotted, urine-soaked sweat boxes.

The cube van sat next to the barn. Two men moved near the front door of the house. They spoke. Sultan couldn't discern what they said. He walked faster, Ashok skipping twice to keep up.

There were no fences, gates, or guards. The place was surrounded, and protected, by apathy. The thought made Sultan's lip curl. Another joke. Allah could be, when he wanted, funnier than anything. If lasers defended your treasure, you'd need an optic specialist to steal it. If your treasure is defended by a general lack of concern, Sultan was your man. He loved this joke. He almost burst out laughing.

"How many men are there?" Ashok asked quietly.

"I do not know," Sultan answered. "The boys know little."

"I am not a fighter."

"You tell me this now?" Sultan looked indignant. "I told your cousin to give me the best fighter in Allahabad. The Indian Jackie Chan, I asked for."

Ashok suddenly looked very concerned. Sultan grinned.

"Stop!" A voice behind them. Taught, masculine, nervous.

Sultan halted and slowly turned at the hips.

"Do not turn around. Do not move at all."

The voice got closer. Sultan fought the need to turn and look.

"Walk!" the voice commanded.

"That's what we were doing," Sultan complained.

"No talking!"

Dull, hard metal on his spine. Sultan stumbled forward, moving before a vertebra cracked. He glanced at Ashok, who looked even more concerned.

They walked into the circle of dirt in front of the main house. The night was quiet and star filled. With the lights coming from inside, there was more than enough light for Sultan to make out the details of his surroundings. The bus-sized house of warped, raw planks. Only a few chips of white paint still clung from years ago. The roof was strangely new and very red. He'd seen it before. He'd never been inside. Raja was just a few meters to his right, curled up and sleeping. Two tufts of grass away. Little islands of green in the sea of gray-puce dirt.

"On your knees!" the man behind them shouted.

"We need—"

Sharp, crunching pain in the back. Sultan lurched forward, losing his footing. Two men emerged from the front door. They ran the place. They brought the thread and took away the carpets and beat you if anything interfered with those two tasks.

"Lock your hands behind your head and get on your knees!"

Ashok put his hands behind his head and dropped to his knees. Sultan followed, watching the two men from the house approach. One had been driving the cube van. He stopped and looked down at Ashok, then Sultan, studying them like they were carpets he might purchase.

"They are not police," he said to the guard behind them. "Shoot them."

CHAPTER 60

MRS. ENFIELD'S THIRD GRADE CLASS

Cathy had stayed up late thinking about ways to work the memory event, to get kids talking and making sure they were adjusted. She met with other teachers, exchanging ideas and breaking union rules. They had plans and theories—and none of it was necessary.

The kids *wanted* class to get back to normal. They forced interest in fractions and sentence parts and photosynthesis. Which was fine with Cathy, and every other teacher sharing the experience. Back to normal. Or as close to it as they could get.

"Is so."

"Is not."

Harsh whispers from the center of the room. The kids were supposed to be reading a passage to themselves, quietly. She looked up.

"Is so."

"Is not."

Alexis and Jared. They had never given her a lick of trouble before. Now Alexis had said more in the last two days than the whole previous school year. Jared had given precise answers when called on. The only topic he had ever previously discussed without prompting was Captain Underpants.

"Is there a problem?" Cathy asked.

"No" and "Yes" came at the same time. Cathy couldn't tell who said what. Half the kids were now distracted, the other half had already lost interest. Daydreaming had been fast and severe this week. As much as they all tried for regular old school, each had someone in the back of his or her head vying for attention.

"You are supposed to be reading," Cathy said. "When everyone's done we'll discuss it."

"Everyone's done," Jared said.

"We've been done for, like, an hour," Alexis added, exaggerating of course, but Cathy glanced at the clock. Twenty-five minutes gone. Huh. Daydreaming apparently wasn't just for kids.

"This story," Jared said. "It's a bit of a problem for me."

"Oh, really?" Cathy got up and rounded her desk.

"The boy has to take the marbles back to the store because stealing is wrong."

"Right."

"But that's not an answer. Stealing isn't always patently wrong."

"I say it is," Alexis said. "It infringes on another's liberties."

"What if he needs the marbles to trade for his sister's life?" Jared asked.

Alexis glowered. "That's ridiculous."

"I've heard of more ridiculous things than that."

Cathy sat back on the edge of her desk. "Stealing is wrong, Jared."

"But always? Stealing bread to feed your family?"

"There can be exceptions," Cathy admitted and regretted immediately. These were eight-year-olds.

Jared turned to Alexis. "See. Exceptions. There are always exceptions."

"What about murder?" Alexis crossed her arms and huffed. "Are there exceptions for murder?"

"What about war? What about the death penalty? That is simply murder under general agreement. It's semantics. There is no objective morality."

"There must be," Alexis said. "There is a common good. There is a just society to which the world can aspire."

"I'm not saying there's not," Jared said. "I'm saying that law needs to become subjective. It must be ready to change with each individual in every circumstance. There are no generalizations. The just society is not the easy society. It is tremendously hard and that's why we do not have one."

"Wow," Cathy said, by accident. "You got all that from Johnny and the marbles?"

"Mrs. Enfield?" Hunter asked from the back row. "Is there going to be a test on any of that sh—"

"Control!" Cathy shot. "Remember we talked about controlling your words."

CHAPTER 61

SUSAN

The table was gruesome. Susan hadn't seen a collection of such smart faces gone dumb since she was an intern. They were all overextending, overthinking, overkilling the subject. None of them had anything new this morning, because there was very little news coming in.

And this was the strain she knew about. It was surface tension. Underneath, she had no idea what might be going on inside any one of them. Her memories were largely benign. She could not say the same for the others. She knew too well the world was full of sociopaths, capable of taking a life as easily as a drink. There was more than job-related stress here and she had no treatment for it.

Susan wanted to kiss Lieutenant Joseph Scott when he entered the conference room, holding a slim stack of papers.

"What do you have?" She did her best not to look like a hungry puppy.

"Not much." He gave her the report. "Postings from some of the med units. This is the trickle."

Susan laid the papers out and took it all in with a single stare. She liked, literally, to get the big picture and then focus on the parts. Focus too soon on the parts, and you could lose sight of the whole.

"'Nonspecific'," Susan said. "What does that mean?"

"An event was experienced and a co-participant could not be identified," Joe explained. "In each of the cases, the subject claimed to have felt something, but the subject did not obtain meaningful data from a named foreign subject."

"Children?" Maria asked. "Like infants?"

"Or fakers," Adam added. "People got left out and wanted so bad to be part of the event they convinced themselves they felt something."

Gary cleared his throat. "Physiologically speaking, why not animals? Somebody please stop me if I'm wrong, but chimp, whale or dolphin brains—just to name a few examples—have brains quite similar to ours. In terms of genes there's only a two percent difference between humans and apes. Structurally, our brains are all the same. Are we positive animals have been excluded?"

Murmurs tumbled across the table. The group had not had any discussion about the rest of Earth's inhabitants. Susan had never thought to invite anyone from a zoological discipline.

Michelle inched to the edge of her chair. "We don't speak dolphin, so the nonspecific reporting subjects could perhaps have received memories that they cannot process."

"There have been no reports of animals going nuts," Casper said. "By now we should have heard reports from farmers and zookeepers and their kin, of odd behaviors."

Michelle shook her head. "If animals can't process human signals...It's still early. In an outbreak of any magnitude, the information comes in fits."

"Quantum packets," Gary added. "Nature repeating itself again. Still, Casper has a point. My grandparents had a dairy farm. They were very close to the animals. They knew about the slightest changes in weather, feed, equipment—anything that might affect the cows. If you spend enough time around animals, you develop a kind of rapport."

"If I may," Joe cut in carefully. "We are monitoring news reports worldwide. I will double-check, but my understanding is there have been no reports of irregularities in animals."

Casper chuckled. "You double-check, Lieutenant. Though it's not like a panda in south China is going to suddenly call CNN and say, 'You won't believe what just happened.'"

Gary said, "That's not what I meant. I fully appreciate the intricacies of human communication. I did not imply a panda would suddenly be able to speak."

"No," Casper pursed his lips.

"No!" Gary became defensive. "I think it is reasonable to assume affected animals may exhibit demonstrably abnormal behavior post event."

"Mad cows?"

"A poor choice of words, I think."

"The cows wouldn't necessarily go mad," Abigail offered. "We didn't. Everyone here at the table seems to have adapted quickly. Sure, I don't know that you're not, like, crying in the shower every night, but... well... you're all here. Functioning."

"Which is remarkable in itself," Gary said.

"People are amazingly resilient," Abigail said. "I've worked with people who've lived through shit you wouldn't ever want to know and come out, basically, all right. Some people whack out over the littlest thing. Most people never whack out even after the biggest, most terrible thing."

"You think animals could adapt like that?" Gary asked. "Without us ever noticing?"

"I haven't done a lot of animal psychology. The way the news is, though, if there was any reason—any story at all— they'd be totally shoving a mic in some baboon's face right now. If animals were involved, you'd expect something, right?"

Adam leaned far over the table. "If animals are not part of the fascinoma, we've got to wonder why. What sets our brains apart?"

"Intelligence," Maria said. "The greatest communication abilities on the planet."

"Which doesn't really explain why just humans? What's in us acting as a catalyst or target for this phenomenon? What's in us that is not in dolphins, cows, or pandas?"

"Or something outside us," Michelle threw in. "Many— most?—I don't know—but Lord knows too many diseases choose us."

"Germs float around looking for us?" Casper scoffed.

"In a way." Michelle beamed, seemingly happy at the scoffing. "Not on an individual basis, but diseases tend to be highly specific, settling in just human intestines, for instance. Not dogs. Never cats."

"I don't think this event is a sickness."

"Oh, no," Michelle said. "But the cause could come from outside."

"Something outside that chose human brains?" Casper exaggerated a look of disbelief. "You know what the word 'choosing' implies. Because viruses don't chose. Lima beans don't chose. You've to move up a bit to have the power of choice."

Casper pressed his lips tight and looked from person to person. Susan watched him, right eyebrow raised, waiting to be challenged. Susan glanced at the others, each letting his last sentence settle in. Except for Abigail. She stared at Casper. *No*, Susan corrected herself. *She studied him*. Abigail observed Casper as she might a patient.

Chapter 62

SULTAN

"I wouldn't shoot me so soon," Sultan said. "There is too much..." Arg! He hated his lack of vocabulary. "Money. Shooting me would make you more poor." That was the best he could do. What a stupid little sentence to balance lives on.

"I will take your money from your dead body," the leader said. Bimal—that was his name. Raja had it in his head somewhere, behind all the blocks he put up in his attempt to never think about this place, these people, or any part of his present life.

"Bimal," Sultan said. The man's head cocked to the side, like he'd been slapped. "I do not have the money with me. Take this phone from my pocket."

"Do I know you?" Bimal stepped closer. Sultan noticed the man next to Bimal look at the man behind Sultan. The one with the gun. They were visibly unhappy about names being spoken out loud.

The tension, the guns, the terror—the memories of this man punching his stomach, burning his blood-soaked fingers so he'd get none on the carpet, cracking a kneecap so hard you could hear the bone splinter—the emotions rolled away, like the surf, ebbing out in a muffled rumble. Knowing Bimal's name, seeing his skinny arms, catching the hint of dissent in his ranks, the tastes of doubt soothed Sultan's mood.

"I am going to stand so that you can get the phone out." Sultan looked at Ashok as he slowly rose. The man's face was blank. Sultan's lip curled. It was a little funny. Ashok had the blankness of enduring a boring lecture, in a class that did not matter.

Bimal almost crashed into Sultan he moved so fast. He ripped the phone out of Sultan's front pocket and stared at it.

"Push one and enter. Hold it to your ear."

"Why?"

"Do it," Sultan commanded in his nicest tone. He knew Bimal was curious, but the other two were nervous.

"How much do you want?" came from the voice on the other end of the call. Sultan was close enough to hear his sister, Anisah's voice.

"What?" Bimal wiggled the phone.

"How much do you want? And what do you want: euros? U.S. dollars?"

"For me," Sultan said. "My friend here, and Raja, one of the boys working here."

"You came to buy a boy?" Bimal asked.

"Raja. Tell the woman on the phone how much money and she will put it in your bank."

"No banks."

"She will wire it, then. Where...you like."

"You trust I will let you go?"

"It will be easier than talking to the police who come looking for us." Sultan bounced his eyebrows once, then added, "Bimal."

The man's mustache crawled at the sound of his own name.

"All you want is one boy."

"Raja is my Other. I am tied to him. He is why I am here."

Bimal sneered and looked at each of the other men. No one said a word. The phone line remained open. There was no breeze. It was for a moment as if the Earth was still, catching its breath. Humans, creatures, time took a long blink. A languid fade to black followed by refocus.

"10,000 euros," Bimal burst. "Cash."

"Yes," Anisah said.

"Tell her where," Sultan said. Bimal gave Anisah an address.

"The phone." Sultan held up his hand. "She needs to know I am good."

Bimal did nothing at first, until Sultan actually reached for the phone. He could see the confusion in the man's eyes. He was one step behind and knew it.

Sultan switched to Arabic. He'd only taught Anisah nine words in Hindi. "How is everything at home?"

"What is going on?" Anisah held back a shout.

"Do you have everything you need?"

"Yes. It seems that way. I'm still working on it."

"I am going to hang up now. Minutes on a satellite phone are a fortune." Sultan handed the phone back to Bimal and reverted to Hindi. "Call. See if your money is in. It may take a few...a little bit. May I see Raja now?"

Bimal bucked his head in the direction of the man near the main house. The man scooted away, into the darkness, toward the chicken coops.

Sultan helped Ashok up and pushed the man's arms down. He finally got a glimpse of the man behind them—dark skin, long, loose black hair, 18 or 19 years old with a smooth, almost featureless face. He had an old wooden rifle with a green canvas strap. It had a lever on the side. Sultan tried to remember what that was called. A bolt. That's right. It was a bolt-action Enfield rifle, the kind you see men on horses carry in all the old pictures.

An old picture, Sultan thought as the other man emerged from the darkness, with a flicker of a person behind him. The boy reminded him of an old photo of himself, the kind you pick up and don't recognize yourself at first. You very gradually pull together all the clues that you are looking at you—another you. This one was twig-thin, unstable, covered with a thin plaster of dust and sweat. Sultan felt his eyes sting, which was revolting. He did not go through all of this to cry like a woman. He put his eyes back on Bimal, let some of the anger back in, then returned his gaze to Raja.

He walked like he was about to fall. He didn't look much taller than a meter, with eyes too big for his head. They caught Sultan like two dark searchlights and he changed direction, loping directly to him.

"I was expecting you earlier," Raja said in Arabic. His accent was odd, as if he'd been drinking.

"We stopped for curry." Sultan grabbed the little boy and hugged him in a way so foreign Sultan grew dizzy, like he'd drawn much too hard on the hookah.

"I knew you would come for me."

"You knew more than I."

"And the others?"

Sultan parted from him, so the boy could watch his mouth, "patience."

Waiting became very difficult. Bimal called the store that took wired money. They had not yet received the order. Ten minutes later he called again, and they had an authorized transfer, but did not have enough cash on hand to cover the amount. They would get it, though, in the morning.

"Good," Sultan said. "We go now." He pointed back up the path, in the direction of the Jeep.

"Not yet," Bimal said. "You know where we are."

"Move," Sultan said.

"You can tell the police before we get away."

"I give my...I promise never to tell the police where you are." Sultan pointed to Ashok. "He will never tell the police where you are. You have our..."

Ashok pressed his lips together, as if fighting to keep his mouth closed. Then he said, "Promise. You have my promise."

"We only came for him." Sultan put his arm around Raja and moved him forward. "We go."

Raja and Ashok both looked like they had a lot more to say. Sultan pushed them down the path. He hopped back, took his phone from Bimal, then skipped to keep up with the others. They did not look back once on their way to the Jeep, into which they jumped, turned and sped as fast as the small motor allowed. *Angry bees*, Sultan thought. *The motor sounds like the crest on the man's shirt, the one who sold me this satellite phone.* Sultan and Raja fit on one seat, Raja took up so little space.

"The other boys," Raja said. Tears poured down his face. The sides of his mouth so tight Sultan thought his cheeks might rip.

Sultan pressed '1' on his phone. "Anisah?"

"Sultan?" She sounded worried.

"I am perfect. Just as you last saw me. We are out of trouble now."

"Comforting."

"Do you have the coordinates?"

"Yes."

"Then there is someone who would very much like to talk to you." Sultan handed the phone to Raja.

"Hello?" his voice was still tight from crying.

"Raja, I have the latitude and longitude for the last call."

"Where I was. The rugmakers."

"Yes. Would you like the phone number for the police in Allahabad?"

Raja struggled to say yes through quivering lips.

Sultan looked over at Ashok. "I never said Raja would not call. Too bad they did not think more of him."

CHAPTER 63

MRS. ENFIELD'S THIRD GRADE CLASS

Samantha Courtie stood in Cathy's doorway, sheep-ish, silent, her past bubbliness flattened. Cathy groaned inside and smiled out.

The markets had opened and telecom company stocks soared as phones continued to jam. Daylong lines at air-ports, full railcars, stuffed buses, and still people actually paid a premium to be treated like farm eggs. The news was seamless, every story flowing from, and then back to, the same central topic. It was exhausting for most people, and off-putting for the rest, like Cathy, who did not plan on ever talking to her Other. She couldn't. There was no physical means of exchanging anything with Choi Shin.

North Korea was isolated. Cathy knew this in the back of her head, the way one knows that Ireland is green or that Antarctica is cold. The adjectives are so old and permanent that their meanings lose their pungency like spices in the back of the cupboard.

"Isolated" never sounded half-bad when an anchor said it on the evening news. She had never considered every-thing the term represented. Her Other, Shin, was not a stupid man. When given a math problem, he knew the approximate answer before doing the work. As a student, he would have driven her nuts. And yet this man had no knowledge of geography, politics, or the twenty-first century. He'd never touched a computer, never googled or e-mailed. His favorite movie was about a radioactive

monster. Obviously a man in a rubber suit, it was nonetheless fantastic, colorful...and the only movie he'd ever
seen.

Shin's flexible, clever mind was filled with ways to get
food. Every day presented a new challenge and every day
that challenge had to be met. He, his wife, and their two
children did not have any fat to fall back on. They had to
scour, claw, and finagle calories just to survive. Each morning, his wife took what money they had down to the train
station, where black-market food might—just might—be
available. Cabbage, rice, rye, oats, never all on the same
day. Some days nothing. Other days, too expensive.

The kids played, begged, or slept on the ground next
to her. They could sleep in the snow when they were weak.
Of all the memories Cathy had withdrawn from Shin's
deposit, the sight of the five- and six-year olds, curled up
together, sleeping on soft sugary snow was the most vivid.
And the most painful. Shin frequently recalled the first time
he had seen it. He had sought his family out, at the rail
station, proud of the money he'd collected. He saw them
lying there and knew his children were dead. Kids didn't
sleep in the snow. They died in the snow and he'd let it
happen and maybe—he hated this part—maybe it was for
the best. When they rose and stretched he nearly passed
out from the strain of not crying in public.

Cathy did not want to discuss any of this with anyone,
least of all an eight year old girl.

"I know things," Samantha said.

"It's OK," Cathy said back.

"I am not safe."

Cathy turned in her chair to face the girl. "Sure you are,
honey. You're not there. You're here, in the United States
of America."

"None of us are safe."

"Come here. Sit down." She motioned Samantha to the
edge of her desk. Cathy had never had a student sit on it,
ever. "The world feels weird right now, but the basics
haven't changed. No one is going to let anything happen
to you."

Samantha's face was stern, like she was laying out her will or discussing plans for a funeral. "Who is your Other?"

A tiny alarm went off in Cathy's head. She'd never heard the alarm before, as it was from North Korea. 'Shut up,' it said. 'You are talking yourself to death.'

"A man," Cathy said. "He lives every day to eat. So his family can eat. He was a printer once, when the factory was open."

"My Other will demand those under him reveal the names of their Others. He will submit those names, and mine, to those above him, and they will decide if we need to be brought in."

"In where, honey?"

"In..." Samantha's eyes zoomed around. "The camps. We probably know too much to be left loose."

"They can't do that."

"Their leader can do anything."

Cathy took Samantha's hands. "He can't. Not here. Not even in his country."

"But he controls everything. Just...everything. My Other, he knows people who were taken right from their beds. Right off the street. Once, a man at the desk next to him—an army officer—was shoved in a black sack and dragged away like trash in the middle of the morning. Taken away and never seen again."

Cathy could see the struggle in the girl's head. The new, terrifying memories, without any context. She didn't have enough life experience to sort them out, give them their proper weight. A mind just letting go of the Easter Bunny was given Kim Jong Il. Nice trade. This poor kid might never sleep again.

"Kim's power is not that great," Cathy said. "My Other defies him everyday. Each morning he walks miles and miles through the woods to a clearing near the Chinese border. The walk is long and hard. It takes him seven hours, and he takes nothing with him but an empty sack. He can't take anything. No water. No food. If stopped, he'd be asked why he has provisions for a long journey. He's been stopped four times by young border guards with old guns. So he takes nothing.

"Once a week, twice if he is lucky, he finds in the clearing a small bag of batteries. Ten, twelve, as many as 24. A man from China drops them there, fresh from the factory. My Other turns and walks back, seven hours, over hills, through mud or snow, avoiding roads and easy places, still with nothing to eat or drink. He can trade the batteries for money or food and keep his family alive.

"The borders are not made of iron," Cathy finished. "The Dear Leader's control is not steel."

"My Other would like this man's name," Samantha said.

"My Other would like to take his family with him one day. To the clearing, then beyond."

"Why doesn't he?"

"He thinks they are still too weak and the journey too hard. Someday, though. If he can fatten them up."

"Fat," Samantha said. "That's funny. I don't think my Other has ever seen a fat person. He was just talking about it the other day. Isn't that funny?"

Cathy nodded. She was glad to see at least the seeds of a smile on the girl's face. It left as quickly as if came.

"There is going to be trouble," Samantha said.

Cathy continued to nod. "But it's not yours. No matter what else you remember, remember that."

CHAPTER 64

CINDY

Cindy sat in an interview room. She wasn't afraid of Brad—and not just because Deputy Pollard was outside the door, listening and occasionally glancing in. Brad was a clawless cat now. She was out of the house. She had a few hundred dollars, the truck, and a place to stay. She could, as needed, put the bastard on his belly and make him squeal. You weren't supposed to enjoy that part. The Swiss Federal Security Service took great care in weeding out people who liked pain and power. They'd never met Brad, though.

Brad Benning wore his best blue going-out shirt, his clean, whiskered jeans and Sunday boots. He smiled at her, blaring those movie-star teeth, and nothing happened. From her knees to her nipples, Cindy felt nothing. The old days were over. Not only wasn't she scared of this guy, she realized she didn't give two shits about him, either.

"Sorry about all this, hon." Brad was wearing the basset hound look, as if he'd just gobbled the last slice of pie.

"Then drop the charges," Cindy said. "If you're so sorry, drop the fool charges."

"You commin' home?"

"Nope."

"Jesus, Cin. Can we get over this?"

"We're through it." Cindy shot her hand to the left. "We're on the other side in a land where we ain't together."

"Come on. Back to your home and your husband."

"Not an option."

"Then what? I got to have you prosecuted?"

Cindy closed her eyes. *What a child!* She opened them slowly, pumping patience into her head. "You told the cops I drugged you and tied you up to die?"

"Yeah, well..."

"A tox screen's going to show you're a big pansy liar. Everyone—and I mean everyone—will learn how I tossed you around."

"Cin—"

"We ain't headed for his and hers rockin' chairs," Cindy continued. "The sooner you realize that the better off we'll both be. I got away, Bradley Benning. I got away. Now I don't care what the fuck you tell your buddies at the bar. Tell 'em I went screwy after the swap. Everyone alive's gonna understand that. Tell 'em you got rid of me. I don't care. All I want from you is dropped charges. And a divorce, but let's try baby steps here, all right?"

Brad stuck his jaw out, gnawing on whatever words sprang into his mouth. He didn't want to eat them, but he knew he had to swallow most of his voice in the police station. Cindy watched the confrontation on his face, a rerun of a show she'd seen too many times.

"I don't think I can do that," Brad said.

It burned her. Where she'd felt nothing before came flames of frustration and clear, gut-punching anger. He'd be able to see it, surely as if he'd colored her face with a red magic marker. *Control was the trick. Check your temper. Focus on the task.* They had taught Florens how to be stone cold. Cindy knew it all, she just had to crank it up. 'Breathe, girl,' she said to herself. Then seal it shut.

"The sheriff is getting, like, 80 calls a day," Cindy started. "He used to get a pair. Since last Thursday, there's a new witness to every crime in the world. New ones, old ones, ones still a gleam in some asshole's eye. This office is getting calls from all over the world. They can't keep up and I can help. I can do something. Help people. How cool is that?"

"Very cool. Really," Brad said. "You want to work. Fine. We can talk about it."

"Talk shit, Bradley. Get your head out of your ass."

Brad's face thinned to a steady sneer. "High and mighty, now, huh? That what you got? Your Other some kind of boy scout? Some kind of kung fu boy scout?"

"There's this guy from France who called. He doesn't speak English and the sheriff hasn't been able to snag a translator. Who knows what he's trying to tell us? Some girl's been kidnapped. There's a body in Bailey Lake. I don't know but I'm gonna find out. The only thing standing in my way—in everybody's way—is you."

"I want my second chance."

"If I come home with you, you'll let me help the sheriff."

"That's the deal."

"Then you are a grade A idiot." Cindy looked through the door's window. Deputy Pollard looked away. A big, bald, mustached man, he was supposed to just stand on the other side, but Cindy understood his attention. His gut was telling him Brad was trouble. Almost anyone's would. She took a few deep breaths. This was going to hurt—no way around it. She laced her hands and stretched out her arms, cracking her knuckles.

"I'll ask you one more time," she said. "Will you drop the charges?"

"That ain't happenin'," Brad returned.

"Then I'm going to have to do this the hard way. Is that what you want?"

"It ain't happenin' any way, Sweetheart."

"I'm gonna beat it out of you," Cindy said. "I'm gonna fuckin' wipe the floor with your pussy ass like I did the other night."

"Not ever again."

"Oh yeah. You're gonna cry like a little girl and beg me to stop the pain. You ready for that?"

"You surprised me before. That's all."

"Surprise has nothin' to do with it." Cindy put her clasped hands on the desk, neat and proper. "You're a pussy now. That's what changed. You got that queer in your head and it's made you a full-fledged, weepy girl pussy."

Brad's jaw muscles bulged through his cheeks. He spoke without parting his teeth. "You go and try it."

"You like it, Bradley? All the memories from the queer? You sittin' at home every night remembering what it's like to take a man's cock in your mouth? You like that, Sweetie?"

"Shut up, Cin."

"Or you more of an ass man now? You like feeling it up there?"

"Shut your filthy mouth."

"Make you hard?"

"Shut up!"

"Or what?"

"I'll get you outside."

Cindy laughed. "You're afraid of me?"

"I don't need cops around."

"Deputy Pollard out there? I told him to look the other way while I whupped your ass. And he will, too. I screwed his brains out last night. Been so long since I had a real man."

Brad flew onto and over the table. Cindy let loose the scream she'd been keeping ready. Brad dove into her like she was a pile of leaves, leading with his hands. She forced herself not to flip him with her feet. It was hard. Letting his hands grab her neck. Crush her neck. They both spilled onto the floor, chair skidding away. Her elbow exploded in pain. All she saw was Brad's sparkling white teeth, crunched together, spit bubbling and spraying. He growled so loud she didn't hear Deputy Pollard burst in. He 'clean and jerked' Brad off her and slammed him against the one-way glass so hard she saw it bow. He was shouting "Larry" and another cop was there a second later, helping to bend Brad's arms into cuffs.

Her neck was chaffed and fiery. In the one-way glass she could see his handprints on her throat. Her whole face was tomato-like.

It only took the sheriff a minute to arrive. He looked concerned, but not fully. He gave her neck a good look. His eyes registered the damage. But there was a tiny smirk somewhere around the mouth.

"You alright?" he asked.

"Fine," Cindy answered and winced. A throat full of sand.

"I take it you want to press charges?"

"Yes, sir."

"Then you'll both be pressin' charges against each other."
The sheriff tapped his chin. "Now I wonder how we can
settle this?"

"I wonder, sir." Cindy coughed. That had hurt more than
she'd expected.

CHAPTER 65

MRS. ENFIELD'S THIRD GRADE CLASS

Cathy wrote 'Empathy' on the chalkboard.

"Can anyone tell my what empathy means?"

The usual hands went up. She scanned passed them, finding a not-so-usual one.

"Hunter." She pointed.

"It's feeling the same thing as someone else."

"Very good."

"Really?" He looked surprised.

"Really. Very well done."

"Jesus Christ, I nailed one." He slapped his hands together.

The class busted out laughing. Cathy closed her eyes. She thought about keeping them that way for a while. For the rest of the day. She was a strong-willed woman. She could stand there for three hours and pretend she was alone. She could.

"I did it again," Hunter said.

Cathy opened her eyes and the laughter quieted. "Yes. That was inappropriate."

"It's just all my memories. They're like me, you know?"

Cathy did know, though it still wasn't an excuse.

"And what are we anyways," Jared chimed in, almost singing, "but a sum total of our memories. Little living libraries of all we've heard, learned, thought, experienced."

"We're people," Alexis said. "We are not collections of information any more than a string of words is a play by Shakespeare."

"You would like to think that," Jared said. "We'd all like to think we're more than silos of thought and ideas, but is there more? Can there be more?"

Alexis looked at Cathy for help, lowering her chin, enlarging her eyes, wordlessly pleading for a little back-up that Cathy wasn't prepared to give. It had been a long time since she had taken any philosophy courses.

"I'm sorry," she said. "This isn't really much more appropriate than Hunter's comment. We need to get—"

"Love," Austin said. Dark skinned, with wild hair Cathy wished his parents would cut by 90 percent. He was much more subdued than he looked. "I love Fluff sandwiches, my brother hates 'em. Why is that? If him and me are just the stuff we've done and read, why don't we both love Fluff sandwiches?"

Jared's mouth took on the shape of an 'n.' He sat back, staring off at the floor.

"I love Fluff, too," someone else said. Another boy agreed. Cathy closed her eyes as the class debated the merits of a marshmallow filling she didn't think any of them should ever have.

"Taste buds," Jared declared, "are physical attributes. Austin, you may very well have a different number, or different quality, of taste buds in your mouth than your brother has. Some people have ten times the number of bitter-sensing buds and dislike coffee because of it. We could all take a bite from the same sandwich and taste different things."

"That doesn't refute his point," Alexis said. "Whatever makes him love Fluff sandwiches is affected by more than his memories. We are more than our memories. We are where they are created, and the creators, and the continuous re-creations."

Jared put his head on his balled-up hand. The whole class hushed and mused. To Cathy, the silence was like a warm bath. With candles. And a new magazine that had nothing to do with education.

"You know a lot about taste buds," Hunter said. "Your Other some kind of tongue doctor or something?"

"No."

"Because that would be cool—being a tongue doctor."

Chapter 66

NIVEN

For his fortieth birthday, Niven's friends took him to a jazz club in Harlem. There weren't many jazz clubs anymore, not like the old days, when he first arrived in the city from the other side of the river. He got to meet Lena Horn. It was easier than it should have been. Niven had met oodles of celebrities. But none had ever taken his hand and pressed it between theirs—cool thinning flesh sliding on bone—and thanked him for wanting to be there, to feel, hear, see. She was, for Niven, a statue brought to life, a breathing piece of art you could touch and talk to, if your mouth worked. He'd never been star-struck before or since.

For his fortieth birthday, Ming's friends took him to Beijing to ride a high speed, bullet-head train. He had spoken often of wanting to touch it and hear it. He could not imagine a train rolling ten times faster than the ones he rode. Laughing, excited as a child, Ming ran his hands down the seamless, slippery side. He felt the hard curly carpet beneath his feet and the skin of warm plastic on the pointless flowing seats. The ride was blank. He never told his friends. He smiled and talked and thanked them for the ride of a lifetime, keeping his disappointment tight inside. The dark hum, the lack of rushing wind, and the struggle to sense any hint that he was even moving. As marvelous as the machine was, it was not the train for a blind man.

A blind man now stood outside the glass. Short, solid, in plain blue work clothes. His face was round and flat, like a plate. Niven had never seen the man before, but knew he was looking at Ming, here in Beijing, for only his second time. Ming didn't like this city. While the high-speed train had been unwelcome sensory deprivation, the rest of the place was sensory overload. Fish burning tire trash. Motorcycle crowd cans hitting concrete. Ming had been scared twice in his life. Once, when he was 11, he'd stumbled, fallen and rolled from the train tracks he'd been following. Until he found those tracks, he had no idea where in the world he stood. Afraid to move, afraid to stay. It took him a lifetime to find the tracks again. The second time he was scared was on his fortieth birthday. He took the wrong way out of a men's room and wandered into the noisy, smelly grit of 10 million people.

Ming's return to Beijing honored Niven. No one had ever done anything like that for him before. His face tightened when he saw Ming, standing at ease in the hallway, staring off to Niven's left. The uniformed man next to him pointed at Niven, a useless gesture, and said he was the one.

"It is very kind of you to come." Niven got off his chair and approached the glass.

"Immigration sent for me," Ming said in English.

Niven inhaled sharply, like he'd been cut. Hearing his voice, from outside the head. Strange and familiar. Odd and right.

"They want me to confirm you are an assassin," Ming continued. "I do not know whether they will jail you or deport you."

"And you couldn't do that over the phone?"

"What is it you say..." Ming started laughing. "Welcome to Chinatown?" He laughed a little harder. Ming turned, fairly accurately, to the guard and switched to Chinese. "This man is not going to kill me. We share no terrible secrets. He is a threat only to himself."

"I will put that in my report." The uniformed man walked away.

"Sorry for the inconvenience," Niven said. "I know the big city is not your cup of tea."

"Why did you come?" Ming asked.

"I don't know," Niven answered. "At first, I told myself I was chasing an idea. A lead I had for a big project. That became irrelevant some time last night...or yesterday morning. I'm not sure what day it is. I'm not sure it was the real reason anyway."

"You tell yourself a lot of things."

Niven cocked his head, the usual signal he was getting ready to rip and tear. The reflex got ahead of him, though. His stash of nasty comments was empty. He couldn't tell this guy about a hard and complicated life.

"What is your problem with me?" Niven tried not to sound snotty, but it was hard to avoid.

Ming's face became serious. "If you have everything in the world and spend all your time worrying about losing it, what is the point of having it in the first place?"

"That's life, isn't it? Getting and keeping."

"I think it is a journey toward happiness."

"Spoken like a true rail monk."

"I can also speak like an art director from New York City. You are a self-absorbed party boy who thinks the priorities of a teenager can lead to happiness in a man."

"Not bad." Niven felt Ming's words, his words—they were in him, spoken by two ex-wives, a half-dozen former girlfriends, his son, and himself. They'd lodged somewhere in his subconscious, which was fine because his conscious wanted nothing to do with them.

"Pious little puke," Niven said. "You think your struggle lets you judge me? You found peace. Goody for you. It's not like you set the bar real high or anything."

"I did not set the bar at all."

"Nor did I. You think I got to pick what made me happy?" Niven spread his arms and leaned against the glass. "I didn't create my talents, my loves, passions, or cravings. I followed them, like tracks across the country-side."

Ming moved to within an inch of the glass barrier. "No one is born craving Salon champagne."

"Ah, but once you've tasted it..."

"If it gushed out of the ground, you would not find it so desirable."

"Got me all figured out, huh? I am the king of gross American consumerism."

"No." Ming's word misted on the glass. "You wish to be the king, and cannot be happy as a lord."

"Seeing is not everything," Niven said.

"I agree."

"You can hate me for not being happy just because I've got all my senses, but it's not what I would call fair."

"I don't hate you." Ming touched his forehead to the glass. "That is, no more than you hate yourself. Did you know your strongest memories are disappointments? Cheating on your first wife. Missing your son's graduation. Telling Marco you can't open an agency with him. Hiring Nicholas. You keep pulling these recollections off the shelf and rereading them. The ones you hate the most were the first to come to me. You spend all your time worrying about things that don't even make you happy. You are what you would call an asshole."

Niven poked a single finger to the glass over Ming's head. "Disappointments and self-loathing don't make me an asshole."

Ming stood straight. "Not changing does."

"I'm almost 60. I'm not changing now."

"You just did," Ming said. "Everyone did. A big switch was thrown and we all moved to different tracks. You can do everything in your power to get back or you can see where the new set takes you."

CHAPTER 67

MRS. ENFIELD'S THIRD GRADE CLASS

Cathy drew three intersecting circles on the chalkboard. She turned to the class, sitting attentively, not yet fully awake.

"Venn diagrams. Yes, your favorite," she announced.

Kylie Stevens raised her hand. A slight, freckly, strawberry blonde who liked drawing and giggling and singing pop songs Cathy would never let her listen to were she her mother, Kylie was never much trouble. Talking in class was it. Cathy didn't hesitate to point to her and say, "Yes."

"Is sex really that good?" Kylie asked.

Cathy froze, shot with a dart from a blow-gun, one of those poisons that relieves you of bodily control, save for her eyebrows, which arched high into her hairline.

"Excuse me?" she said.

"Sex. It's all this guy thinks about. My Other, that is."

The rest of the class remained silent. No grinning, no laughing. They were nothing but unsure.

Cathy rolled her head around, breaking her own trance. "The...ah...I'm pretty sure this is inappropriate."

"You said there are no stupid questions."

"The district restricts—" Cathy stopped. That wasn't a good answer. "Perhaps we can talk about this later."

"Oh, sure. That's OK," Kylie said. "I just know I'm not the only one who's wondering, you know?"

"I don't know," Cathy mumbled. She panned the room, all eyes on her. There were very few times in her teaching career that she'd had this quality and quantity of attention.

"It's just..." Kylie tapped her chin, "my Other remembers liking sex, but I can't seem to remember why, exactly. The memory is not the thing, I guess."

"My Other thinks a lot about sex, too," Alexis said. "He's Italian."

"Mine, too," yelled another voice from the back. "All his memories are of either these great dinners that go on forever, or sex he had with a woman he never seems to know much about."

"Mine hates the sex," Cameron said. It was the first thing he'd said since asking to be moved from the window.

"Then you ain't doin' it right," Hunter shouted.

Cathy shouted, "Whoa, whoa!" over top of the rising noise.

The door rattled. Cathy stepped over to it, thrilled for the distraction, but not wanting to open it and let anyone else sample the class discussion. She cracked the door and Mrs. Danvers smiled from the other side.

"Could I take your room for a bit?" she asked. "Debbie needs you down in the office."

Debbie. Deborah Shilling, the principal. Great. What, was she listening through the loudspeaker or something?

"Sure." Cathy slipped through the crack, into the hall. "It's all yours. Is there a problem?"

"All I know is that Samantha Courtie girl was sent down."

Troubling, but whatever it was, it had to be better than this. Cathy breezed down the corridor.

Chapter 68

SUSAN

"That's not science!" Adam shouted.

"It's new science for a new world," Gary shot back.

"I understand if you prefer deductive methods to empirical. We've all learned the classics. But you, friend...you are offering something completely different. An adductive method." Adam turned away from the table, dismissing the whole group with the wave of a hand. "I don't care for it."

"I don't care for it, either," Gary continued. "I don't think you realize we're on the same side, here. The difficulty I'm facing is my inability to invalidate the idea."

"You can use common sense," Casper offered.

"No." Gary turned to him. Susan thought he looked fearful. "I can't. Common sense tells me none of this could have happened. It's uncommon sense I need now. What is your specialty, Casper?"

"I make a very good puttanesca."

"What you do for DARPA? Please. I don't think you're a physicist."

"Does it show? When I use phrases like 'common sense,' perhaps."

Gary crunched his lips and glared at the man.

"He's an engineer," Susan said. "There—I've outted him."

"I suspected," Gary said. "Good. Then maybe you can help me out on this."

"Electric Universe Theory," Casper said, "is for backyard astronomers and Art Bell fans."

"I want a dollar from each of you," Abigail ordered. "In clean, unmarked bills."

Casper took out his wallet. Adam and Gary both slid bills to Abigail.

"Do you have change for a fifty?" Casper asked.

"How about we run a tab until you're through? I might not need change."

"Certainly," Casper smirked. "I'm to explain the silliness, then? Fine. Always wanted to try stand up.

"Electric Universe Theory, such that it is, states that electromagnetic forces are stronger and more prevalent in our lives and in the cosmos than current atomic theory suggests. Electricity becomes god of the gaps, answering all the questions quantum theory can't or won't. Jets of plasma from galaxies, for instance. Or the apparent stability of the universe. It does have the advantage of relieving us from time/space, allowing an amicable divorce, and it does get rid of Einstein's idea that gravity is a divot in space. That never sat well with me. Ha. Gravity well, get it? That is as far as it goes."

Maria Serrano sat forward. She had not spoken in a day. "Why the attitude? So what if electricity is stronger than everyone thought?"

"So what, indeed?" asked Casper. "I don't care one way or another. I am as far from entrenched academia as one can get. Those who believe that the sun is a ball of lightning need to give me evidence. Those that believe it's a nuclear furnace have been doing so for decades."

"There might be more to it," Maria said. "If there was a theory out there before Cinco de Mayo that may have allowed for the event, I want to hear it, no matter how silly."

"Then why don't we get Rupert Sheldrake on the phone? I'm sure he'll tell us how dogs predicted the event. He must be grinning ear to ear with evidence of a morphic field running between all of us. Is that what you want? I have met many crackpots who would like to waste your time. Pyramids, dousers, alien abductees—this event can be adapted to any idea that wasn't solid to begin with. That is the danger."

"New data—" Maria sat back, "—means we re-evaluate. I've got to do it all the time. We all do, I bet."

"But Casper doesn't re-evaluate." Abigail's voice was soft, like she was saying it in her head, but it somehow snuck out of her mouth.

All noise stopped.

Susan looked at the young lady, slumped in her chair. A small tingle escalated in the back of her head. Abigail was a psychologist. Susan did not harbor any prejudice against them. She worked with them every day. She had a healthy amount of respect for the field. But the psychologists she worked with had a nasty habit of seeing things she didn't, things other people didn't know they were showing and, in some uncomfortable instances, didn't want to be shown.

"Casper shoots things down," Abigail said.

Casper smiled, as usual.

"You have not liked one idea that's been presented."

"There haven't been any good ones," he replied.

"Even the opposites—the combating ideas. You never pick a side. You shoot at everything."

"It's a living."

"But the reasonable science stuff? Like 'get more data'? You didn't even like that one." Abigail didn't look at Casper. She stared into the table. She wasn't talking to him, or to anybody. She sat quiet for a moment, then she looked at Susan.

"Did you invite him?" she asked.

Susan felt a rush of blood. She was thankful her skin would hide any blushing. "Not exactly."

The group broke out in murmurs and questions. *How did he get here? This was invitation only? Handpicked? Who was he anyway?*

Susan tried to push the noise down with her hands. "He's welcome. Casper has been more than welcome. We needed a devil's advocate."

"Who sent you?" Adam asked him directly.

"I can't say," Casper answered.

"Why are you here?"

"To participate."

"To collect, is more like it. Did your bosses send you here to collect ideas and bring them back so they can start building memory drains? Is that your plan? Find the scientists who can build mind-suckers. We know they're possible now, just not how."

Adam's voice had too much malice in it for Susan's liking. Everyone looked mean. She didn't feel very friendly herself.

"We're done for the day," she announced. "Thank you for your time."

Most jumped up to leave. They each needed a stretch or breath or, gauging from the their expressions, to punch something. *Everyone wanted out of the room—probably off the whole damn campus,* Susan thought.

She did. It wasn't anger, it was fatigue. She didn't know how much energy the brain used, but she knew everyone had limits. No one could think full out, at his or her best, all the time. Her staff frequently spoke of the need to recharge, as if they were all batteries, or said they needed to chill, as if they were overheating. She wasn't fond of metaphors. While she believed medicine was as much an art as it was a science—full of technique, practice, nuance, and sense—she did not believe it was poetry. If you felt your tank was low, she wanted to know what you were really talking about. Sugar levels? Lack of oxygen? Circulation? Why, what, how?

Abigail was like that, too. Susan did not know the woman personally, but there was a connection. She didn't need to swap memories with her to recognize Abigail's inquisitiveness and intelligence. The woman would not have made it this far lacking those traits.

The difference was that Abigail studied specifics while she had been studying the whole. Specifically, Abigail had studied Casper. Without asking, Susan knew why. Casper was salient. He jutted out from the rest. Susan had always found it attractive, but to Abigail it had been something else.

He didn't fit. It was no more complicated than that. He did not sit well at the table. He did not even match up to the Casper she had known two years ago. She should have recognized the oddity. *I would have*, she told herself, *if I weren't so distracted all the time. Antonio. Grammie. The world in shock.*

Not that it was a huge difference. Casper had always been the contrarian. It was his personality and his talent. DARPA used him for it, but the other way. He brought them the ideas from beyond the mainstream. The brain scramblers, robot flies, electromagnetic pulse rifles.

And yet, here he was, knocking down every idea as fast as it got up.

Abigail asked her if she had invited him. What an interesting question. What made her ask that? How did she know he wasn't on her guest list?

"You're not going to find complicity here." Adam pointed at Caper's chest. "You're mining the wrong vein."

"Adam," Susan said. "Please. Let's call it a day."

"I thought we were at least trying to do some good."

"We are. We will. We'll talk later."

Adam stormed toward the door.

"You," Susan turned to Casper. "I'll talk to you right now."

CHAPTER 69

MRS. ENFIELD'S THIRD GRADE CLASS

Cathy zipped through the main office and into Debbie's—Mrs. Shilling's—private office. Samantha sat facing the principal, looking as disturbed as everyone who had to sit in that seat. She had a sparkly purple notebook on her lap.

"Thanks, Mrs. Enfield," Debbie said. Rotund, fake-blonde, with gold glasses on a gold chain, Cathy always thought Debbie was trying too hard to look like a grammar school principal. She wore lots of vests and holiday-themed sweaters. She was close to retirement. To her credit, she was not one of those 'sweep it under the carpet,' 'hide it until I'm gone' administrators. Cathy liked her, admired her, and silently wished she'd get a hair cut different from her grandmother.

"No problem." Cathy sat down next to Samantha and turned to her. "Hi, Samantha." There was no point in not sounding chipper.

The girl smiled back.

"Samantha," Debbie said. "Would you show Mrs. Enfield your notebook?"

Samantha drummed her fingers across the purple cover. The subtle bouncing made the metallic flecks flicker under the florescent lights. She watched it. Or, at least, pointed her eyes in the direction of the dazzle. Cathy couldn't say what she was actually seeing.

She leaned toward Samantha. "It's OK."

Samantha looked at Cathy, looked right into her eyes, her own eyes narrow, probing, like tools. There was no sense that this was a popular girl, who played with Barbies and loved horses. Her face was Wonderbread white, spotless, fresh. Cathy saw a mask. She dragged the notebook from the girl's hands.

Inside were lists of names. Kids and their Others. Details. Where they lived, how and when they came and went. The first name was Cathy's, followed by a dash, followed by everything she'd told her about Shin and the batteries. Then another dash and times and dates. Cathy's class times. Her lunch times. The time she left the school yesterday. That alarm deep inside her head sounded again, the little device that had been grown in Shin's brain and sent to hers. It was loud and cold and slowed time. She gazed into the Samantha mask. Now Cathy's eyes narrowed and drilled. Her instinct was to slam shut, board up as if a tsunami had struck.

But it wasn't her instinct—it was a memory of someone else's mechanism for survival. It was Shin's way. That way was so important and so powerful it was as available to her as the words to the North Korean national anthem.

She could, however, overcome it. She knew what that signal was. She was 28. Samantha was that, minus 20.

Cathy turned to Debbie. "Yes?"

"This seems highly inappropriate, don't you think?" Debbie asked.

"'Inappropriate' has been my favorite word lately. I have seen a lot of it in last few days. This wouldn't make my top ten. No offense, but it wouldn't make my top ten in the last ten minutes."

Debbie's lips bunched up. "As you are a subject of Ms. Courtie's interests, I thought you should be informed."

"Oh," Cathy turned to Samantha. "You didn't call for me."

Samantha shook her head without looking up.

Cathy returned to the principal. "We need a minute."

Debbie recoiled, mouth open, like she'd been called petty, controlling, or fat. Cathy didn't move her eyes or add another word. This was not the opening of a discussion. She felt a little prickle on the back of her neck and her sweat glands wake.

"Certainly." Debbie got up, giving the impression that she was going to fetch them some tea. "I'll be right back."

As the door closed, Cathy whipped the notebook against the wall. It splattered and slid out of sight. Samantha bolted upright.

"That's not you, Samantha Courtie," Cathy spat. "Not you at all. That's from someone else in you and he can't have you. Got that?"

The girl stared at her. "That wasn't my notebook."

"The nonsense. The spying. That's over there—not here? Do you understand?"

"I don't know what you're talking about."

"You are your own person," Cathy said. "You have a life, your life, spread out ahead. Would you ever let someone else choose your favorite color? Insist that you like dogs more than cats? Would you ever let someone else tell you your favorite store or movie is? No. Never. And you're not going to let someone else make you a rat."

Samantha's mouth contorted and her eyes went watery.

"Do you understand?"

She nodded, fighting with her mouth, holding back a good cry.

Cathy clutched the girl's hands. "You like school and soccer. You're good at public speaking. You love Christmas and riding your bike. All the rest of that, it goes in back. It's a TV show you don't watch anymore. Can you do that, Sam? Can you?"

The girl started to cry, head pumping up and down, eyes crinkly red slits. Cathy hugged her tight as she could and let her cry.

"Why?" Samantha whined. "Why did God do this?"

Cathy squeezed her again. She didn't talk about God in the public school. *Giant lizards. Bags of batteries. Two children sleeping in the snow. Emptiness.* God was not in Cathy's memories of North Korea.

"You know what I think?" Cathy asked in reply. "I think this was the answer to someone's prayer. Every prayer gets answered. Every stinking one. So many get answered every second that you can't always see the single answers clearly. Does that make any sense?"

Samantha shook her head against Cathy's shoulder. "I pray for my team to win, you pray for yours. Sometimes you think your prayer was answered, other times you don't. What happens—whatever the outcome—it's God being fair. The world is always as it should be, though it might not seem so. I think somebody prayed that the rest of the world would notice what was happening in his county. Maybe somebody else prayed that he'd remember what it was like to be eight years old again. God answered all the prayers, and this time we saw it."

Cathy pushed Samantha back so she could look into her bloating, ripe tomato eyes. "Do you remember what it's like to be eight years old?"

The girl nodded and Cathy nodded along. *They both needed to remember what it was like to be eight. Everyone did,* Cathy thought. And continued to think, until it was a full-fledged idea.

CHAPTER 70

ARCHIE

They never found out what was wrong with Archie. After 26 years, they pretty much figured they never would. He was a swift and lively child until around the age of four, when the seizures stated coming. The first one was like a stab in Lilly's heart. Any mother would have been pained, but Lilly was young, inexperienced, and determined to be perfect. The second seizure was a hatchet in her gut.

Archie missed developmental landmarks. His sentences got no longer. Math became a mystery. He didn't progress the way everyone else did. His body continued to grow long and lean, all bone and tendon, like most beanpole boys his age. His brain seemed to have found a spot to rest, though. It nestled into short, two-syllable words and gave up altogether on writing, adding, and playing with puzzles. Archie giggled, cried, ran, climbed up the back of the sofa, and periodically fell sideways to the floor, wriggling like a downed power line.

Doctors, tests, doctors, tests. He wasn't autistic. He wasn't epileptic. He wasn't anything in any book. His brain had a tendency to misfire. The tendency increased and, like weeds in a garden, the sparks prevented anything else in the brain from growing.

By the time Archie was eight, he'd stopped talking. Lilly and her husband George did, as well.

"That's it?" George said on a Monday night, staring at a recently thawed Salisbury steak and a pile of canned peas.

"You like—"

"Not the dinner," he cut Lilly off. "That's all we can talk about? Archie did this, Archie didn't do that? That's all we've got to say anymore?"

"No, it's just...that's my day. What do you want me to say?"

"Nothing." George put his balding head in his calloused hands. "If it's about Archie, don't say it."

They said nearly nothing to each other for seven months.

Archie helped them get back together by almost dying. He stopped breathing for while, after a particularly dark seizure. He lived, but in a regressed state, giving up walking and any potty training he'd mastered.

George learned to make ramps and affix handrails to studs. They didn't work so well screwed to drywall. He sold his precious Buick Grand National and bought a conversion van, complete with a lift and wheelchair tie-downs.

They learned to live with their silent partner.

"I don't know how you do it," Lilly's sister said late one Christmas night as she watched Lilly pull turkey meat from the carcass.

"It's not tragic," Lilly said. "That's what's tough to explain to people. There are times when Archie sees something or hears something and belts one out, one of his roars and it just cracks us up. Roaring at a squirrel. We were watching this stupid talking heads show when a guy from the National Rifle Association said guns were making America safe and Archie, out of nowhere, blows this raspberry." Lilly laughed. "That's comedy. You can't get that on the Home Box."

Lilly looked over at Archie, staring out at the sparkling night-blue grass. His face drawn, thin because the muscles did so little, his eyes moved like someone kept shaking his head.

"He laughs," she said. "What else is there, really?"

For George, work was work and home was work. Fix this, trim that, sit with Archie.

For Lilly, home was the world. Get up, clean Archie. Feed him. Clean him again. Clean the house from the mess she'd just made. Then lunch, then dinner, then George. Zip out if he's in a good mood, get more food and cleaning supplies. Talk to someone on the phone, read a little, watch TV, sleep. Repeat. There was no holiday, there was no different day. George was around on the weekends; that was the only thing separating one day from the next.

The local hospice saved their marriage. They took Archie once in a while, for a Saturday and Sunday. It broke their hearts, but not completely. Just little chips in the corners. They needed to visit a different world and doing it together helped to keep them that way—together. Dinner at a chain restaurant and a terrible movie was enough to revive them as a couple, as people, not just Archie's support system.

This continued through May 8. Mother's Day.

Lilly and George made lunch after church. Lilly opened her present 'from Archie.' A jogging suit two sizes too big, in a color she'd never dream of wearing. She laughed to herself. George was so terrible at this. He'd be better off actually letting Archie pick the gift.

On the following Wednesday, the doorbell rang. Lilly went, expecting to buy donuts from a little league team.

The man at the door didn't look like he'd ever held a baseball in his life. Shocking silver hair, tanned wrinkles, a blue sports coat that fit without a ripple over a brilliant yellow shirt. None of which impressed Lilly as much as the ascot. She'd never seen a red silk—or any—ascot in person. The man bit the end of black sunglasses.

Next to the man was a tall blonde woman in her mid-twenties. Lilly didn't know what to make of her. She had stripper hair, but a red polka dot sundress. The two went together like salt and paper.

"Can I help you?" Lilly asked.

The man pulled the sunglasses from his mouth. He looked at Lilly, longer than she thought was polite. He smiled so wide his eyes disappeared.

"*Vous êtes la mère d'Archie,*" he said.

"You are Archie's mom," the woman translated. Lilly recognized her accent. The man sounded French, but the woman sounded like she was from about five feet from here.

"*Excusez-moi,*" he continued. "*C'est comme si je vous connais.*"

"Excuse me," the woman echoed. "It is as if he knows you."

Lilly's eyes caught on first. They blurred. Her hands trembled. "George!" she called out before her throat got too tight.

"*Je m'apelle Jean Herval.*" The man took Lilly's hand and kissed it. "Archie's Other."

"Hi," the woman said. "I'm Cindy Benning from the Attala County Sheriff's Office. I'm translatin' for Mr. Herval."

George and Lilly sat on the couch. Cindy took a chair.

Jean went right to Archie. Archie flailed around, whipping his fore arms and lower legs in little circles with such force he looked like he might spin out of his wheelchair. She couldn't recall ever seeing him this excited.

Lilly cried. She had no idea why, or even what emotion was causing the gush. Tears came out and that is all she could really say about the matter. She knew George wanted to cry too, but wouldn't, not with this other guy in the house. George was getting a headache right now from holding everything in. In a half hour he'd ask her where the Tylenol was.

Archie shouted something that sounded like "Jean."

"*Oui,*" Jean said, moving behind the young man. "Archie, Archie, Archie." He looked to Lilly and George. "*Il aime son nom beaucoup. Il aime entendre son nom.*"

Cindy said, "He likes his name very much. He likes hearing his name."

Jean dug his fingers into Archie's scalp and Archie began to hum.

"*Vous avez su ceci étiez son favori?*" Jean asked. "*Il l'aime quand vous lavez les cheveux.* Shampoo, Archie. Shampoo."

"Did you know this was his favorite?" Cindy asked. "He loves it when you wash his hair."

"Jean," Archie pushed out. It was the first full word he'd said in more than ten years.

George could no longer keep his tears inside. Lilly let a steady stream fall. Neither said a word. They did not want to stop Jean for anything. *Keep him talking, what is it like in there, in Archie's head?* Lilly had more questions than air in her lungs.

"*Il aime des promenades,*" Jean directed to George.

"He loves walks," Cindy said.

"*Jour. Nuit. Pluie. Froid.*"

"Day. Night. Rain. Cold,"

"*Il aime des sensations.*"

"He loves sensations...feelings," Cindy added.

Jean stopped rubbing Archie's head. He took the boy's hand and patted it.

"What..." Lilly started. "What are his memories like?"

Jean smiled, seeming to understand the question without an interpretation. Any mother would probably have the same question. Any person, period. He squeezed Archie's hand and motioned to a highback chair next to the couch.

"Please," Lilly said.

Jean sat down and explained all he could. Cindy, in her Sunday-best voice, tried to relay it all.

"Archie's memories are emotions. They are pure feelings. Love, hate, frustration, fear, silliness. I have had to put words to them. He has memories of being young and knowing the words. The words, they no longer come. They are in another room, in his mind. The door slams shut if he goes to it. He cannot reach that room. He cannot reach many rooms in his mind."

Lilly made the slightest of gasps, as if she had just surfaced. George took her hand.

"He likes music," Cindy continued. "All kinds. Loud is better. He remembers buttered popcorn. The smell is happiness. Bacon. That is happiness, too. I have many memories of smells. I wish...there were more words for them. The scent of purple flowers in a yard. Lilacs perhaps? Those are heaven to Archie. The smell of the sea. That is the smell of fun. Water. Both of you smile at the smell of the sea, and that makes Archie happiest. He loves you both very much."

"You can tell that?" Lilly managed to get out.

"*Vous pouvez pemser que?*" Cindy asked Jean.

Jean answered and Cindy turned to Lilly and George.

"That is why I am here," Cindy translated. "Archie wishes he could throw his love at you, like a ball or a pillow. To hit you with it so you could feel him. Affection. Appreciation. All of the love that he has."

Jean said more, quickly, and Cindy continued. "He has given me much. Much new and much that I had lost. I came to convey his love and I came to thank him for what he's given me. He hit me with memories of pure love."

Archie smiled on as everyone cried. Cindy wasn't even sure why she'd let loose. It was good, like a shower. The opposite of a shower. She washed all her dinginess out and away. She hadn't solved a murder or protected a child from abuse, but she'd done something just the same. She thought, quite simply, it was the best thing she'd ever done.

CHAPTER 71

SUSAN

"If you wanted to be alone with me," Casper said, "there were far easier ways."

Susan smiled and sat down next to him. She turned her chair so she could put her feet up. She exhaled loudly and gazed at the ceiling.

"There is no great story about me," she said. "I'm curious by nature and there's nothing more worthy of curiosity than the human brain."

"I'm thinking Thai tonight." Casper crossed his legs and shouldered close to Susan.

"How about you?" she asked. "You got a story?"

"Boy meets girl."

"While trying to build a machine that scrambles brains. I know that one. What about before that? How does one decide he wants to get into the business of disrupting neural networks?"

"My best friend was mistakenly shot dead. If the police had nonlethal weapons at the time, he'd be alive today."

"You never had a best friend."

"Oh, Susan, that was harsh."

"Is everything you've told me a lie?"

"Hardly anything."

Susan smiled again. "That's because you haven't said much. You deflate. Poke holes in everyone else's balloons. Now why is that, do you think?"

Casper bent down the corners of his mouth, feigning ignorance.

"I think you shoot everything down so we don't know when we hit the right one."

"Huh," Casper said. "That sounds counterproductive."

"Not if you already know what's happened. The answer. The fascinoma of May 5th is not a fascinoma to you."

"Now that is an interesting hypothesis. Are the Knights Templar involved? I love when they tie in."

Susan said, "You came here to make sure this group didn't stumble onto anything real."

"You do realize how paranoid that sounds. You've been inside. You should know better. A bunch of old men straining to stay one step ahead of the comic book writers. And losing, I might add."

"You're ahead of the rest of the world, covering your tracks."

"I shall take that as a compliment. I do so want to impress you."

"You have," Susan said, "but in the wrong way. I thought you were curious like me. Not a saboteur. Not someone so willing to play me."

Casper lost his smile. "I never played you."

"What do you call it, then? Using a personal relationship to stay inside my group?"

"We both know I could have had the president place me here. I didn't use you."

"A presidential appointment would not have been subtle enough for you. You wanted to worm your way in with smoke and mirrors."

"You're mixing your metaphors."

"No," Susan said. "You've got all the tricks. A little flirting, a little sarcasm, some direct refutation when needed. Come to think of it, it's kind of desperate."

Casper flicked his hand. "Now you're just getting nasty."

"What do you know, Casper Yan?"

He burrowed backward into his chair, a tired dog on an old porch.

"You're protecting something," Susan pushed. "It's obvious. Something we got to or something we've yet to discuss."

"I wish—"

"I don't have a story. I'm just curious. Relentlessly curious."

"Thai food."

"I'm kicking you out. Bringing in a few others. My report to the secretary will reflect DARPA's lack of cooperation."

"A drink."

"You can test your clout. Should be fun for you. This whole think-tank thing was getting old anyway. I wasn't sure there was an answer. Now that I know there is, we'll really go at it, starting with the Department of Defense."

"We'll talk over drinks." Casper winked.

"I don't think so." Susan got up. She glanced around, but she had brought nothing to the meeting, not even her purse.

"We'll just drink, then."

"So long, Casper." Susan strolled around the table, on the right side.

Casper leaped up and rounded on the left. He beat her to the door.

"Do you really believe in grand conspiracies?" Casper blocked Susan's way. "The Masons rule the world. The Trilateral Commission sank Atlantis. There are no secrets. There never were any, and even less so now."

"When we met you believed in at least the possibility of remote viewing," Susan said. "You did work on déjà vu. You relished the fact that everyone thought you were a bit nuts and now...now it's all garbage? Now that the whole world has had a taste of the truly weird, you've become the resident skeptic? As my Grammie used to say, that duck don't waddle."

Casper notched back, eyes popping, mouth forming a small 'o.' "What does that mean?"

Susan jammed her fists on her hips. "Which part?"

"The duck part."

"It means Abigail was right. You don't add up and I've had enough shifty men in my life."

Casper's lips twitched. He moved his head, as if there were other people in the room and he wanted to see if they were listening. He closed his eyes tightly, like paparazzi were snapping photos, then he opened them and looked at Susan. She was standing straight and still.

"I came to hear what others were thinking. My motives are no more complicated than that. I heard what you were putting together and knew it would be interesting. This was no safari, and certainly no defensive maneuver."

Susan crossed her arms. "But?"

"But nothing."

"You haven't told me *your* hypothesis."

"Yes..." he drew out, glancing at the floor as if there might be some hole to jump down. "There is that."

Susan stood solid, arms tight, gaze unflinching, stern and patient. In her career she had performed several long surgeries. She made sure, just by her face, that Casper understood her capacity for standing and staring.

"You've heard my hypothesis," Casper said. "They said it."

"Which one?"

"All of them. I like them all, rolled up together like a juicy roulade."

Casper motioned for Susan to sit, than pulled out the end-most chair and sat himself. *He suddenly looks tired,* Susan thought. She suddenly felt tired. All the madness, the tension, the uncertainty—it was ending, bleeding out of her and taking its energetic hormones along.

"Here is the great problem with modern science: it is the study of repetition. Newton drops an apple, it falls to the ground. You drop an apple, it falls to the ground. I drop an apple, same thing. We get a theory and it predicts those results for everyone forever."

Casper bent forward, putting his elbows on his knees. "But what about a woman in Siberia who drops an apple only to have it hang there, mid-air? She rushes to get her husband and they watch it hover, ignorant of its duty to plummet. They gape at it and go get some others. Everyone sees the floating apple, so they call the local newspaper. The reporter shows up and splat. Sauce on the tile.

"The anomaly is quickly forgotten because it could not be repeated. It was one-in-a-quadrillion event, so statistically insignificant that it doesn't exist."

Susan narrowed her eyes. "So you're tossing out everyone else's hypotheses because you secretly hate science?"

"No," Casper said. "I've been tossing them, but onto a bigger heap. Your team hasn't been thinking big enough. Not that I hold them at fault—I've been at this a lot longer. I've learned to expand my realm of possibility. There is a wide world of nonrepeating events. It's out there, here, around and through us. We're just not good at seeing it. In fact, I think we've evolved to experience it less and less. We're pattern recognition critters, you and me and all of humankind. We've gotten so good at it we see faces on Martian mountains and saints on potato chips. Experiences that don't fit patterns are much tougher for us to discern."

"I'm not following you," Susan said.

"Your string theory, with us all being connected. It's right. We are. Michelle's tipping point? Real. We are all filled and spilled like some kind of clepsydra running on mental energy. Jung was right, he just couldn't prove it. Again, laboratory conditions prevent results. Electric Universe theory is right, although misapplied. Poor saps can't get out of their own way. Did we talk about Sheldrake and morphic fields?"

"I don't recall."

"We touched on it, I'm sure. All of these conversations must pass by there, like visiting the Liberty Bell when in Philadelphia. More necessary than rewarding. Matters not—Sheldrake is right, too. He can't prove it. Proof precludes an outcome. And then there's the next stop on our inevitable journey. Aliens. Little green men that snatch us in the middle of the night."

Susan didn't hold back her scowl. As free and open as she'd wanted these sessions to go, there were, she felt, boundaries. Aliens, Nessie, and Bigfoot were on the other side.

"Pout away," Casper sat back in his chair, flicking his hands again. "They are real. Misunderstood, as are ghosts, elves, and gnomes. Real just the same."

"Please, Casper." Susan had reached her sarcasm limit over an hour ago. She needed him to turn off the acid drip and speak to her basically, without hint or hue.

"Stay with me," Casper requested. "I have never told another living person my idea. You are the first. You may be the last. I never talk about it because it is difficult for me to accept. The only thing more difficult is ridding myself of it. The idea keeps coming back, resurfacing, like a bobbing apple. And I'd even stopped bobbing. Until last Thursday.

"OK, so here's one of my pet peeves: the so-called search for life in the galaxy. Every time NASA launches a probe to find water on Mars or one of Jupiter's moons I chuckle. What's the point? Water equals life? There can be no life *sans* water? Well that's rather narrow-minded to the point of absurdity, don't you think? Every life form on this planet is a Pachinko machine for energy. Some forms hold the energy for years, some minutes, but every bug, bear, and Betty is a net of interconnecting energy. We see the matter: the fur, scales, and—ahem—other things. We don't see the energy. So we look for the matter. Dumb. It's the energy that matters. The fast, intricate cascades of charges charging through our brains. That is life. Not the four hundred dollars worth of chemicals in these capacitors we call bodies."

Casper took a breath. Susan hoped it would be a long one. She needed a second to catch up, to make sure that there was nothing completely asinine in his last statement.

"You've seen it, Susan." Casper used a reverent voice. "That moment when the body suddenly becomes just a mass of chemicals. One second you've got a person, the next moment a corpse. The energy is gone. The life. You've witnessed it."

"A few too many times."

"Whatever that twinkle is, that spark of life, the actual energy that makes a person more than an organic sculpture—I think there is more of it out there."

"More life? Like after-life?"

"Like energy. The mighty science of physics can only account for about 10% of the matter/energy in the universe.

They keep revising, recounting, and relying on dark substances to fill their gaps. God of the gaps—it would be funny if it wasn't so frightening. We know there is energy out there that we have no way of detecting. I'm pretty convinced it has detected us."

Casper sat back and swallowed. Susan watched him, waiting for the grin, the strain of trying not to smile and to finally break into laughter. She wanted him to show her this was his last, best fib.

Casper didn't break. "Circuits of energy devoid of visible material conduits. Enormous networks, with billions of nodes. Intelligent. Conscious. Is it any more difficult to conceive of a sentient ball of energy than it is to conceive of us? Sentient bags of water and carbon. We are, I dare say, the less likely in many respects."

Susan shook her head. *Aliens*. This wasn't what she wanted to hear. Her anger with Casper had been driven by the thought that he actually knew something. That the government knew something. The anger and the hope blew out.

"Too much, eh?" Casper said.

"'Fraid so."

"You can see why I have never had this discussion with anyone."

"What about your Other? He or she any help?"

"Long discussions over the phone? No. A third-grader in Lockport, New York. I wouldn't want to disturb him more than I already have. I'm quite envious of him. I want to go back to building really cool model planes."

"You should." Susan smiled.

"And I will... as soon as I am sure you don't think I'm nuts."

"I don't."

Casper crinkled his lips. "Wrong answer. You must or you would not have said that."

He held up two fingers, in a 'V.' A peace sign or victory sign, depending on your point-of-view. "Two people. Myself and this kid in Lockport. Yourself and the man in Guatemala. Always two. Binary."

"Like a computer," Susan confirmed.

"Like a pattern, a design. Some congestion of energy has looked at this planet the way we've look at those rocks on Mars and saw a face. It saw a reflection of itself—a network of billions of binary nodes. So it tried contact. Maybe it's been trying for thousands of years, which is why we get these fleeting moments of paranormal activity. Maybe it's a great tumbleweed, rolling through space, and glommed on to us for one-point-five seconds last Thursday. I don't know. I do know that what happened was not an accident. It was a connection, with us and with everything."

"You know?" Susan pumped her eyebrows. "You really know this?"

"It's the only answer." Casper cocked his head. *A slight taunt*, Susan thought.

"You don't think that's a little premature?"

"I'm never premature." He let out a tiny grin. "I'm just quick witted. I can't help it. Besides, like I said, I've been at this a long time. I've been to Tunguska, Siberia, and felt the tug on my mind. I've read the KGB files on their mentalists, sending thoughts to each other across thousands of miles. I've been privy to Chinese studies of twins and their uncanny ability to know what the other is feeling, despite distance, concrete, and steel. Our own remote viewing program had spotty results. Should it have had any? The military abandoned it because it wasn't turnkey. I took up the study for that very reason—the sporadic nature of it all."

"And you couldn't let the group in on this hypothesis of yours?"

"I'm not ready to retire. I don't want to leave DARPA and my work, yet."

Susan let her face show her confusion.

"Energy," Casper exhaled. "I'm not supposed to discuss *that* topic at all. Sentient or not, everyone's very interested in energy. If you want to rock the status quo, just talk about an unlimited, universally available energy source. Energy that doesn't come through a pipe someone already owns. Oh, that keeps you off the 'A' list."

Casper spread out over his chair, a balloon finally out of air. He stared over Susan's shoulder, eyes glassy, either open too long or on the verge of tears. She could not decide. She couldn't decide anything. Him, truth, trust. Deflation, avoidance, fear. Warm, gentle fear for his reputation, his lifestyle, a rapidly eroding status quo. She'd read once that people were less likely to adopt new tastes and ideas after the age of 25. The food and music of your youth would always be your favorites. She now decided that was absolutely true. She had no taste for this much newness.

Not that it was completely new. The Susan of last week would have dismissed Casper's lunacy, written him off as either dishonest or senile. None of his ravings would have fit the patterns of her experience.

Her experiences had recently doubled.

She was slowly realizing that not all her memories came in packets, like old letters in a shoe box. She had some memories like that, events that could be read over and over. Her mother saying good-bye, as she left for the parole hearing for the man who killed Susan's father. Grammie crying and singing and rocking side-to-side, trying to tell Susan mommy wasn't coming back. *Antonio's boat had flipped once. An instant, wicked wind—a xocomil—drove him into the lake and whipped up waves higher than his head and shoulders. He surfaced, and the evil wind shoved water down his throat. It was the wind that carries away sin. Today, it would take him. He was dead. Then he was back on his up-turned boat. Clutching the slimy bottom like a newborn opossum on her mother's back.*

These were sorted, packaged recollections. They were not the totality of one's memories. There were other experiences strewn throughout, a stratum of life that made her nod in agreement, feel at home, understand in terms of her experience. Antonio would hug Casper around the shoulder and offer him a drink. He'd love the fact that a European—anyone who wasn't from the highlands around Lake Atitlan was a European—understood the mystery. Mother Earth is as Casper described: a great tumbleweed in space, huge and alive. We live on a wise and attentive ball of interconnected energy. No one ever said we had the only one. Antonio would have no problem with the fact that we couldn't see this other globe. He thought we couldn't see but a fraction of this one.

Memories, experience, acceptance, place.

"That's it?" Susan said. To Casper and to herself. "That's all we're going to get?"

"People's stories don't end in resolution," Casper said. "That's why we find death so sad. It's always abrupt, always too soon. Life as a whole is continuous. But you know that. Did you want things to be different this time?"

"This time?" Susan flinched, as if the question were a gnat. "Was there ever another time?"

"Funny you should ask that. I actually think there might have been. The story of the Tower of Babel always struck me as odd. The Old Testament God had a natural modus operandi—the deluge or locust—except that one time when he messes with everyone's heads. Gives them different languages. Kind of like Thursday, don't you think? Lots of people got lots of new languages rammed into their heads. Only this time, people had more context. We know more about the globe. Those people building the tower didn't know there were other continents, let alone people scratching out a life upon them.

"That is not, however, at all what I meant." Casper softened his voice. "Your mystery. Your story, the one you claim you don't have. Did you want to solve this one, because you can't solve the other?"

Susan heard the *nuwals* humming. It was the plodding spiritual Grammie sang hanging sheets in the backyard or thumbing the skin off steaming potatoes.

"Here's another thing I've never told another person," Casper began. "I looked him up—the man who killed your father."

"What—"

Casper raised his hand. "You know, the opportunity presented itself. That's hardly an excuse. I told myself I couldn't be looking into your private life, if it was at things you didn't even know. I thought maybe I could understand. You. Or by corollary, us, or the lack thereof."

"You thought my past might tell you why we broke up? Lord, you poor man. You ever think it was just you? The same you 3who does things like dig into my past. Were you ever going to tell me?"

"There was nothing to tell," Casper said.

"Nothing? The whole intelligence community on your speed dial and you learned nothing?"

"Thats becaus there is no answer, Susan. That's what I learned, and it was no further than you ever got. John McCorely killed your father for some perceived slight. His gang probably killed your mother to make some kind of statement. It was lunacy. Stupid, wasteful lunacy. I never had the appetite to contact you and tell you that your lifelong desire to make sense of things would fail to culminate in understanding a multiple murderer."

"And now I have another 'event' that I'm never going to understand." Susan felt cold, like her chair had descended to a lower, damper place.

"No." Casper dropped to his knees before Susan and took her hands, balling hers with his own. "You *do* understand. You *have* figured it all out. You look and you look hard, and you help other people along the way. How many lives has your curiosity saved? How many more before you're done? It doesn't matter what goes on in the heads of vermin like McCorely. It doesn't even matter if the planet's just been whisked through a veil of dark energy. You make the world better and there is no higher calling. What was it you said the other day? About the sun?"

"We all help the sun cross the sky."

"I like that phrase. I believe I shall adopt it as my new motto."

CHAPTER 72

MRS. ENFIELD'S THIRD GRADE CLASS

Cathy saw the circle from her window: four boys around one. She didn't usually go outside until all the lovelies were off: on their buses, in their minivans, or three blocks down the street. There was always work to do and the more she did here, the less she had to do at home. She could read patterns, though. Millions of years of evolution and six years of teaching had given her the ability to notice a human bonfire. She ran outside.

The boy in the middle had a coat, gloves, and hat. Those around him pointed and jeered. Other kids—walkers, not busers or mini-vanners—gathered in an outer circle to see what would happen. She heard words like 'frosty' and 'freak' as she neared. She also heard words in a nasally language she couldn't fathom. It was twangy, she thought, like someone making fun of Korean. The boy didn't notice her. The one laughing and twanging moved first. Fingers splayed, he moved to shove the boy in gloves. It was the type of pushing Cathy had seen a thousand times. Aggressive, but ultimately harmless. She jogged toward the kids, repeatedly yelling "Hey!"

The boy with the gloves punched upward, through the other's jaw. The twangy boy's head flew back. He lost his footing. Another boy jumped in, maybe to help the hurt one, Cathy couldn't tell. The gloved boy tripped him and cut across his face with his elbow.

Cathy ran, screaming. Bystanders parted. The gloved boy cocked his arm back, fist balled. Cathy grabbed his wrist, like snagging an angry rattlesnake. He repositioned, brought his other fist around, and stopped.

"What's going on here?" Cathy snapped.

Kids yelled all kinds of nothings and disclaimers: he did this, he did that. Cathy put her body between the two most riled of the boys.

"Sorry," the gloved boy said.

"Do I need to bring you all inside?"

"No!" The boy wrenched his hand away. "I won't go in." Cathy had never seen such a look of horror. Not at all. And certainly not from the threat of going to the office.

"He's a maniac," the boy on the ground screeched.

"All right," she huffed. "All right. Let's all calm down." The boy on the ground was bleeding from the mouth. He, at least, was going back inside.

The gloved boy stood, watching the blood like it was his own. "It's not my fault," he muttered, "that I don't want to be cold. Once you've been cold inside...it's not my fault."

She decided to get the other one down to the nurse's office.

"Here," said a tiny voice next to her. It belonged to a tiny girl Cathy didn't know, a first grader maybe. The girl held up a tooth. "An upper central incisor," she continued. "Avulsed by trauma to the head."

"Oh." Cathy took the small, blood-stumped tooth.

"If you put it in milk it will keep better. A decent dentist can re-implant it."

CHAPTER 73

ALISTAIR

Valerie seemed shocked to see Alistair get out of the car. He'd called her from the road. He said he was heading home, everything was fine. Apparently she hadn't believed any of it until he actually hugged her, so tight she thought he pulled something.

He let go only to sneak into the girls' bedroom and stroke their sleeping heads. He stayed for half an hour, quietly letting the tears snuff the fire in his head. He'd never cried that way, with the burning in the corner of his eyes, face creased, forehead like an iron. John had been wrong. Alistair knew how happy he was and how happy he wanted to stay—how happy he wanted his whole gang to stay.

They went back downstairs.

"So it's over?" Valerie asked. She sat on her favorite chair, cradling a cup of chamomile tea she'd yet to sip.

"All done." Alistair sat on the floor, hugging her left leg.

"How did you get out of the prison?"

"I bought my way out. I gave a hundred thousand dollars cash to the first guard I saw and told him we had to clean John's cell. I gave another hundred grand to the guy who ran the cameras to scrub any record of me."

"Any left? Did I just ask that? It's not—"

"Lots." Alistair kissed her knee. "And I'm not sure it's enough, what with me being a serial killer—"

"Your killing days are over," she said gently.

"True," Alistair replied. "Blood in, blood out."

CHAPTER 74

NIVEN

"He's really happy you're here." Annabelle's curls jumped about all by themselves, brilliant blonde, in the kind of cut one didn't see without a taste for screwball comedies from the 30s. Lithe and snappy, she made the hair work. Niven knew why Pierce had fallen for her. She dared you not to.

Niven watched his son through the pass-through, tossing orders to the sous chefs, barking, tasting, swiping, and cutting.

"The crowd looks good," Niven said.

"Coming back." Annabelle examined the room. Two empty tables, but it was still early.

Niven leaned in. "Don't tell Pierce, but I'm trying to generate a little more buzz. This is a wonderful restaurant. It deserves—"

"He wouldn't—"

Niven waggled an index finger over his wine. "Of course he wouldn't. He's going to make it all on his own. I'm telling you because you are the more reasonable of the lot."

"Besides..." The voice made Annabelle and Niven look across the table. Ming continued, "Niven is going to need something to do with his time. He doesn't fish or play golf."

They all chuckled. Ming sat back in his silk shirt and short, spiked hair. Candlelight did the shimmy on his black glasses.

"The tomatoes in Campari are excellent today," Ming went on.

"I'll tell the chef," Annabelle said. "They're from the new guy. He'll be thrilled. Before Cinco de Mayo he was driving a gypsy cab. Then he swapped with a famous chef. He won't tell us who. But his stuff speaks for itself."

"It's nice of you to take a chance on him," Niven said.

"I had nothing to do with it," Annabelle replied. "That's all Pierce. Nice guy, once you get to know him."

Niven snickered and stopped the waiter. "If you don't mind, I'd like to send a bottle over to that table—the one with the priest."

"Make it a bottle of Salon," Ming said.

"Why not. Thank you, Ming," Niven said.

"You're in a good mood," said Annabelle.

"A new mood," Niven replied, "and I don't know how long it will last."

CHAPTER 75

MRS. ENFIELD'S THIRD GRADE CLASS

Screeching, dancing, running, happy kids. Grouping, pointing, tagging, dripping sauce and melted cheese, spanking cans of powdered sugar and, best of all, laughing. To Cathy, the gym had never looked grander or been put to better use. The entrance said 'Welcome to the World Carnival.' She loved the mixture of meanings in the sliding syntax. She'd thought of the international festival idea, but a fifth-grader had come up with the name. He deserved extra credit for making Cathy smile.

The children of Public School 23 had put together and run the carnival. Booths with foods from all over the world. Games children play in other lands. Pictures, paintings, and models of places the kids now knew, but had never visited. Cathy convinced the administration to cough up the money for supplies and really let the kids do it up right. They had agreed at the speed of sound.

"Did you ever study judo?"

Cathy looked down. Jared stood next to her, arms crossed, surveying the party like a two-thirds scale vice-principal.

"Judo?" she asked.

"The art of redirecting energy. You're good at it. Taking all of this garbage we have in our heads and pushing it through a narrow, and decidedly juvenile jet is genius. Pure genius."

"Why thank you."

"No, thank you. You're wasting your talents here. Have you ever thought of a career in politics, the ultimate arena of redirection?"

"Politics? No," Cathy said. "I want to work for a living. Besides, after this year I'd consider it a step backwards."

"Truly."

"Did you make anything for the carnival?"

"I helped build a few of the booths," Jared said. "My Other's an engineer of sorts. American. He did not provide me with exotic recipes for roulade or kimchi."

"Being able to build things is wonderful. I bet you have a fun summer."

"I believe so. I could build a nuclear-powered tree house if I could get my hands on a few esoteric items."

Cathy looked at Jared, eyes thin.

He laughed. "Don't worry. I know...and I know better."

"I would hate to see you blow yourself up."

They both gazed out at the stripes and streamers. Salt maps of Thai beaches, a bamboo hut, a cauldron of simmering oatmeal against a red tartan backdrop.

"So much has changed," Cathy said.

Jared shook his head. "I think the better word might be 'revealed.'"

Our titles are available at major book stores and local independent resellers who support Science Fiction and Fantasy readers like you.

EDGE Science Fiction
and Fantasy Publishing

Tesseract Books

www.edgewebsite.com

Our titles are available at major book stores and local independent resellers who support Science Fiction and Fantasy readers like you.

Alphanauts by J. Brian Clarke (tp) - ISBN: 978-1-894063-14-2
Apparition Trail, The by Lisa Smedman (tp) - ISBN: 978-1-894063-22-7
As Fate Decrees by Denysé Bridger (tp) - ISBN: 978-1-894063-41-8
Avim's Oath (Part Six of the Okal Rel Saga) by Lynda Williams (pb)
    - ISBN: 978-1-894063-35-7

Black Chalice, The by Marie Jakober (hb) - ISBN: 978-1-894063-00-7
Blue Apes by Phyllis Gotlieb (pb) - ISBN: 978-1-895836-13-4
Blue Apes by Phyllis Gotlieb (hb) - ISBN: 978-1-895836-14-1

Children of Atwar, The by Heather Spears (pb) - ISBN: 978-0-88878-335-6
Cinco de Mayo by Michael J. Martineck (pb) - ISBN: 978-1-894063-39-5
Cinkarion - The Heart of Fire (Part Two of The Chronicles of the Karionin)
    by J. A. Cullum - (tp) - ISBN: 978-1-894063-21-0
Clan of the Dung-Sniffers by Lee Danielle Hubbard (pb) - ISBN: 978-1-894063-05-0
Claus Effect, The by David Nickle & Karl Schroeder (pb) - ISBN: 978-1-895836-34-9
Claus Effect, The by David Nickle & Karl Schroeder (hb) - ISBN: 978-1-895836-35-6
Courtesan Prince, The (Part One of the Okal Rel Saga) by Lynda Williams (tp)
    - ISBN: 978-1-894063-28-9

Dark Earth Dreams by Candas Dorsey & Roger Deegan (comes with a CD)
    - ISBN: 978-1-895836-05-9
Darkness of the God (Children of the Panther Part Two)
    by Amber Hayward (tp) - ISBN: 978-1-894063-44-9
Distant Signals by Andrew Weiner (tp) - ISBN: 978-0-88878-284-7
Dreams of an Unseen Planet by Teresa Plowright (tp) - ISBN: 978-0-88878-282-3
Dreams of the Sea (Part 1 of Tyranaël) by Élisabeth Vonarburg (tp)
    - ISBN: 978-1-895836-96-7
Dreams of the Sea (Part 1 of Tyranaël) by Élisabeth Vonarburg (hb)
    - ISBN: 978-1-895836-98-1
Druids by Barbara Galler-Smith and Josh Langston (tp)
    - ISBN: 978-1-894063-29-6

Eclipse by K. A. Bedford (tp) - ISBN: 978-1-894063-30-2
Even The Stones by Marie Jakober (tp) - ISBN: 978-1-894063-18-0
Evolve: Vampire Stories of the New Undead edited by Nancy Kilpatrick (tp)
    - ISBN: 978-1-894063-33-3

Far Arena (Part Five of the Okal Rel Saga) by Lynda Williams (tp)
    - ISBN: 978-1-894063-45-6
Fires of the Kindred by Robin Skelton (tp) - ISBN: 978-0-88878-271-7
Forbidden Cargo by Rebecca Rowe (tp) - ISBN: 978-1-894063-16-6

Game of Perfection, A (Part 2 of Tyranaël) by Élisabeth Vonarburg (tp)
  - ISBN: 978-1-894063-32-6
Gaslight Grimoire: Fantastic Tales of Sherlock Holmes
  edited by Jeff Campbell & Charles Prepolec (pb)
  - ISBN: 978-1-8964063-17-3
Gaslight Grotesque: Nightmare Tales of Sherlock Holmes
  edited by Jeff Campbell & Charles Prepolec (pb)
  - ISBN: 978-1-8964063-31-9
Green Music by Ursula Pflug (tp) - ISBN: 978-1-895836-75-2
Green Music by Ursula Pflug (hb) - ISBN: 978-1-895836-77-6

Healer, The (Children of the Panther Part One) by Amber Hayward (tp)
  - ISBN: 978-1-895836-89-9
Healer, The (Children of the Panther Part One) by Amber Hayward (hb)
  - ISBN: 978-1-895836-91-2
Hell Can Wait by Theodore Judson (tp) - ISBN: 978-1-978-1-894063-23-4
Hounds of Ash and other tales of Fool Wolf, The by Greg Keyes (pb)
  - ISBN: 978-1-894063-09-8
Hydrogen Steel by K. A. Bedford (tp) - ISBN: 978-1-894063-20-3

i-ROBOT Poetry by Jason Christie (tp) - ISBN: 978-1-894063-24-1
Immortal Quest by Alexandra MacKenzie (pb) - ISBN: 978-1-894063-46-3

Jackal Bird by Michael Barley (pb) - ISBN: 978-1-895836-07-3
Jackal Bird by Michael Barley (hb) - ISBN: 978-1-895836-11-0
JEMMA7729 by Phoebe Wray (tp) - ISBN: 978-1-894063-40-1

Keaen by Till Noever (tp) - ISBN: 978-1-894063-08-1
Keeper's Child by Leslie Davis (tp) - ISBN: 978-1-894063-01-2

Land/Space edited by Candas Jane Dorsey and Judy McCrosky (tp)
  - ISBN: 978-1-895836-90-5
Land/Space edited by Candas Jane Dorsey and Judy McCrosky (hb)
  - ISBN: 978-1-895836-92-9
Lyskarion: The Song of the Wind (Part One of The Chronicles of the Karionin)
  by J.A. Cullum (tp) - ISBN: 978-1-894063-02-9

Machine Sex and other stories by Candas Jane Dorsey (tp)
  - ISBN: 978-0-88878-278-6
Maërlande Chronicles, The by Élisabeth Vonarburg (pb)
  - ISBN: 978-0-88878-294-6
Moonfall by Heather Spears (pb) - ISBN: 978-0-88878-306-6

Of Wind and Sand by Sylvie Bérard (translated by Sheryl Curtis) (pb)
  - ISBN: 978-1-894063-19-7
On Spec: The First Five Years edited by On Spec (pb)
  - ISBN: 978-1-895836-08-0
On Spec: The First Five Years edited by On Spec (hb)
  - ISBN: 978-1-895836-12-7
Orbital Burn by K. A. Bedford (tp) - ISBN: 978-1-894063-10-4
Orbital Burn by K. A. Bedford (hb) - ISBN: 978-1-894063-12-8

Pallahaxi Tide by Michael Coney (pb) - ISBN: 978-0-88878-293-9
Passion Play by Sean Stewart (pb) - ISBN: 978-0-88878-314-1
Petrified World (Determine Your Destiny #1) by Piotr Brynczka (pb)
  - ISBN: 978-1-894063-11-1
Plague Saint by Rita Donovan, The (tp) - ISBN: 978-1-895836-28-8
Plague Saint by Rita Donovan, The (hb) - ISBN: 978-1-895836-29-5
Pock's World by Dave Duncan (tp) - ISBN: 978-1-894063-47-0
Pretenders (Part Three of the Okal Rel Saga) by Lynda Williams (pb)
  - ISBN: 978-1-894063-13-5

Reluctant Voyagers by Élisabeth Vonarburg (pb) - ISBN: 978-1-895836-09-7
Reluctant Voyagers by Élisabeth Vonarburg (hb) - ISBN: 978-1-895836-15-8
Resisting Adonis by Timothy J. Anderson (tp) - ISBN: 978-1-895836-84-4
Resisting Adonis by Timothy J. Anderson (hb) - ISBN: 978-1-895836-83-7
Righteous Anger (Part Two of the Okal Rel Saga) by Lynda Williams (tp)
  - ISBN: 897-1-894063-38-8

Silent City, The by Élisabeth Vonarburg (tp) - ISBN: 978-1-894063-07-4
Slow Engines of Time, The by Élisabeth Vonarburg (tp)
  - ISBN: 978-1-895836-30-1
Slow Engines of Time, The by Élisabeth Vonarburg (hb)
  - ISBN: 978-1-895836-31-8
Stealing Magic by Tanya Huff (tp) - ISBN: 978-1-894063-34-0
Strange Attractors by Tom Henighan (pb) - ISBN: 978-0-88878-312-7

Taming, The by Heather Spears (pb) - ISBN: 978-1-895836-23-3
Taming, The by Heather Spears (hb) - ISBN: 978-1-895836-24-0
Ten Monkeys, Ten Minutes by Peter Watts (tp) - ISBN: 978-1-895836-74-5
Ten Monkeys, Ten Minutes by Peter Watts (hb) - ISBN: 978-1-895836-76-9
Tesseracts 1 edited by Judith Merril (pb) - ISBN: 978-0-88878-279-3
Tesseracts 2 edited by Phyllis Gotlieb & Douglas Barbour (pb)
  - ISBN: 978-0-88878-270-0
Tesseracts 3 edited by Candas Jane Dorsey & Gerry Truscott (pb)
  - ISBN: 978-0-88878-290-8
Tesseracts 4 edited by Lorna Toolis & Michael Skeet (pb)
  - ISBN: 978-0-88878-322-6
Tesseracts 5 edited by Robert Runté & Yves Maynard (pb)
  - ISBN: 978-1-895836-25-7
Tesseracts 5 edited by Robert Runté & Yves Maynard (hb)
  - ISBN: 978-1-895836-26-4
Tesseracts 6 edited by Robert J. Sawyer & Carolyn Clink (pb)
  - ISBN: 978-1-895836-32-5
Tesseracts 6 edited by Robert J. Sawyer & Carolyn Clink (hb)
  - ISBN: 978-1-895836-33-2
Tesseracts 7 edited by Paula Johanson & Jean-Louis Trudel (tp)
  - ISBN: 978-1-895836-58-5
Tesseracts 7 edited by Paula Johanson & Jean-Louis Trudel (hb)
  - ISBN: 978-1-895836-59-2
Tesseracts 8 edited by John Clute & Candas Jane Dorsey (tp)
  - ISBN: 978-1-895836-61-5
Tesseracts 8 edited by John Clute & Candas Jane Dorsey (hb)
  - ISBN: 978-1-895836-62-2

Tesseracts Nine edited by Nalo Hopkinson and Geoff Ryman (tp)
  - ISBN: 978-1-894063-26-5
Tesseracts Ten: A Celebration of New Canadian Speculative Fiction
  edited by Robert Charles Wilson and Edo van Belkom (tp)
  - ISBN: 978-1-894063-36-4
Tesseracts Eleven: Amazing Canadian Speulative Fiction
  edited by Cory Doctorow and Holly Phillips (tp)
  - ISBN: 978-1-894063-03-6
Tesseracts Twelve: New Novellas of Canadian Fantastic Fiction
  edited by Claude Lalumière (pb)
  - ISBN: 978-1-894063-15-9
Tesseracts Thirteen: Chilling Tales from the Great White North
  edited by Nancy Kilpatrick and David Morrell (tp)
  - ISBN: 978-1-894063-25-8
Tesseracts 14: Strange Canadian Stories
  edited by John Robert Colombo and Brett Alexander Savory (tp)
  - ISBN: 978-1-894063-37-1
Tesseracts Q edited by Élisabeth Vonarburg & Jane Brierley (pb)
  - ISBN: 978-1-895836-21-9
Tesseracts Q edited by Élisabeth Vonarburg & Jane Brierley (hb)
  - ISBN: 978-1-895836-22-6
Throne Price by Lynda Williams and Alison Sinclair (tp)
  - ISBN: 978-1-894063-06-7
Time Machines Repaired Whie-U-Wait by K. A. Bedford (tp)
  - ISBN: 978-1-894063-42-5

Limited Edition Available

If you collect limited editions of books, you need to check out the special "COFFIN" edition of *EVOLVE: Vampire Stories of the New Undead*.

Protected in a magnetically sealed miniature pine coffin; packaged in an open ended black bag; identified by a unique wax seal; and certified as an original; is a hardcover copy of *EVOLVE: Vampire Stories of the New Undead*.

Each of these "COFFIN" editions is identified by unique number: on the lid, the box and the book. Each book is signed by all of the authors, the cover artist, the editor and the publisher.

Only 50 copies of this limited edition are available. You must order your copy directly from the publisher. Limited to one copy per customer. We expect the COFFIN edition to sell out quickly. Act fast to avoid disappointment.

Limited "COFFIN" edition — $230.00 US plus shipping and taxes.

"If you're into vampires at all, this is a collection
of stories you'll love." — Lisa C.